P9-DBY-871

PRINCE OF CHAOS

AVON BOOKS • NEW YORK

AVON BOOKS
A division of
The Hearst Corporation
1350 Avenue of the Americas
New York, New York 10019

Published in hardcover by William Morrow and Company, Inc.; for information address Avon Books.

First Avon Books Printing: November 1992

AVON TRADEMARK REG. U.S. PAT. OFF. AND IN OTHER COUNTRIES, MARCA REGISTRADA, HECHO EN U.S.A.

Printed in the U.S.A.

RA 10 9 8 7 6

To Jane Lindskold—

Gramercy, lady, for your help.
This one was yours from the start.

PRINCE OF CHAOS

I

See one coronation and you've seen them all. Sounds cynical and probably is, especially when the principal is your best friend and his queen's your inadvertent lover. But there's generally a procession, with a lot of slow music, and uncomfortable, colorful garb, incense, speeches, prayers, the ringing of bells. They are tedious, generally hot, and requiring of one an insincere attention, as at weddings, commencements, and secret initiations.

And so Luke and Coral became the sovereigns of Kashfa, in the same church where we'd fought almost— but, unfortunately, not quite—to the death with my mad brother Jurt but a few hours before. As Amber's only representative at the event—albeit of, technically, unofficial status—I was accorded a ringside standing-place, and eyes were often drifting my way. So I had to keep alert and mouth appropriate responses. While Random would not permit formal status to my presence at the ceremony, I knew he'd be irritated if he heard that my behavior was less than diplomatically sound.

So I wound up with hurting feet, a stiff neck, and colorful garments soaked with sweat. That's show biz. Still, I wouldn't have had it any other way. Luke and I go back through some of the damnedest times, and I couldn't help but think of them—from sword's point to track meets, from art galleries and into Shadow—as I stood there sweltering and wondering what would become of him now he wore a crown. Such an occurrence had changed my uncle Random from a happy-go-lucky musician, footloose and degenerate, into a sage and responsible monarch—though I've only my relatives' reports when it comes to knowing about the first. I found myself hoping it wouldn't mellow Luke out all that much. Still—again—Luke was a very different person than Random, not to mention ages younger. Amazing what years can do, though—or is it just the nature of events? I realized myself to be a lot different than I had been not so very long ago, from all that had happened to me recently. A lot different than I'd been yesterday, come to think of it.

During the recessional Coral managed to pass me a note, saying that she had to see me, giving a time and a place, even including a small map. It proved an apartment to the rear of the palace. We met there that evening and wound up spending the night. She and Luke had been married as kids, by proxy, I learned then, part of the diplomatic arrangement between Jasra and the Begmans. It didn't work out, though—the diplomatic part, that is—and the rest kind of fell by the wayside. The principals had sort of forgotten about the marriage, too, till recent events served as a reminder. Neither had seen the other in years. Still, the record showed that the prince had been married. While it was an annullable thing, she could also be crowned with him. If there were anything in it for Kashfa.

And there was: Eregnor. A Begman queen on the

Kashfan throne might help smooth over that particular real estate grab. At least, that had been Jasra's thinking, Coral told me. And Luke had been swayed by this, particularly in the absence of the guarantees from Amber and the now-defunct Golden Circle Treaty.

I held her. She was not well, despite what seemed an amazing postoperative recovery. She wore a black patch over her right eye and was more than a little reactive should my hand stray near it—or even if I looked at it for too long. What might have led Dworkin to replace the damaged eye with the Jewel of Judgment, I could not even guess. Unless he somehow considered her proof against the forces of the Pattern and the Logrus in their attempts to recover it. My expertise in this area, though, was nonexistent. Having finally met the diminutive mage, I had become convinced of his sanity—though this feeling in no way served to penetrate those enigmatic qualities that ancient wise men tend to possess.

"How does it feel?" I asked her.

"Very strange," she replied. "Not pain—exactly. More like the way a Trump contact feels. Only it's with me all the time, and I'm not going anywhere or talking to anyone. It's as if I'm standing in some sort of gateway. Forces are moving about me, through me."

In an instant I was at the center that was the gray ring with its wheel of many-spoked reddish metal. From the inside, here, it was like a great web. A bright strand pulsed for my attention. Yes, it was a line to a very potent force in distant Shadow, one that might be used for probing. Carefully, I extended it toward the covered jewel she wore in her eye socket.

There was no immediate resistance. In fact, I felt nothing as I extended the line of power. An image came to me of a curtain of flame, however. Pushing through the fiery veil, I felt my extension of inquiry slowing, slowing, halted. And there I hovered, as it were, at the edge of a void. This was not the way of attunement, as I understood it, and I was loath to invoke the Pattern, which I understood to be a part of it, when employing other forces. I pushed forward and felt a terrible coldness, draining the energies I had called upon.

Still, it was not draining the energy directly from me, only from one of the forces I commanded. I pushed it farther, and I beheld a faint patch of light like some distant nebula. It hung against a background the deep red of port wine. Closer still, and it resolved itself into a form—a complex, three dimensional construct, half-familiar—which must be the pathway one takes in attuning oneself to the Jewel, from my father's description. All right, I was inside the Jewel. Should I essay the initiation?

"Go no further," came an unfamiliar voice, though I realized it to be Coral who was making the sounds. She seemed to have slipped into a trance state. "You are denied the higher initiation."

I drew back on my probe, not eager for any demonstrations that might come my way along it. My Logrus sight, which had remained with me constantly since recent events in Amber, gave me a vision of Coral now fully enfolded and penetrated by the higher version of the Pattern.

"Why?" I asked it.

But I was not vouchsafed a reply. Coral gave a little jerk, shook herself, and stared at me.

"What happened?" she asked.

"You dozed off," I replied. "No wonder. Whatever Dworkin did, plus the day's stress . . ."

She yawned and collapsed back on the bed.

"Yes," she breathed, and then she was really asleep.

I pulled off my boots and discarded my heavier garments. I stretched out beside her and drew a quilt over us. I was tired, too, and I just wanted someone to hold.

How long I slept I do not know. I was troubled by dark, swirling dreams. Faces—human, animal, demonic, moved about me, none of them bearing particularly cheerful expressions. Forests fell and burst into flame, the ground shook and split, the waters of the sea rose in gigantic waves and assailed the land, the moon dripped blood and there came up a great wailing. Something called my name. . . .

A great wind rattled the shutters till they burst inward, flapping and banging. In my dream, a creature entered then and came to crouch at the foot of the bed, calling softly to me, over and over. The room seemed to be shaking, and my mind went back to California. It seemed that an earthquake was in progress. The wind rose from a shriek to a roar, and I heard crashing sounds from without, as of trees falling, towers toppling. . . .

"Merlin, Prince of the House of Sawall, Prince of Chaos, rise up," it seemed to say. Then it gnashed its fangs and began again.

At the fourth or fifth repetition it struck me that I might not be dreaming. There were screams from somewhere outside, and steady pulses of lightning came and went against almost musical rolls of thunder.

I raised a protective shell before I moved, before I opened my eyes. The sounds were real, as was the broken shutter. So was the creature at the foot of the bed.

"Merlin, Merlin. Rise up, Merlin," it said to me—it being a long-snouted, pointed-eared individual, well-fanged and clawed, of a greenish-silver cast of complexion, eyes large and shining, damp leathery wings folded against its lean sides. From its expression, I couldn't tell whether it was smiling or in pain. "Awaken, Lord of Chaos."

"Gryll," I said, naming an old family servant from the Courts.

"Aye, Lord," it replied. "The same as taught you the bonedance game."

"I'll be damned."

"Business before pleasure, Lord. I've followed the black thread a long and horrid way to come calling."

"The threads didn't reach this far," I said, "without an awful lot of push. Maybe even not then. Do they now?"

"It's easier now," he replied.

"How so?"

"His Majesty Swayvill, King of Chaos, sleeps this night with the ancestors of darkness. I was sent to fetch you back for the ceremonies."

"Now?"

"Now."

"Yeah. Well, okay. Sure. Just let me get my stuff together. How'd it happen, anyhow?"

I pulled on my boots, donned the rest of my garments, buckled on my blade.

"I am not privy to any details. Of course, it is common knowledge that his health was poor."

"I want to leave a note," I said.

He nodded.

"A brief one, I trust."

"Yes."

I scrawled on a piece of parchment from the writing table, *Coral, Called away on family business. I'll be in touch,* and I laid it beside her hand.

"All right," I said. "How do we do this?"

"I will bear you upon my back, Prince Merlin, as I did long ago."

I nodded as a flood of childhood memories returned to me. Gryll was immensely strong, as are most demons. But I recalled our games, at Pit's-edge and out over the darkness, in burial chambers, caves, still-smoking battlefields, ruined temples, chambers of dead sorcerers, pri-

vate hells. I always seemed to have more fun playing
with demons than with my mother's relatives by blood
or marriage. I even based my main Chaos form upon
one of their kind.

He absorbed a chair from the room's corner for extra
mass, changing shape to accommodate my adult size. As
I climbed upon his elongated torso, catching a firm hold,
he exclaimed, "Ah, Merlin! What magics do you bear
these days?"

"I've their control, but not full knowledge of their
essence," I answered. "They're a very recent acquisi-
tion. What is it that you feel?"

"Heat, cold, strange music," he replied. "From all
directions. You have changed."

"Everyone changes," I said as he moved toward the
window. "That's life."

A dark thread lay upon the wide sill. He reached out
and touched it as he launched himself.

There came a great rushing of wind as we fell downward, moved forward, rose. Towers flashed past, wav-
ering. The stars were bright, a quarter moon just risen,
illuminating the bellies of a low line of clouds. We
soared, the castle and the town dwindling in an eyeblink.
The stars danced, became streaks of light. A band of
sheer, rippling blackness spread about us, widening. The
Black Road, I suddenly thought. It is like a temporary
version of the Black Road, in the sky. I glanced back.
It was not there. It was as if it were somehow reeling in
as we rode. Or was it reeling us in?

The countryside passed beneath us like a film played
at triple speed. Forest, hill, and mountain peak fled by.
Our black way was a great ribbon heaving before us,
patches of light and dark like daytime cloud shadows
sliding past. And then the tempo increased, staccato. I
noted of a sudden that there was no longer any wind.
Abruptly, the moon was high overhead, and a crooked

mountain range snaked beneath us. The stillness had a
dreamlike quality to it, and in an instant the moon had
fallen lower. A line of light cracked the world to my
right and stars began to go out. There was no feeling of
exertion in Gryll's body as we plunged along that black
way; and the moon vanished and light grew buttery yellow along a line of clouds, acquiring a pink cast even
as I watched.

"The power of Chaos rises," I remarked.

"The energy of disorder," he replied.

"There is more to this than you've told me," I said.

"I am but a servant," Gryll responded, "and not
privy to the councils of the mighty."

The world continued to brighten, and for as far ahead
as I could see our black ribbon rippled. We were passing
high over mountainous terrain. And clouds blew apart
and new ones formed at a rapid rate. We had obviously
begun our passage through Shadow. After a time, the
mountains wore down and rolling plains slid by. Suddenly the sun was in the middle of the sky. We seemed
to be passing just above our black way, Gryll's toes
barely grazing it as we moved. At times his wings hardly
fluttered before me, at other times they thrummed like
those of a hummingbird, into invisibility.

The sun grew cherry-red far to my left. A pink desert
spread beneath us. . . .

Then it was dark again and the stars turned like a great
wheel.

Then we were low, barely passing above the tops of
the trees. . . .

We burst into the air over a busy downtown street,
lights on poles and the fronts of vehicles, neon in windows. The warm, stuffy, dusty, gassy smell of city rose
up about us. A few pedestrians glanced upward, barely
seeming to note our passage.

Even as we flashed across a river, cresting the house-tops of suburbia, the prospect wavered and we passed over a primordial landscape of rock, lava, avalanche, and shuddering ground, two active volcanoes—one near, one far—spewing smoke against a blue-green sky.

"This, I take it, is a shortcut?" I said.

"It is the shortest cut," Gryll replied.

We entered a long night, and at some point it seemed that our way took us beneath deep waters, bright sea creatures hovering and darting both near at hand and in the middle distance. Dry and uncrushed, the black way protected us.

"It is as major an upheaval as the death of Oberon," Gryll volunteered. "Its effects are rippling across Shadow."

"But Oberon's death coincided with the re-creation of the Pattern," I said. "There was more to it than the death of a monarch of one of the extremes."

"True," Gryll replied, "but now is a time of imbalance among the forces. This adds to it. It will be even more severe."

We plunged into an opening in a dark mass of stone. Lines of light streaked past us. Irregularities were limned in a pale blue. Later—how long, I do not know—we were in a purple sky, with no transition that I can recall from the dark sea bottom. A single star gleamed far ahead. We sped toward it.

"Why?" I asked.

"Because the Pattern has grown stronger than the Logrus," he replied.

"How did that happen?"

"Prince Corwin drew a second Pattern at the time of the confrontation between the Courts and Amber."

"Yes, he told me about it. I've even seen it. He feared Oberon might not be able to repair the original."

"But he did, and so now there are two."

"Yes?"

"Your father's Pattern is also an artifact of order. It served to tip the ancient balance in the favor of Amber."

"How is it you are aware of this, Gryll, when no one back in Amber seems to know it or saw fit to tell me?"

"Your brother Prince Mandor and the Princess Fiona suspected this and sought evidence. They presented their findings to your uncle, Lord Suhuy. He made several journeys into Shadow and became persuaded that this is the case. He was preparing his findings for presentation to the king when Swayvill suffered his final illness. I know these things because it was Suhuy who sent me for you, and he charged me to tell them to you."

"I just assumed it was my mother who'd sent for me."

"Suhuy was certain she would—which is why he wanted to reach you first. What I have told you concerning your father's Pattern is not yet common knowledge."

"What am I supposed to do about it?"

"He did not entrust me with that information."

The star grew brighter. The sky was filled with splashes of orange and pink. Shortly, lines of green light joined them, and they swirled like streamers about us.

We raced on, and the configurations came to dominate the sky fully, like a psychedelic parasol rotating slowly. The landscape became a total blur. I felt as if a part of me dozed, though I am certain I did not lose consciousness. Time seemed to be playing games with my metabolism. I grew enormously hungry and my eyes ached.

The star brightened. Gryll's wings took on a prismatic shimmer. We seemed to be moving at an incredible pace now.

Our strand curved upward at its outer edges. The process continued as we advanced until it seemed we were moving in a trough. Then they met overhead, and it was as if we sped down a gun barrel, aimed at the blue-white star.

"Anything else you're supposed to tell me?"

"Not so far as I know."

I rubbed my left wrist, feeling as if something should have been pulsing there. Oh, yes. Frakir. Where was Frakir, anyway? Then I recalled leaving her behind in Brand's apartment. Why had I done that? I—my mind felt cloudy, the memory dreamlike.

This was the first time since the event that I had examined that memory. Had I looked earlier I would have known sooner what it meant. It was the clouding effect of glamor. I had walked into a spell back in Brand's apartment. I'd no way of knowing whether it had been specific to me or merely something I'd activated in poking about. It could, I supposed, even have been something more general, enlivened by the disaster—possibly even an unintentional side effect of something that had been disturbed. Somehow I doubted the latter, however.

For that matter, I doubted any generality about the business. It was just too *right* to have been a booby-trap Brand had left lying about. It had confounded a trained sorcerer, me. Perhaps it was only my present distancing from the vicinity of its occurrence that had helped to clear my mind. As I reviewed my actions from the time of exposure I could see that I had been moving in something of a haze since then. And the more I reviewed the more I felt the spell to have been specifically tailored to enfold me. Not understanding it, I could not consider myself free of it with this knowledge either.

Whatever it was, it had caused me to abandon Frakir without thinking twice about it, and it had caused me to feel—well—strange. I could not tell exactly how it might have influenced, might still be influencing, my thoughts and my feelings, the usual problem when one is caught up inside a spell. But I didn't see how it could possibly have been the late Brand himself who had set the thing up against such an unpredictable occurrence as my having rooms next to his old ones years after his death, from which I would be prompted to enter his quarters in the disastrous aftermath of an improbable confrontation between the Logrus and the Pattern in an upper hall of Amber Castle. No, it seemed that someone else had to be behind it. Jurt? Julia? It didn't seem too likely that they'd be able to operate undetected in the heart of Amber Castle. Who then? And could it have had anything to do with that episode in the Hall of Mirrors? I drew blanks. Were I back there now I might be able to come up with a spell of my own to ferret out the one responsible. But I wasn't, and any investigation at that end of things would have to wait.

The light ahead flashed more brightly now, winking from heavenly blue to baleful red.

"Gryll," I said. "Do you detect a spell upon me?"

"Aye, m'lord," he replied.

"Why didn't you mention it?"

"I thought it one of your own—for defense, perhaps."

"Can you lift it? I'm at a disadvantage, here on the inside."

" 'Tis too tangled in your person. I wouldn't know where to begin."

"Can you tell me anything about it?"

"Only that it's there, m'lord. Does seem rather heavy about the head, though."

"Could be coloring my thoughts a certain way, then?"

"Aye, a pale blue."

"I wasn't referring to your manner of perceiving it. Only to the possibility that it could be influencing my thinking."

His wings flashed blue, then red. Our tunnel expanded

suddenly and the sky grew bright with the crazy colors of Chaos. The star we followed now took on the proportions of a small light—magically enhanced, of course—within a high tower of a sepulchral castle, all gray and olive, atop a mountain the bottom and middle of which had been removed. The island of stone floated above a petrified forest. The trees burned with opal fires—orange, purple, green.

"I'd imagine it could be disentangled," Gryll observed. "But its unraveling be a bafflement to this poor demon."

I grunted. I watched the streaking scenery for a few moments. Then, "Speaking of demons . . ." I said.

"Yes?"

"What can you tell me about the sort known as a *ty'iga*?" I asked.

"They dwell far out beyond the Rim," he replied, "and may be the closest of all creatures to the primal Chaos. I do not believe they even possess true bodies of the material sort. They have little to do with other demons, let alone anyone else."

"Ever know any of them—uh—personally?"

"I have encountered a few—now and then," he replied.

We rose higher. The castle had been doing the same. A fall of meteors burned its way, brightly, silently, behind it.

"They can inhabit a human body, take it over."

"That doesn't surprise me."

"I know of one who has done this thing, several times. But an unusual problem has come up. It apparently took control of one on the human's deathbed. The passing of the human seemed to lock the *ty'iga* in place. It cannot vacate the body now. Do you know of any way it might escape?"

Gryll chuckled.

"Jump off a cliff, I suppose. Or fall on a sword."

"But what if it's tied to its host so closely now that this doesn't free it?"

He chuckled again.

"That's the breaks of the game, in the body-stealing business."

"I owe this one something," I said. "I'd like to help her—it."

He was silent for a time, then replied, "An older, wiser *ty'iga* might know something about these matters. And you know where they are."

"Yeah."

"Sorry I can't be more help. They're an old breed, *ty'iga*."

And now we bore down upon that tower. Our roadway under the shifting kaleidoscope that was the sky dwindled before us to but the tiniest of streaks. Gryll beat his way toward the light in the window and I peered past him.

I glanced downward. The prospect was dizzying. From some distant place a growling sound came up, as if portions of the earth itself were moving slowly against each other—a common enough occurrence in this vicinity. The winds beat at my garments. A strand of tangerine clouds beaded the sky to my left. I could make out detail work in the castle walls. I caught sight of a figure within the room of the light.

Then we were very near, and then through the window and inside. A large, stooped, gray and red demonic form, horned and half-scaled, regarded me with elliptically pupiled yellow eyes. Its fangs were bared in a smile.

"Uncle!" I cried as I dismounted. "Greetings!"

Gryll stretched and shook himself as Suhuy rushed forward and embraced me—carefully.

"Merlin," he said at last, "welcome home. I regret

the occasion but rejoice in your presence. Gryll has told you . . . ?''

''Of the passing of His Highness? Yes. I'm sorry.''

He released me and stepped back a pace.

''It is not as if it were unanticipated,'' he said. ''Just the opposite. Too much so, in fact. Yet there is no proper time for such an event.''

''True,'' I replied, massaging a certain stiffness out of my left shoulder and groping in my hip pocket after a comb.

''And he had been ailing for so long that I had grown used to it,'' I said. ''It was almost as if he'd come to terms with the weakness.''

Suhuy nodded. Then, ''Are you going to transform?'' he asked.

''It's been a rough day,'' I told him. ''I'd as soon save my energy, unless there's some demand of protocol.''

''None at all, just now,'' he replied. ''Have you eaten?''

''Not recently.''

''Come then,'' he said. ''Let's find you some nourishment.''

He turned and walked toward the far wall. I followed him. There were no doors in the room, and he had to know all the local Shadow stress points, the Courts being opposite to Amber in this regard. While it's awfully hard to pass through Shadow in Amber, the shadows are like frayed curtains in the Courts—often, you can look right through into another reality without even trying. And, sometimes, something in the other reality may be looking at you. Care must be taken, too, not to step through into a place where you will find yourself in the middle of the air, underwater, or in the path of a raging torrent. The Courts were never big on tourism.

Fortunately, the stuff of Shadow is so docile at this

end of reality that it can be easily manipulated by a shadowmaster—who can stitch together their fabrics to create a way. Shadowmasters are technicians of locally potent skill, whose ability derives from the Logrus, though they need not be initiates. Very few are, although all initiates are automatically members of the Shadow-master Guild. They're like plumbers or electricians about the Courts, and their skills vary as much as their counterparts on the Shadow Earth—a combination of aptitude and experience. While I'm a guild member I'd much rather follow someone who knows the ways than feel them out for myself. I suppose I should say more about this matter. Maybe I will sometime.

When we reached the wall, of course, it wasn't there. It just sort of grew misty and faded away; and we passed through the space where it had been—or, rather, a dif-ferent analogous space—and we were passing down a green stairway. Well, it wasn't exactly a stairway. It was a series of unconnected green discs, descending in spiral fashion, proper riser and tread distance apart, sort of floating there in the night air. They passed about the exterior of the castle, finally stopping before a blank wall. Before we reached that wall we passed through several moments of bright daylight, a brief flurry of blue snow, and the apse of something like a cathedral without an altar, skeletons occupying pews at either hand. When we finally came to the wall we passed through it, emerg-ing in a large kitchen. Suhuy led me to the larder and indicated I should help myself. I found some cold meat and bread and made myself a sandwich, washing it down with tepid beer. He nibbled at a piece of bread himself and sipped at a flagon of the same brew. A bird appeared overhead in full flight, cawing raucously, vanishing again before it had passed the entire length of the room.

"When are the services?" I asked.

"Redsky next, almost a whole turning off," he replied. "So you've a chance to sleep and collect yourself before then—perhaps."

"What do you mean, 'perhaps'?"

"As one of the three, you're under black watch. That's why I summoned you here, to one of my places of solitude." He turned and walked through the wall. I followed him, still bearing my flagon, and we seated ourselves beside a still, green pool beneath a rocky overhang, umber sky above. His castle contained places from all over Chaos and Shadow, stitched together into a crazy-quilt pattern of ways within ways. "And since you wear the spikard you've added resources for safety," he observed.

He reached out and touched the many-spoked wheel of my ring. A faint tingling followed in my finger, hand, and arm.

"Uncle, you were often given to cryptic utterances when you were my teacher," I said. "But I've graduated now, and I guess that gives me the right to say I don't know what the hell you're talking about."

He chuckled and sipped his beer.

"On reflection, it always became clear," he said.

"Reflection . . ." I said, and I looked into the pool.

Images swam amid the black ribbons beneath its surface—Swayvill lying in state, yellow and black robes muffling his shrunken form, my mother, my father, demonic forms, all passing and fading, Jurt, myself, Jasra and Julia, Random and Fiona, Mandor and Dworkin, Bill Roth and many faces I did not know . . . .

I shook my head.

"Reflection does not clarify," I said.

"It is not the function of an instant," he replied.

So I returned my attention to the chaos of faces and forms. Jurt returned and remained for a long time. He was dressing himself, in very good taste, and he appeared to be relatively intact. When he finally faded

there returned one of the half-familiar faces I had seen
earlier. I knew he was a noble of the Courts, and I
searched my memory. Of course. It had been a long
while, but now I recognized him. It was Tmer, of the
House of Jesby, eldest son of the late Prince Rolovians,
and now lord himself of the Ways of Jesby—spade
beard, heavy brow, sturdily built, not unhandsome, in a
rugged sort of way; by all report a brave and possibly
even sensitive fellow.

Then there was Prince Tubble of the Ways of Chanicut, phasing back and forth between human and swirling demonic forms. Placid, heavy, subtle; centuries old
and very shrewd; he wore a fringed beard, had wide,
innocent, pale eyes, was master of many games.

I waited, and Tmer followed Jurt followed Tubble into
vanishment amid the coiling ribbons. I waited longer,
and nothing new occurred.

"End of reflection," I announced at last. "But I still
don't know what it means."

"What did you see?"

"My brother Jurt," I replied, "and Prince Tmer of
Jesby. And Tubble of Chanicut, among other attrac-
tions."

"Most appropriate," he responded. "Entirely appropriate."

"And so?"

"Like you, Tmer and Tubble are both under black
watch. I understand Tmer is at Jesby, though I believe
Jurt has gone to earth somewhere other than Dalgarry."

"Jurt's come back?"

He nodded.

"He could be at my mother's Fortress Gantu," I
mused. "Or, Sawall did have a second stead—the Ways
of Anch, at the very Rim."

Suhuy shrugged.

"I do not know," he said.

"But why the black watch—for any of us?"

"You went off into Shadow to a fine university," he said, "and you have dwelled in the Court of Amber, which I would deem highly educational. Therefore, I bid you take thought. Surely, a mind so well honed—"

"I realize the black watch means we face some sort of danger. . . ."

"Of course."

". . . But its nature eludes me. Unless . . ."

"Yes."

"It has to do with Swayvill's death. So it must involve some sort of political settlement. But I've been away. I don't know what matters are hot just now."

He showed me row upon row of worn but still nasty fangs.

"Try the matter of the succession," he said.

"Okay. Say the Ways of Sawall are supporting one possible successor, Jesby the other, Chanicut the other. Say we're at each other's throats over the matter. Say I've come back into the middle of a vendetta. So whoever's giving the orders right now has declared us under watch as a matter of keeping things from getting messy. I appreciate it."

"Close," he said, "but it's already gone further than that."

I shook my head.

"I give up," I said.

From somewhere there came up a wailing sound.

"Think about it," he replied, "while I welcome a guest."

He rose and stepped into the pool, vanishing immediately.

I finished my beer.

II

It seemed but moments later that a rock to my left shimmered and emitted a bell-like tone. Without conscious intent my attention gathered itself at my ring, which Suhuy had referred to as a spikard. I realized in that instant that I was preparing to use it to defend myself. Interesting, how familiar I felt with it now, how adapted I seemed to have become to it in so short a time. I was on my feet, facing the stone, left hand extended in its direction when Suhuy stepped through the shining place, a taller, darker figure at his rear. A moment later and that figure followed him, emerging into substantiality and shifting from an octopal ape form to that of my brother Mandor, humanized, wearing black as when last I had seen him, though the garments were fresh and of a slightly different cut, his white hair less tousled. He quickly scanned the area about us and gave me a smile.

"I see that all is well," he stated.

I chuckled as I nodded toward his arm in its sling.

"As well as might be expected," I replied. "What happened in Amber after I left?"

"No fresh disasters," he answered. "I stayed only long enough to see whether there was anything I could do to be of assistance. This amounted to a little magical clearing of the vicinity and the summoning of a few planks to lay over holes. Then I begged leave of Random to depart, he granted it, and I came home."

"A disaster? At Amber?" Suhuy asked.

I nodded.

"There was a confrontation between the Unicorn and the Serpent in the halls of Amber Palace, resulting in considerable damage."

"What could have occasioned the Serpent's venturing that far into the realm of Order?"

"It involved what Amber refers to as the Jewel of Judgment, which the Serpent considers its missing eye."

"I must hear the entire tale."

I proceeded to tell him of the complicated encounter, leaving out my own later experiences in the Corridor of Mirrors and Brand's apartments. While I spoke, Mandor's gaze drifted to the spikard, to Suhuy, and back. When he saw that I noted this he smiled.

"So Dworkin is himself once more . . . ?" Suhuy said.

"I didn't know him before," I replied. "But he seemed to know what he was about."

". . . And the Queen of Kashfa sees with the Eye of the Serpent."

"I don't know that she sees with it," I said. "She's still recovering from the operation. But that's an interesting thought. If she could see with it, what might she behold?"

"The clear, cold lines of eternity, I daresay. Beneath all Shadow. No mortal could bear it for too long."

"She is of the blood of Amber," I said.

"Really? Oberon's?"

I nodded.

"Your late liege was a very active man," he observed. "Still, it would be quite a burden of seeing, though I speak only from guesswork—and a certain knowledge of principles. I've no idea what may come of this. Only Dworkin could say. Be he sane, there is a reason for it. I acknowledge his mastery, though I've never been able to anticipate him."

"You know him, personally?" I asked.

"I knew him," he said, "long ago, before his troubles. And I do not know whether to rejoice or despair in this. Recovered, he may be working for the greater good. Then again, his interests may be totally partisan."

"Sorry I can't enlighten you," I said. "I find his actions cryptic, too."

"I'm baffled also," Mandor said, "by the disposition of the Eye. But it still sounds pretty much a local matter, involving Amber's relations with Kashfa and Begma. I don't see that there is anything to be gained at this point by speculation. It's better keeping most of our attention for more pressing local matters."

I felt myself sigh.

"Such as the succession?" I suggested.

Mandor quirked an eyebrow.

"Oh, Lord Suhuy has briefed you already?"

"No," I replied. "No, but I heard so much from my father of the succession in Amber, with all its cabals, intrigues, and double crosses, that I almost feel an authority on the subject. I imagine it could be that way here, too, among the Houses of Swayvill's descendants, there being many more generations involved."

"You have the right idea," he said, "though I think the picture might be a bit more orderly here than it was there."

"That's something, anyway," I said. "For me, I intend to pay my respects and get the hell out. Send me a postcard telling me how it gets settled."

He laughed. He seldom laughs. I felt my wrist prickle where Frakir usually rides.

"He really doesn't know," he said, glancing at Suhuy.

"He's just arrived," Suhuy answered. "I hadn't the time to tell him anything."

I groped in my pocket, located a coin, withdrew it, and flipped it.

"Heads," I announced, on inspection. "You tell me, Mandor. What's going on?"

"You're not next in line for the throne," he said.

It being my turn to laugh, I did.

"I already knew that," I said. "You told me not that long ago, over dinner, how long the line was before me—if someone of my mixed blood could be considered at all."

"Two," he said. "Two stand before you."

"I don't understand," I said. "What happened to all the others?"

"Dead," he replied.

"Bad year for the flu?"

He gave me a nasty smile.

"There has been an unprecedented number of fatal duels and political assassinations recently."

"Which sort dominated the field?"

"The assassinations."

"Fascinating."

". . . And so you three are under black watch protection of the Crown, and were given into the care of your respective Houses' security."

"You're serious."

"Indeed."

"Was this sudden thinning of the ranks a matter of many people simultaneously seeking advancement? Or was it a smaller number, removing roadblocks?"

"The Crown is uncertain."

"When you say 'the Crown,' who, exactly, are you referring to, right now? Who's making decisions in the interim?"

"Lord Bances of Amblerash," he replied, "a distant relative and longtime friend of our late monarch."

"I sort of recall him. Could he have an eye on the throne himself, and be behind any of the—removals?"

"The man's a priest of the Serpent. Their vows bar them from reigning anywhere."

"There are usually ways around vows."

"True, but the man seems genuinely uninterested in such a thing."

"That needn't preclude his having a favorite, and maybe helping him along a bit. Is anybody near the throne particularly fond of his Order?"

"To my knowledge, no."

"Which doesn't mean someone mightn't have cut a deal."

"No, though Bances isn't the sort of man one would approach easily with a proposition."

"In other words, you believe he's above whatever's going on?"

"In the absence of evidence to the contrary."

"Who is next in line?"

"Tubble of Chanicut."

"Who's second?"

"Tmer of Jesby."

"Top of the line, your pool," I said to Suhuy.

He showed me his teeth again. They seemed to rotate.

"Are we at vendetta with either Chanicut or Jesby?" I asked.

"Not really."

"We're all just taking care then, huh?"

"Yes."

"How did it all come to this? I mean, there were a

lot of people involved, as I recall. Was it a night of the long knives, or what?''

''No, the deaths have been occurring steadily for some time. There wasn't a sudden bloodbath when Swayvill took his turn for the worse—though a few did occur just recently.''

''Well, there must have been some investigation. Do we have any of the perps in custody?''

''No, they either escaped or were killed.''

''What of those who were killed? Their identities might indicate their political affiliations.''

''Not really. Several were professionals. A couple of others were general malcontents, arguably among the mentally ill.''

''You're saying there are no clues as to who might be behind it all?''

''That's right.''

''What about suspicions then?''

''Tubble himself is of course suspect, though it is not a good idea to say it aloud. He stood to benefit the most, and now he's in a position to do so. Also, there is much in his career of political connivance, double-dealing, assassination. But that was long ago. Everyone has a few skeletons in the cellar. He has been a quiet and conservative man for many years.''

''Tmer, then—He's close enough to generate suspicion. Is there anything to connect him with the bloody business?''

''Not really. His affairs are hardly open. He's a very private man. But he was never associated with such extremes in the past. I do not know him all that well, but he has always struck me as a simpler, more direct person than Tubble. He seems the sort who'd simply attempt a coup if he wanted the throne badly enough, rather than spend a lot of time intriguing.''

''There could, of course, be a number of people involved, each acting in his own interest—''

''And now that the matter is imminent they'll have to surface soon?''

''It would seem so, wouldn't it?''

A smile. A shrug.

''No reason for a coronation to end it all,'' he said. ''A crown does not automatically make a person dagger-proof.''

''But the successor would come to power with a lot of bad baggage.''

''It wouldn't be the first time in history. And if you stop to think about it, some very good monarchs have come to power under such a cloud. By the way, has it occurred to you that the others might be speculating along these lines about you?''

''Yes, and it makes me uncomfortable. My father wanted the throne of Amber for a long time, and it really messed up his life. He was only happy when he said the hell with it. If I learned anything from his story, that's it. I have no such ambition.''

But for a moment, I wondered. What would it feel like to control a massive state? Every time I complained about politics, here, in Amber, back in the States on the Shadow Earth, there was the automatic corollary of considering the way I'd manage situations if I were in charge.

''I wonder?'' Mandor repeated.

I glanced downward.

''Perhaps the others are looking into their own scrying pools just now,'' I said, ''hoping for clues.''

''Doubtless,'' he responded. ''What if Tubble and Tmer did meet untimely ends? What would you do?''

''Don't even think about it,'' I said. ''It won't happen.''

''Suppose.''

''I don't know.''

"You really should make some sort of decision, just to have it out of the way. You're never at a loss for words when you know your own mind."

"Thanks. I'll remember that."

"Tell me more of your story, since last we met."

And so I did, Pattern ghosts and all.

Somewhere near the end the wailing sound began again. Suhuy moved toward the rock.

"Excuse me," he said, and the rock parted and he passed within.

Immediately, I felt Mandor's gaze heavy upon me.

"We probably only have a moment," he said. "Not enough time, really, to go into everything I wanted to cover with you."

"Very private, huh?"

"Yes. So you must arrange to dine with me before the funeral. Say, a quarter-turning hence, bluesky."

"All right. Your place, or the Ways of Sawall?"

"Come to me at Mandorways."

The rock phased again as I nodded, and a lithe demonic figure entered, shimmering bluely within a veil of cloud. I was on my feet in an instant, then bowing to kiss the hand she extended.

"Mother," I said. "I hadn't anticipated the pleasure—this soon."

She smiled, and then it went away in a swirl. The scales faded, the contours of her face and form flowed. The blue went away into a normal though pale flesh color. Her hips and shoulders widened as she lost something of height, though still remained tall. Her brown eyes grew more attractive as the heavy brow ridges receded. A few freckles became visible across her now-human, slightly upturned nose. Her brown hair was longer than when last I had seen her in this form. And she was still smiling. Her red tunic became her, simply belted; a rapier hung at her left hip.

"My dear Merlin," she said, taking my head between her hands and kissing me upon the lips. "I am pleased to see you looking so well. It has been quite a while since last you visited."

"I've had a very active existence of late."

"To be sure," she said. "I've heard some report of your various misadventures."

"I'd imagine you would have. It's not everyone has a *ty'iga* following him about, periodically seducing him in various forms, and making life, in general, very complicated with unwanted efforts at protection."

"It shows that I care, dear."

"It also shows that you have no respect for my privacy nor trust in my judgment."

Mandor cleared his throat.

"Hello, Dara," he said then.

"I suppose it must seem that way to you," she stated. Then, "Hello, Mandor," she went on. "What happened to your arm?"

"A misunderstanding involving some architecture," he replied. "You've been out of sight, though hardly out of mind, for some time."

"Thank you, if that's a compliment," she said. "Yes, I go a bit reclusive every now and then, when the weight of society becomes troublesome. Though you're hardly the one to talk, sir, vanishing for long stretches as you do in the labyrinths of Mandorways—if that be indeed where you take yourself."

He bowed.

"As you say, lady, we appear to be creatures of a kind."

Her eyes narrowed, though her voice was unchanged, as she said, "I wonder. Yes, I can sometimes see us as kindred spirits, perhaps even more than in our simplest cycles of activity. We've both been out and about a lot of late, though, haven't we?"

"But I've been careless," said Mandor, indicating his injured arm. "You, obviously, have not."

"I never argue with architecture," she said.

"Or other imponderables?" he asked.

"I try to work with what is in place," she told him.

"Generally, I do, too."

"And if you cannot?" she asked.

He shrugged.

"Sometimes there are collisions."

"You've survived many in your time, haven't you?"

"I can't deny it, but then it has been a long while. You seem made of very survivable stuff yourself."

"So far," she responded. "We really must compare notes on imponderables and collisions one day. Wouldn't it be strange if we were similar in all respects?"

"I should be very much surprised," he answered.

I was fascinated and slightly frightened by the exchange, though I could go only by feeling and had no notion of specifics. They were somehow similar, and I'd never heard generalities delivered with quite that precision and emphasis outside of Amber, where they often make a game of talking that way.

"Forgive me," Mandor said then, to the company in general, "but I must absent myself to recuperation. Thank you for your hospitality, sir." He bowed to Suhuy. "And for the pleasure of crossing—paths with you"—this to Dara.

"You've barely arrived," Suhuy said, "and you've taken no refreshment. You make me a poor host."

"Rest assured, old friend, there is none could perform such a transformation," he stated. He looked at me as he backed toward the opening way. "Till later," he said, and I nodded.

He passed into the way, and the rock solidified with his vanishment.

"One wonders at his deliveries," my mother said, "without apparent rehearsal."

"Grace," Suhuy commented. "He was born with an abundance."

"I wonder who will die today?" she said.

"I am not certain the implication is warranted," Suhuy replied.

She laughed.

"And if it is," she said, "they will certainly expire in good taste."

"Do you speak in condemnation or envy?" he asked.

"Neither," she said. "For I, too, am an admirer of grace—and a good jest."

"Mother," I said, "just what's going on?"

"Whatever do you mean, Merlin?" she replied.

"I left this place a long time ago. You sent a demon to find me and take care of me. Presumably, it could detect someone of the blood of Amber. So there was some confusion between myself and Luke. So it settled by taking care of both of us—until Luke began his periodic attempts to kill me. Then it protected me from Luke and tried to determine which of us was the proper party. It even lived with Luke for a time, and later pursued me. I should have guessed at something of this because it was so eager to learn my mother's name. Apparently, Luke was just as closemouthed about his parentage."

She laughed.

"It makes a beautiful picture," she began. "Little Jasra and the Prince of Darkness—"

"Don't try to change the subject. Think how embarrassing that is for a grown man—his mother sending demons to look after him."

"The singular. It was just one demon, dear."

"Who cares? The principle's the same. Where do you get off with this protective business? I resent—"

"The *ty'iga* probably saved your life on more than one occasion, Merlin."

"Well, yes. But—"

"You'd rather be dead than protected? Just because it was coming from me?"

"That's not the point!"

"Then what is the point?"

"It seems you just assumed I couldn't take care of myself, and—"

"Well, you couldn't."

"But you had no way of knowing that. I resented your starting with the assumption that I needed chaperoning in Shadow, that I was naive, gullible, careless—"

"I suppose it would hurt your feelings if I said that you were, going to a place as different from the Courts as that Shadow is."

"Yes, I can take care of myself!"

"You weren't doing that great a job of it. But you are making a number of unwarranted assumptions yourself. What makes you think that the reasons you gave are the only possible ones for my taking such an action?"

"Okay. Tell me that you knew that Luke was going to try to kill me every April thirtieth. And if the answer is yes, why didn't you just tell me?"

"I did not know that Luke was going to try to kill you every April thirtieth."

I turned away. I clenched my fists and relaxed them.

"So you just did it for the hell of it?"

"Merlin, why do you find it so difficult to admit that other people might sometimes know things you don't?"

"Start with their unwillingness to tell me these things."

She was silent a long moment. Then, "I'm afraid there is something to what you say," she replied. "But there were strong reasons for not talking of such matters."

"Then start with the inability to tell me. Tell me now why you didn't trust me then."

"It wasn't a matter of trust."

"Is it okay to tell me now what it was?"

Another, longer silence followed.

"No," she finally said. "Not yet."

I turned toward her, keeping my features composed and my voice level.

"Then nothing has changed," I said, "nor ever shall. You still do not trust me."

"That is not true," she answered, glancing at Suhuy. "It is just that this is not the proper time or the proper place to go into these matters."

"Might I fetch you a drink or something to eat, Dara?" Suhuy said immediately.

"Thank you no," she replied. "I cannot stay much longer."

"Mother, tell me, then, something about the *ty'iga*."

"What do you wish to know?"

"You conjured it from someplace beyond the Rim."

"That is correct."

"Such beings are bodiless themselves, but capable of taking over a living host for their own purposes."

"Yes."

"Supposing such a being took over the body of a person at or near the moment of death, making it the sole animating spirit and controlling intelligence?"

"Interesting. Is this a hypothetical question?"

"No. It's really happened with the one you sent after me. It doesn't seem able to quit that body now. Why not?"

"I am not really certain," she said.

"It is trapped now," Suhuy offered. "It can only come and go by reacting with a resident intelligence."

"The body, with the *ty'iga* in control, recovered from the illness that killed its consciousness," I said. "You mean it's stuck there now for life?"

"Yes. So far as I know."

"Then tell me this: Will it be released when that body dies, or will it die with it?"

"It could go either way," he replied. "But the longer it remains in the body, the more likely it is that it will perish along with it."

I looked back at my mother.

"There you have the end of its story," I stated.

She shrugged.

"I've done with this one and released it," she said, "and one can always conjure another should the need arise."

"Don't do it," I told her.

"I shan't," she said. "There is no need to, now."

"But if you thought there were, you would?"

"A mother tends to value her son's safety, whether the son likes it or not."

I raised my left hand, extending the forefinger in an angry gesture, when I noticed that I was wearing a bright bracelet—it seemed an almost-hologramatic representation of a woven cord. I lowered my hand, bit back my first response, and said, "You know my feelings now."

"I knew them a long time ago," she said. "Let us dine at the Ways of Sawall, half a turning hence, purplesky. Agreed?"

"Agreed," I said.

"Till then. Good turning, Suhuy."

"Good turning, Dara."

She took three paces and was gone, as etiquette prescribed, out the same way by which she had entered.

I turned and strode to the pool's edge, stared into its depths, felt the muscles in my shoulders slowly unknot. Jasra and Julia were down there now, back in the citadel of the Keep, doing something arcane in the lab. And then the strands were flowing over them, some cruel truth beyond all order and beauty, beginning to form themselves into a mask of fascinating, frightening proportion.

I felt a hand on my shoulder.

"Family," Suhuy said, "intrigues and maddens. You are feeling the tyranny of affection at the moment, are you not?"

I nodded.

"Something Mark Twain said about being able to choose your friends but not your relatives," I answered.

"I do not know what they are up to, though I have my suspicions," he said. "There is nothing to do now but rest and wait. I would like to hear more of your story."

"Thanks, Uncle. Yeah," I said. "Why not?"

So I gave him all the rest of my tale. Partway through it, we adjourned to the kitchen for further sustenance, then took another way to a floating balcony above a lime-colored ocean breaking upon pink rocks and beaches under a twilit or otherwise indigo sky without stars. There, I finished my telling.

"This is more than a little interesting," he said, at last.

"Oh? Do you see something in it all that I don't?" I asked.

"You've given me too much to consider for me to give you a hasty judgment," he said. "Let us leave it at that for now."

"Very well."

I leaned on the rail, looked down at the waters.

"You need rest," he said after a time.

"I guess I do."

"Come, I'll show you to your room."

He extended a hand and I took hold of it. Together, we sank through the floor.

And so I slept, surrounded by tapestries and heavy drapes, in a doorless chamber in the Ways of Suhuy. It might have been in a tower, as I could hear the winds passing beyond the walls. Sleeping, I dreamt. . . .

I was back in the castle Amber, walking the sparkling length of the Corridor of Mirrors. Tapers flickered in tall holders. My footsteps made no sound. The mirrors came in all manner of shapes. They covered the walls at either hand, big ones, little ones. I passed myself within their depths, reflected, distorted, sometimes re-reflected. . . .

I was halted before a tall, cracked mirror to my left, framed in tin. Even as I turned toward it I knew that it would not be me whom I regarded this time.

Nor was I mistaken. Coral was looking at me from out of the mirror. She had on a peach-colored blouse and was not wearing her eyepatch. The crack in the mirror divided her face down the middle. Her left eye was the green I remembered, her right was the Jewel of Judgment. Both seemed to be focused upon me.

"Merlin," she said. "Help me. This is too strange. Give me back my eye."

"I don't know how," I said. "I don't understand what was done."

"My eye," she went on, as if she had not heard. "The world is all swarming forces in the Eye of Judgment, cold—so cold!—and not a friendly place. Help me!"

"I'll find a way," I said.

"My eye . . ." she continued.

I hurried by.

From a rectangular mirror in a wooden frame carved at its base in the form of a phoenix, Luke regarded me.

"Hey, old buddy," he said, looking slightly forlorn, "I'd sure like to have my dad's sword back. You haven't come across it again, have you?''

'' 'Fraid not,'' I muttered.

''It's a shame to get to hold your present for such a short period of time. Watch for it, will you? I've a feeling it might come in handy.''

''I'll do that,'' I said.

''After all, you're kind of responsible for what happened,'' he continued.

''Right,'' I agreed.

''. . . And I'd sure like to have it back.''

''Yeah,'' I said, moving away.

A nasty chuckle emerged from a maroon-framed ellipse to my right. Turning, I beheld the face of Victor Melman, the shadow Earth sorcerer I had confronted back when my troubles were beginning.

''Son of perdition!'' he hissed. '' 'Tis good to see you wander lost in Limbo. May my blood lie burning on your hands.''

''Your blood is on your own hands,'' I said. ''I count you as a suicide.''

''Not so!'' he snapped back. ''You slew me most unfairly.''

''Bullshit,'' I answered. ''I may be guilty of a lot of things, but your death is not one of them.''

I began to walk away, and his hand emerged from the mirror and clutched at my shoulder.

''Murderer!'' he cried.

I brushed his hand away.

''Bugger off!'' I said, and I kept going.

Then, from a wide, green-framed mirror with a greenish haze to the glass, Random hailed me from my left, shaking his head.

''Merlin! Merlin! What are you up to, anyway?'' he asked. ''I've known for some time that you haven't been keeping me abreast of everything that's afoot.''

''Well,'' I replied, regarding him in an orange T-shirt

and Levi's, "that's true, sir. Some things I just haven't had time to go into."

"Things that involve the safety of the realm—and you haven't had time?"

"Well, I guess there's something of a judgmental factor involved."

"If it involves our safety, I am the one to do the judging."

"Yes, sir. I realize that—"

"We have to have a talk, Merlin. Is it that your personal life is mixed with this in some way?"

"I guess that's true—"

"It doesn't matter. The kingdom is more important. We must talk."

"Yes, sir. We will as soon as—"

"'As soon as,' hell! Now! Stop screwing around at whatever you're up to and get your ass back here! We have to talk!"

"I will, as soon as—"

"Don't give me that! It verges on the traitorous if you're withholding important information! I need to see you now! Come home!"

"I will," I said, and I hurried away, his voice joining a continuing chorus of the others, repeating their demands, their pleas, their accusations.

Out of the next one—circular, with a blue braided frame—Julia regarded me.

"And there you go," she said, almost wistfully. "You knew I loved you."

"I loved you, too," I admitted. "It took me a long time to realize it. I guess I messed up, though."

"You didn't love me enough," she said. "Not enough to trust me. And so you lost my trust."

I looked away.

"I'm sorry," I said.

"Not good enough," she responded. "Thus, we are become enemies."

"It doesn't have to be that way."

"Too late," she said. "Too late."

"I'm sorry," I repeated, and I hurried away.

Thus, I came to Jasra, in a red, diamond frame. Her bright-nailed hand reached out and caressed my cheek.

"Going somewhere, dear boy?" she asked.

"I hope so," I said.

She smiled crookedly and pursed her lips.

"I've decided you were a bad influence on my son," she said. "He lost his edge when he became friends with you."

"Sorry about that," I said.

". . . Which may make him unfit to rule."

"Unfit or unwilling?" I asked.

"Whichever, it will be your fault."

"He's a big boy now, Jasra. He makes his own decisions."

"I fear you've taught him to make the wrong ones."

"He's his own man, lady. Don't blame me if he does things you don't like."

"And if Kashfa crumbles because you've softened him?"

"I decline the nomination," I said, taking a step forward. It was good that I was moving, for her hand shot out, nails raking at my face, barely missing. She threw expletives after me as I walked away. Fortunately, they were drowned amid the cries of the others.

"Merlin?"

Turning to my right again I beheld the face of Nayda within a silver mirror, its surface and curled frame of a single piece.

"Nayda! What are *you* down on me for?"

"Nothing," the *ty'iga* lady replied. "I'm just passing through, and I need directions."

"You don't hate me? How refreshing!"

"Hate you? Don't be silly. I could never do that."

"Everyone else in this gallery seems irritated with me."

"It's only a dream, Merlin. You're real, I'm real, and I don't know about the others."

"I'm sorry my mother put you under that spell to protect me—all those years ago. Are you really free of it now? If you're not, perhaps I can—"

"I'm free of it."

"I'm sorry you had so much trouble fulfilling its terms—not knowing whether it was Luke or me you were supposed to be guarding. Who'd have known there'd be two Amberites in the same neighborhood in Berkeley?"

"I'm not sorry."

"What do you mean?"

"I came for directions. I want to know how I can find Luke."

"Why, in Kashfa. He was just crowned king the other day. What do you need him for?"

"Hadn't you guessed?"

"No."

"I'm in love with him. Always was. Now that I'm free of the *geas* and have a body of my own, I want him to know that I was Gail—and how I feel. Thanks, Merlin. Good-bye."

"Wait!"

"Yes?"

"I never said thanks for your protecting me all those years—even if it was only a compulsion for you, even if it got to be a big bother for me. Thanks, and good luck."

She smiled and faded away. I reached out and touched the mirror.

"Luck," I thought I heard her say.

Strange. It was a dream. Still—I couldn't awaken, and it felt real. I—

"You made it back to the Courts in time for all the scheming, I see"—this from a mirror three paces ahead, black-bound and narrow.

I moved to it. My brother Jurt glared out at me.

"What do you want?" I asked.

His face was an angry parody of my own.

"I want you never to have been," he said. "Failing that, I'd like to see you dead."

"What's your third choice?" I asked.

"Your confinement to a private hell, I guess."

"Why?"

"You stand between me and everything I want."

"I'll be glad to step aside. Tell me how."

"There's no way you can or will, on your own."

"So you hate me?"

"Yes."

"I thought your bath in the Fountain destroyed your emotions."

"I didn't get the full treatment, and it only made them stronger."

"Any way we can forget the whole thing and start over again, be friends?"

"Never."

"Didn't think so."

"She always cared more about you than me, and now you're going to have the throne."

"Don't be ridiculous. I don't want it."

"Your desires have nothing to do with the matter."

"I won't have it."

"Yes, you will—unless I kill you first."

"Don't be stupid. It's not worth this."

"One day soon, when you least expect it, you will turn and see me. It will be too late."

The mirror grew entirely black.

"Jurt!"

Nothing. Aggravating, having to put up with him in dream as well as waking.

I turned my head toward a fire-framed mirror several paces ahead and to my left, knowing—somehow—it was next on my route. I moved toward it.

She was smiling.

"And there you have it," she said.

"Aunty, what's going on?"

"It seems to be the sort of conflict generally referred to as 'irreducible,'" Fiona replied.

"That's not the sort of answer I need."

"Too much is afoot to give you a better one."

"And you're a part of it?"

"A very small one. Not one who can do you much good just now."

"What am I to do?"

"Learn your options and choose the best one."

"Best for whom? Best for what?"

"Only you can say."

"Can you give me a hint?"

"Could you have walked Corwin's Pattern that day I took you to it?"

"Yes."

"I thought so. It was drawn under unusual circumstances. It can never be duplicated. Our Pattern would never have permitted its construction had it not been damaged itself and too weak to prevent its coming into being."

"So?"

"Our Pattern is trying to absorb it, incorporate it. If it succeeds, it will be as disastrous as it would have been were the Pattern of Amber destroyed at the time of the war. The balance with Chaos will be totally upset."

"Isn't Chaos strong enough to prevent this? I'd thought they were equally potent."

"They were until you repaired the Shadow Pattern and Amber's was able to absorb it. This increased its strength beyond that of Chaos. Now it is able to reach for your father's against the power of the Logrus."

"I don't understand what is to be done."

"Neither do I, yet. But I charge you to remember what I have said. When the time comes you must make a decision. I've no idea what it will involve, but it will be very important."

"She's right," came a voice from behind my back.

Turning, I saw my father within a shining black frame, a silver rose set at its top.

"Corwin!" I heard Fiona say. "Where are you?"

"In a place where there is no light," he said.

"I thought you somehow in Amber, Father, with Deirdre," I said.

"The ghosts play at being ghosts," he answered. "I have not much time, for my strength is low. I can tell you only this: Trust not the Pattern, nor the Logrus either, nor any of their spawn, till this matter be settled."

He began to fade.

"How can I help you?" I asked.

The words ". . . in the Courts" came to me before he vanished.

I turned again.

"Fi, what did he mean by that?" I asked her.

She was frowning.

"I get the impression that the answer lies somewhere in the Courts," she replied slowly.

"Where? Where should I look?"

She shook her head and began to turn away.

"Who would know best?" she said.

Then she, too, was gone.

Voices were still calling to me, from behind, from ahead. There was weeping and laughter, and my name being repeated. I rushed ahead.

"Whatever happens," Bill Roth said, "if you need a good lawyer, I'll handle it—even in Chaos."

And then there was Dworkin, squinting at me from out of a tiny mirror with a twisted frame.

"Nothing to be alarmed about," he remarked, "but all sorts of imponderables are hovering about you."

"What am I to do?" I cried.

"You must become something greater than yourself."

"I don't understand."

"Escape the cage that is your life."

"What cage?"

He was gone.

I ran, and their words rang around me.

Near the end of the hall was a mirror like a piece of yellow silk stretched upon a frame. The Cheshire Cat grinned at me from within.

"It's not worth it. The hell with them all," he said. "Come to the cabaret, old chum. We'll tip a few brews and watch the man paint."

"No!" I cried. "No!"

And then there was only a grin. This time I faded, too. Merciful, black oblivion and the sound of the wind, somewhere, passing.

III

How long I slept, I do not know. I was awakened by Suhuy's repeating my name.

"Merlin, Merlin," he said. "The sky is white."

"And I've a busy day," I answered. "I know. I'd a busy night, too."

"It reached you, then."

"What?"

"A small spell I sent, to open your mind to some enlightenment. I hoped to lead you to answers from within, rather than burden you with my guesswork and suspicions."

"I was back in the Corridor of Mirrors."

"I knew not what form it might take."

"Was it real?"

"As such things go, it should have been."

"Well, thanks—I guess. It reminds me that Gryll said something about your wanting to see me before my mother did."

"I wanted to see how much you knew before you faced her. I wanted to protect your freedom of choice."

44

"What are you saying?"

"I'm sure she wants to see you on the throne."

I sat up and rubbed my eyes.

"I suppose that's possible," I said.

"I don't know how far she's willing to go to effect this. I wanted to give you a chance to know your own mind before you're exposed to her plans. Would you care for a cup of tea?"

"Yes, thanks."

I accepted a mug he proffered and raised it to my lips.

"What are you saying about her beyond a guess at her wishes?" I asked.

He shook his head.

"I don't know how active her program might be," he said, "if that is what you mean. And whether she was connected with it or another, the spell you came wearing has faded now."

"Your doing?"

He nodded.

I took another swallow.

"I never realized how close I'd gotten to the head of the line," I added. "Jurt *is* number four or five in the succession, isn't he?"

He nodded.

"I've a feeling it's going to be a very busy day," I said.

"Finish your tea," he told me, "and follow me when you would."

He walked away through a dragon tapestry on the far wall.

As I raised the mug again, the bright bracelet on my left wrist came free and drifted before me, losing its braided outline, becoming a circle of pure light. It hovered above the steaming brew, as if enjoying its cinnamony aroma.

"Hi, Ghost," I said. "Why'd you weave yourself about my wrist that way?"

"To look like that piece of rope you usually wear," came the reply. "I thought you must be fond of the effect."

"I mean, what were you up to the whole time?"

"Just listening, Dad. Seeing how I might be of help. These people are all your relatives, too?"

"The ones we've met so far, yes."

"Is it necessary to go back to Amber to speak ill of them?"

"No, it works here in the Courts, too." I took another sip of tea. "Any special ill you have in mind? Or was that a general question?"

"I don't trust your mother or your brother Mandor, even if they are my grandmother and uncle. I think they're setting you up for something."

"Mandor's always been good to me."

". . . And your uncle Suhuy—he seems eminently stable, but he reminds me a lot of Dworkin. Might he be sitting on all sorts of internal turmoils and ready to flip out anytime?"

"I hope not," I said. "He never has."

"Oh-oh, it's been building, and this is a time of stress."

"Where are you getting all this pop psychology, anyway?"

"I've been studying the great psychologists of the Shadow Earth. It's part of my ongoing attempt to understand the human condition. I realized it was time I learned more about the irrational parts."

"What brought all this on?"

"The higher order edition of the Pattern I encountered in the Jewel, actually. There were aspects of it I simply could not understand. This led to considerations of chaos theory, then to Menninger and all the others for its manifestations in consciousness.''

"Any conclusions?''

"I am wiser therefor.''

"I mean, concerning the Pattern.''

"Yes. Either it possesses an element of irrationality itself, like living things, or it is an intelligence of such an order that some of its processes only seem irrational to lesser beings. Either explanation amounts to the same thing from a practical standpoint.''

"I never had the opportunity to apply some of the tests I'd designed, but can you say from self-knowledge whether you fall into such a category yourself?''

"Me? Irrational? The notion never occurred to me. I can't see how it could be.''

I finished my tea and swung my legs over the side of the bed.

"Too bad,'' I said. "I think some measure of it is what makes us truly human—that, and recognizing it in ourselves, of course.''

"Really?''

I rose and began dressing myself.

"Yes, and controlling it within oneself may have something to do with intelligence and creativity.''

"I'm going to have to study this very closely.''

"Do that,'' I said, pulling on my boots, "and let me know your findings.''

As I continued dressing, he asked, "When the sky turns blue you will breakfast with your brother Mandor?''

"Yes,'' I said.

"And later you will take lunch with your mother?''

"That's right.''

"Later still, you will attend the late monarch's funeral?''

"I will.''

"Will you need me to protect you?''

"I'll be safe with my relatives, Ghost. Even if you don't trust them."

"The last funeral you attended got bombed."

"That's true. But it was Luke, and he's sworn off. I'll be okay. You want to sightsee, go ahead."

"All right," he said. "I do."

I rose and crossed the chamber, to stand before the dragon.

"Can you tell me the way to the Logrus?" Ghost asked.

"Are you joking?"

"No," he stated. "I've seen the Pattern, but I've never seen the place of the Logrus. Where do they keep it?"

"I thought I gave you better memory functions than that. In your last encounter with the thing, you pissed it off in the max."

"I suppose I did. Do you think it would hold a grudge?"

"Offhand, yes. Upon consideration, yes. Stay away from it."

"You just advised me to study the chaos factor, the irrational."

"I didn't advise you to commit suicide. I put a lot of work into you."

"I value myself, too. And you know I have a survival imperative, the same as organic beings."

"It's your judgment I wonder about."

"You know a lot about my abilities."

"It's true you're good at getting the hell out of places."

"And you owe me a decent education."

"Let me think about it."

"That's just stalling. I suppose I can find it myself."

"Fine. Go ahead."

"It's that hard to locate?"

"You gave up on omniscience, remember?"

"Dad, I think I need to see it."

"I haven't the time to take you there."

"Just show me the way. I'm good at concealing my-self."

"I'll give you that. All right. Suhuy is Keeper of the Logrus. It lies in a cavern—somewhere. The only way I know to it begins in this place."

"Where?"

"There are something like nine turnings involved. I'll lay a seeing upon you, to lead you."

"I don't know whether your spells would work on something like me—"

I reached out through the ring—pardon me, spikard—superimposed a series of black asterisks upon a map of the ways he must follow, hung it in the space of my Logrus vision before him, and I said, "I designed you, and I designed this spell."

"Uh, yes," Ghost replied. "I feel as if I suddenly possess data that I can't access."

"It will be presented to you at the appropriate times. Form yourself into the likeness of a ring upon my left index finger. We will quit this room in a moment and pass through others. When we are near the proper way I will indicate it by pointing. Proceed in that direction and you will pass through something along your route which will conduct you into another place. Somewhere in that vicinity you will find a black star indicating the next direction you must take—to another place and an-other star and so on. Eventually, you will emerge in a cavern that houses the Logrus. Conceal yourself as com-pletely as you can and make your observations. When you wish to retreat, reverse the process."

He shrank himself and flew to my finger.

"Look me up later and let me know your experi-ences."

"I was planning to," came his tiny voice. "I would not wish to add to your probable present paranoia."

"Keep it up," I said.

I crossed the room and entered the dragon.

I emerged in a small sitting room, one window looking out over mountains; the other, a desert. There was no one about, and I stepped out into a long hallway. Yes, just as I recalled.

I moved along it, passing a number of other rooms, till I came to a door on my left, which I opened to discover a collection of mops, brooms, buckets, brushes, a heap of cleaning cloths, a basin. Yes, as I remembered. I pointed to the shelves on my right.

"Find the black star," I said.

"You're serious?" came the small voice.

"Go and see."

A streak of light proceeded from my index finger, grew distorted as it neared the shelves, folded itself into a line so thin it was no longer present.

"Good luck," I breathed, and then I turned away.

I closed the door, wondering whether I had done the right thing, consoling myself with the thought that he would have gone looking and doubtless located the Logrus eventually, anyway. Whatever was to be on this front, would be. And I was curious as to what he might learn.

I turned and took myself back up the hallway to the little sitting room. It might be my last opportunity at being alone for a time, and I was determined to take advantage of it. I seated myself on a pile of cushions and withdrew my Trumps. A quick run through the deck turned up the one I had hastily sketched of Coral on that recent hectic day back in Amber. I studied her features till the card grew cold.

The image became three-dimensional, and then she

slipped away and I saw myself, walking the streets of Amber on a bright afternoon, holding her hand as I led her around a knot of merchants. Then we were descending the face of Kolvir, sea bright before us, gulls passing. Then back in the cafe, table flying against the wall. . . .

I covered the card with my hand. She was asleep, dreaming. Odd, to enter another's dreams that way. Odder, to find myself there—unless, of course, the touch of my mind had prompted unconscious reminiscence. . . . One of life's smaller puzzles. No need to awaken the poor lady, just to ask her how she was feeling. I supposed I could call Luke and ask him how she was doing. I began searching for his card, then hesitated. He must be pretty busy, his first few days on the job as monarch. And I already knew she was resting. As I toyed with Luke's card, though, finally pushing it aside, the one beneath it was revealed.

Gray and silver and black. . . . His face was an older, somewhat harder version of my own. Corwin, my father, looked back at me. How many times had I sweated over that card, trying to reach him, till my mind tied itself into aching knots, with no result? The others had told me that it could mean he was dead, or that he was blocking the contact. And then a funny feeling came over me. I recalled his own story, in particular when he'd spoken of the times they had tried to reach Brand through his Trump, being at first unable to because he had been imprisoned in such a distant shadow. Then I remembered his own attempts to reach through to the Courts, and the difficulty imposed by the great distance. Supposing that, rather than being dead or blocking me, he was greatly removed from the places I had been when I had made the efforts?

But then, who was it had come to my aid that night in Shadow, bearing me to that peculiar place between shadows and the bizarre adventures that befell me there? And though I was totally uncertain as to the nature of his appearance to me in the Corridor of Mirrors, I had later encountered indications of his presence in Amber Castle itself. If he'd been in any of those places, it would seem he hadn't really been too far off. And that would mean he'd simply been blocking me, and another attempt to reach him would probably prove equally fruitless. Still, what if there were some other explanation for all these occurrences and . . .

The card seemed to grow cold beneath my touch. Was it just my imagination, or was the strength of my regard beginning to activate it? I moved forward in my mind, focusing. It seemed to grow even colder as I did so.

"Dad?" I said. "Corwin?"

Colder still, and a tingling feeling in my fingertips that touched it. It seemed the beginning of a Trump contact. It could be that he was much nearer to the Courts than to Amber, within a more reachable range now. . . .

"Corwin," I repeated. "It's me, Merlin. Hello."

His image shifted, seemed to move. And then the card went totally black.

Yet, it remained cold, and a sensation like a silent version of contact was present, like a telephone connection during a long pause.

"Dad? Are you there?"

The blackness of the card took on the aspect of depth. And deep within it, something seemed to be stirring.

"Merlin?" The word was faint, yet I was certain it was his voice, speaking my name. "Merlin?"

The movement within the depth was real. Something was rushing toward me.

It erupted from the card into my face, with a beating of black wings, cawing, crow or raven, black, black.

"Forbidden!" it cried. "Forbidden! Go back! Withdraw!"

It flapped about my head as the cards spilled from my hand.

"Stay away!" it screeched, circling the room. "Forbidden place!"

It passed out the doorway and I pursued it. It seemed to have vanished, though, in the moments it was lost to my sight.

"Bird!" I cried. "Come back!"

But there was no reply, no further sounds of beating wings. I peered into the other rooms and there was no sign of the creature in any of them.

"Bird . . . ?"

"Merlin! What's the matter?"—this from high overhead.

I looked up to behold Suhuy, descending a crystal stair behind a quivering veil of light, a sky full of stars at his back.

"Just looking for a bird," I replied.

"Oh," he said, reaching the landing and stepping through the veil which then shook itself out of existence, taking the stair along with it. "Any particular bird?"

"A big black one," I said. "Of the talking sort."

He shook his head.

"I can send for one," he said.

"This was a special bird," I said.

"Sorry you lost it."

We walked out into the hallway and I turned left and headed back to the sitting room.

"Trumps all over the place," my uncle remarked.

"I was attempting to use one and it went black and the bird flew out of it, shouting, 'Forbidden'! I dropped them at that point."

"Sounds as if your correspondent is a practical joker," he said, "or under a spell."

We knelt and he helped me to gather them.

"The latter seems more likely," I said. "It was my

father's card. I've been trying to locate him for a long
while now, and this was the closest I've come. I actually
heard his voice, within the blackout, before the bird interrupted and cut us off.''

"Sounds as if he is confined to a dark place, perhaps
magically guarded as well.''

"Of course!'' I said, squaring up the edges of my
deck and recasing it.

One cannot shift the stuff of Shadow in a place of
absolute darkness. It is as effective as blindness in stopping one of our blood from escaping confinement. It
added an element of rationality to my recent experience.
Someone wanting Corwin out of commission *would*
have to keep him in a very dark place.

"Did you ever meet my father?'' I asked.

"No,'' Suhuy replied. "I understand that he did visit
the Courts briefly, at the end of the war. But I never had
the pleasure.''

"Did you hear anything of his doings here?''

"I believe he attended a meeting with Swayvill and
his counselors, along with Random and the other Amberites, preliminary to the peace treaty. After that, I understand he went his own ways, and I never heard where
they might have led him.''

"I'd heard as much in Amber,'' I said. "I wonder.
. . . He'd killed a noble—a Lord Borel—near the end
of the final battle. Any chance Borel's relatives might
have gone after him?''

He clicked his fangs twice, then pursed his lips.

"The House of Hendrake . . .'' he mused. "I think
not. Your grandmother was Hendrake. . . .''

"I know,'' I said. "But I didn't have much to do with
them. Some disagreement with Helgram. . . .''

"Hendrake Ways is very much of the military sort,''
he went on. "Glory of battle. Martial honor, you know.

I can't see them as holding a peacetime grudge for a wartime happening.''

Recalling my father's story, I said, "Even if they considered the killing less than honorable?''

"I don't know," he said to that. "It's hard to guess attitudes on specific questions.''

"Who is head of the House of Hendrake now?''

"The Duchess Belissa Minobee.''

"The duke, her husband—Larsus. . . . What happened to him?''

"He died at Patternfall. I believe Prince Julian of Amber slew him.''

"And Borel was their son?''

"Yes.''

"Ouch. Two of them. I didn't realize.''

"Borel had two brothers, a half brother and a half sister, many uncles, aunts, cousins. Yes, it's a big House. And the women of Hendrake are as doughty as the men.''

"Yes, of course. There are songs, such as 'Never Wed a Hendrake Lass.' Any way of finding out whether Corwin had any doings with Hendrake while he was here?''

"One could ask about a bit, though it's been a long while. Memories fade, trails grow cold. Not easy.''

He shook his head.

"How long till bluesky?'' I asked him.

"Fairly soon,'' he said.

"I'd better be heading for Mandorways then. I promised my brother I'd breakfast with him.''

"I'll see you later,'' he said. "At the funeral, if not before.''

"Yes,'' I said. "I guess I'd better clean up and change clothes.''

I headed back through the way to my room, where I summoned a basin of water, soap, toothbrush, razor; also, gray trousers, black boots and belt, purple shirt and gloves, charcoal cloak, fresh blade and scabbard. When I had made myself presentable, I took a way through a forested glade to the receiving room. From there, I exited onto a thruway. A quarter mile of mountain trail later, ending abruptly at a chasm, I summoned a filmy and crossed upon it. Then I bore right to Mandorways, traveling a blue beach beneath a double sun for perhaps a hundred yards. I turned right, passing through a remembered archway of stone, moving briefly past a bubbling lava field and through a black obsidian wall, which took me to a pleasant cavern, over a small bridge, through a corner of a graveyard, a few steps along the Rim and into the receiving area of his Ways.

The entire wall to my left was composed of slow flame; that to my right, a non-returnable way, save for light, giving sight of some sea-bottom trench where bright things moved about and ate one another. Mandor was seated humanformed before a bookcase directly ahead, wearing black and white, feet propped on a black ottoman, a copy of Robert Hass's *Praise,* which I had given him, in his hand.

He smiled as he looked up.

" 'Death's hounds feared me,' " he said. "Nice line, that. How are you this cycle?"

"Rested, finally," I said. "Yourself?"

He placed the book upon a small, legless table that floated near just then, and rose to his feet. The fact that he had obviously been reading it because I was coming in no way detracted from the compliment. He had always been that way.

"Quite well, thank you," he replied. "Come, let me feed you."

He took my arm and steered me toward the wall of fire. It fell away as we drew near and our footsteps sounded in a place of momentary darkness, succeeded almost immediately by a small lane, sunlight filtered through arching branches overhead, violets blooming at either hand. The lane took us to a flagged patio, a green and white gazebo at its farther end. We mounted a few stairs to a well-set table within, frosted pitchers of juice and baskets of warm rolls near at hand. He gestured and I seated myself. At his gesture a carafe of coffee appeared beside my setting.

"I see you recall my morning predeliction," I said, "from the Shadow Earth. Thank you."

He smiled faintly as he nodded, seating himself across from me. Birdsongs I could not identify sounded from the trees. A gentle breeze caused leaves to rustle.

"What are you up to these days?" I asked him as I poured a cup of coffee and broke a roll.

"Observing the scene, mainly," he replied.

"Political scene?"

"As always. Though my recent experience in Amber has led me to regard it as part of an even larger picture."

I nodded.

"And your investigations with Fiona?"

"Those, too," he answered. "These are shaping up into very unusual times."

"I've noticed."

"It seems almost as if the Pattern-Logrus conflict were making itself manifest in mundane affairs, as well as on the cosmic scale."

"I feel that way, too. But then I'm prejudiced. I got caught up in the cosmic part early, and without a scorecard. I've been run all over the place and manipulated every which way recently—to the point where all of my affairs seemed part of their bigger picture. I don't like it a bit, and if I had some way to make them back off I'd use it."

"Hm," he said. "And what if your whole life were a study in manipulation?"

"I wouldn't feel good about it," I said. "I guess I'd

feel just the way I do now, only perhaps more intensely.''

He gestured and an amazing omelet appeared before me, followed, moments later, by a side dish of fried potatoes, mixed with what appeared to be green chilies and onions.

''All of this is hypothetical,'' I said as I began eating, ''isn't it?''

There followed a long pause as he took his first mouthful, then, ''I think not,'' he said.

''I think the Powers have been moving madly for a long while now,'' he went on, ''and we're finally nearing endgame.''

''What makes you privy to these matters?''

''It began with a careful consideration of events,'' he said. ''Then followed the formulation and testing of hypotheses.''

''Spare me a lecture on the use of the scientific method in theology and human politics,'' I said.

''You asked.''

''True. Go ahead.''

''Do you not feel it somewhat odd that Swayvill expired just when he did, when so many things are coming to fruition simultaneously, after having hung on for so long?''

''He had to go sometime,'' I said, ''and all the recent stresses probably proved too much.''

''Timing,'' Mandor said. ''Strategic placement. Timing.''

''For what?''

''To place you on the throne of Chaos, of course,'' he replied.

IV

Sometimes you hear an unlikely thing and that's all it is. Other times, you hear something improbable and it strikes an echo. There is an immediate feeling of having known it, or known something very like it, all along, and just not having bothered to pick it up and examine it. By rights, I should have choked at Mandor's pronouncement, then snorted something such as "Preposterous!" Yet, I'd a peculiar feeling about this business— whether his conclusion was right or wrong—as if there were something more than conjecture involved, as if there just might be some overall plan moving me toward the circle of power in the Courts.

I took a long, slow drink of coffee. Then, "Really?" I said.

I felt myself smiling as he sought my eyes, studied my face.

"Are you consciously party to the effort?"

I raised my coffee cup again. I had been about to say, "No, of course not. This is the first I've heard of the notion." Then I recalled my father's telling me how he had duped Aunt Flora into giving him vital information his amnesia had washed away. It was not the cleverness with which he had done it that had impressed me so much as the fact that his mistrust of relatives transcended consciousness, existed as a pure existential reflex. Not having been through all the family rivalries Corwin had, I lacked responses of such intensity. And Mandor and I had always gotten along particularly well, even though he was a few centuries older and had very different tastes in some areas. But, suddenly, discussing such a high-stakes matter as we were, that small voice Corwin referred to as his worse-if-wiser self suggested, "Why not? You could use the practice, kid," and as I lowered the cup again I decided to try it out, just to see how it felt, for a few minutes.

"I don't know whether we both have the same thing in mind," I said. "Why don't you tell me about the middle game—or perhaps even the opening—for what you see rushing to conclusion now."

"Both the Pattern and the Logrus are sentient," he said. "We've both seen evidence of that. Whether they are manifestations of the Unicorn and the Serpent or the other way around makes no real difference. Either way, we are talking about a pair of greater-than-human intelligences with vast powers at their disposal. Whichever came first is also one of those useless theological points. We need only concern ourselves with the present situation, as it affects us."

I nodded.

"A fair assessment," I agreed.

"The forces they represent have been opposed but fairly evenly matched for ages," he went on, "and thus a kind of balance has been maintained. They have constantly sought small victories over each other, each attempting to add to its own domain at the expense of the other. It appears to be a zero-sum game. Both Oberon

and Swayvill were their agents for a long while, with
Dworkin and Suhuy as their intermediaries with the
powers themselves.''

''So?'' I said as he took a sip of juice.

''I believe that Dworkin had touched the Pattern too
closely,'' he continued, ''and so became subject to manipulation. He was sufficiently sophisticated, however,
that he realized this and resisted. This resulted in his
madness, with a reciprocal damaging effect on the Pattern itself because of their close connection. This, in
turn, caused the Pattern to leave him alone, rather than
risk further trauma. The damage was done, though, and
the Logrus gained a small edge. This allowed it to act
in the realm of order when Prince Brand began his ex-
periments to increase his personal abilities. I believe he
laid himself open to control and became an unwitting
agent of the Logrus.''

''That's a lot of supposition,'' I said.

''Consider,'' he responded, ''that his aims seemingly
became those of a madman. They make much more
sense when seen as the goal of something wanting to
destroy all order, to restore the universe to chaos.''

''Continue,'' I said.

''At some point, the Pattern discovered—or perhaps
possessed all along—the ability to create 'ghosts,' short-
lived simulacra of those who had negotiated it. Fascinating concept, that. I was very interested to learn of it.
It provided a major mechanism, supporting my thesis of
the Pattern's and possibly the Logrus's, direct action in
the promotion of physical events. Might they have figured in the setting up of your father as the Pattern's
champion against Brand? I wonder.''

''I don't follow,'' I said. ''Setting him up, you say?''

''I've a feeling he was really the Pattern's choice as
the next King of Amber, easy to promote, too, as it
seemed to coincide with his own wishes. I've wondered

about his sudden recovery in that Shadow Earth clinic, and particularly about the circumstances surrounding the accident that put him there, when even with differing time streams it seemed possible that Brand might have had to be in two places at the same time—imprisoned and looking down the sights of a rifle. Of course, Brand is no longer available to clarify the matter."

"More supposition," I said, finishing my omelet. "But not uninteresting. Please continue."

"Your father had second thoughts about the throne, however. Still, he *was* Amber's champion. Amber *did* win the war. The Pattern *was* repaired. The balance *was* restored. Random was the second choice as monarch—a good maintainer of the status quo—and that choice *was* made by the Unicorn, not by the Amberites following any of their versions of the Rules of Succession."

"I never looked at it all that way," I said.

"And your father—inadvertently, I believe—provided a bonus. Afraid that the Pattern had not been repaired, he drew another. Only, it *had* been repaired. Thus, there were two artifacts of order, rather than one. Though, as a separate entity, it probably did not add to the Pattern's strength, it added to order, as such, diminishing the effects of the Logrus. So your father set the balance right, then proceeded to tip it again—in the other direction."

"This is your conclusion from the investigations you and Fiona made of the new Pattern?"

He nodded slowly, took a sip of juice.

"Hence, more Shadow storms than usual, as a mundane effect," he said, "bringing us up to present times."

"Yes, present times," I said, pouring more coffee. "We've noted they've grown interesting."

"Indeed. Your story of the girl Coral, asking the Pattern to send her to an appropriate place, is a case in point. What did it immediately do? It sent her to a

Shadow Pattern and turned out the lights. Then it sent you to rescue her, repairing that edition of itself in the process. Once it was repaired it was no longer a Shadow Pattern, but another version of itself that it was then able to absorb. It probably absorbed that entire shadow as well, adding considerably to its own energies. Its edge over the Logrus increased even more. The Logrus would need a big gain to restore the balance after that. So it risked an incursion into the Pattern's domain, in a desperate effort to obtain the Eye of Chaos. That ended in a stalemate, though, because of the intervention of that bizarre entity you call Ghostwheel. So the balance remains tipped in the Pattern's favor, an unhealthy state of affairs.''

''For the Logrus.''

''For everybody, I'd say. The Powers will be at odds, the shadows in turmoil and disorder in both realms till things have been righted.''

''So something should be done to benefit the Logrus?''

''You already know that.''

''I suppose I do.''

''It communicated with you directly, didn't it?''

I recalled my night in the chapel in the place between shadows, where I had been faced with a choice between the Serpent and the Unicorn, the Logrus and the Pattern. Resenting the bullying in such a forced format, I had refused to choose either.

''Yes, it did,'' I answered.

''It wanted you for its champion, didn't it?''

''I suppose it did,'' I said.

''And . . . ?''

''. . . And here we are,'' I replied.

''Did it indicate anything that might support my thesis?''

I thought about that trek through the Undershadow,

mixing menace with ghosts—Pattern, Logrus, or both.

"I suppose it did," I repeated.

But, ultimately, it had been the Pattern I had served at the end of that journey, albeit unwittingly.

"You are prepared to execute its design for the good of the Courts?"

"I'm prepared to seek resolution of this matter, for everybody's peace of mind."

He smiled.

"Is that a qualification or an agreement?"

"It's a statement of intent," I said.

"If the Logrus has chosen you, it has its reasons."

"I daresay."

"It almost goes without saying that having you on the throne would strengthen the House of Sawall immensely."

"The thought had occurred to me, now you mention it."

"For one with your background, of course, it would become necessary to determine where your ultimate loyalty lies—with Amber or with the Courts."

"Do you foresee another war?"

"No, of course not. But anything you do to strengthen the Logrus will arouse the Pattern and provoke some response from Amber. Hardly to the point of war, but possibly to that of retaliation."

"Could you be more specific as to what you have in mind?"

"I'm only dealing in generalities at the moment, to give you opportunity to assess your reactions."

I nodded.

"Since we're talking generalities I'll just repeat my statement: I'm prepared to seek a resolution—"

"All right," he said. "We understand each other to this extent. In the event you make it to the throne, you want the same thing we do—"

" 'We'?" I interrupted.

"The House of Sawall, of course. —But you don't want anyone dictating specifics to you."

"That says it nicely," I replied.

"But of course we're speaking hypothetically, there being a couple of others about with stronger claims."

"So why argue contingencies?"

"If the House were able to see you crowned, however, do you acknowledge you would owe consideration for this?"

"Brother," I said, "you *are* the House, for all major purposes. If you're asking for a commitment before taking out Tmer and Tubble, forget it, I'm not all that eager to sit on a throne."

"Your wishes are not paramount in this," he said. "There is no reason for squeamishness when you consider that we've long been at odds with Jesby, and Chanicut's always been a troublemaker."

"Squeamishness has nothing to do with it," I said. "I never said I wanted the throne. And, frankly, I think either Tmer or Tubble would probably do a better job."

"They are not designates of the Logrus."

"And if I am, I should make it without any help."

"Brother, there is a big gap between its world of principles and ours of flesh, stone, and steel."

"And supposing I have my own agenda and it does not include your plan?"

"What is it, then?"

"We're speaking hypothetically, remember?"

"Merlin, you're being obstinate. You've a duty in this, to the House as well as to the Courts and the Logrus."

"I can assess my own duties, Mandor, and I have— so far."

"If you've a plan to set things right, and it's a good

one, we'll help you to effectuate it. What have you in mind?''

''I do not require help at this point,'' I said, ''but I'll remember that.''

''What do you require right now?''

''Information,'' I said.

''Ask me. I have a lot.''

''All right. What can you tell me about my mother's maternal side, the House of Hendrake?''

He pursed his lips.

''They're into soldiering, professionally,'' he said. ''You know they're always off fighting in Shadow wars. They love it. Belissa Minobee's been in charge since General Larsus's death. Hm.'' He paused. Then, ''Do you ask because of their rather odd fixation involving Amber?''

''Amber?'' I said. ''What do you mean?''

''I recall a social visit to the Ways of Hendrake one time,'' he said, ''when I wandered into a small, chapellike room. In a niche in one wall there hung a portrait of General Benedict, in full battle regalia. There was an altarlike shelf below it bearing several weapons, and upon which a number of candles were burning. Your mother's picture was there, too.''

''Really?'' I said. ''I wonder whether Benedict knows? Dara once told my father she was descended from Benedict. Later, he figured this an out-and-out lie. . . . Do you think people like that would hold a grudge against my father?''

''For what?''

''Corwin slew Borel of Hendrake at the time of the Patternfall War.''

''They tend to take such things philosophically.''

''Still, I gather it was a somewhat less than kosher engagement from the way he described it—though I don't believe there were any witnesses.''

"So let sleeping wyverns lie."

"I've no intention of rousing them. But what I was wondering was that if they had somehow heard details they might have been out to clear some debt of honor on his behalf. Do you think they could have been behind his disappearance?"

"I just don't know," he replied, "how that would fit in with their code. I suppose you could ask them."

"Just come out and say, 'Hey, are you responsible for whatever happened to my dad?' "

"There are more subtle ways of learning a person's attitudes," he responded. "As I recall, you had a few lessons in them in your youth."

"But I don't even know these people. I mean, I might have met one of the sisters at a party, now I think of it—and I recall having seen Larsus and his wife in the distance a few times—but that's it."

"Hendrake will have a representative at the funeral," he said. "If I were to introduce you, perhaps you could apply a little glamour to obtain an informal audience."

"You know, that may be the way to go," I told him.

"Probably the only way. Yes, do that, please."

"Very well."

He cleared the table with a gesture, filled it with another. This time, paper-thin crepes with a variety of fillings and toppings appeared before us; and fresh rolls, variously spiced. We ate for a time in silence, appreciating the balminess and the birds, the breezes.

"I wish I could have seen something of Amber," he said at length, "under less restricted circumstances."

"I'm sure that can be arranged," I replied. "I'd like to show you around. I know a great restaurant in Death Alley."

"That wouldn't be Bloody Eddie's, would it?"

"It would, though the name gets changed periodically."

"I've heard of it, and long been curious."

"We'll do that one day."

"Excellent."

He clapped his hands and bowls of fruit appeared. I freshened my coffee and swirled a Kadota fig in a bowl of whipped cream.

"I'll be dining with my mother later," I remarked.

"Yes. I overheard."

"Have you seen much of her recently? How's she been?"

"As she said, rather reclusive," he replied.

"Do you think she's up to something?"

"Probably," he said. "I can't recall a time when she hasn't been."

"Any idea what?"

"Why should I guess when she'll probably tell you outright?"

"You really think she will?"

"You have an advantage over everyone else, in being her son."

"Also a drawback, for the same reason."

"Still, she's more likely to tell you things than she would anyone else."

"Except, perhaps, Jurt."

"Why do you say that?"

"She always liked him better."

"Funny, I've heard him say the same thing about you."

"You see him often?"

"Often? No."

"When was the last time?"

"About two cycles ago."

"Where is he?"

"Here, in the Courts."

"At Sawall?" I had visions of him joining us for

lunch. I wouldn't put something like that past Dara either.

"One of its byways, I think. He's rather reticent concerning his comings and goings—and stayings."

There being something like eight byway residences to Sawall that I knew of, it would be difficult to run him down through byways that could lead well into Shadow. Not that I'd any desire to, at the moment.

"What brings him home?" I asked.

"The same thing as yourself, the funeral," he said, "and all that goes with it."

All that goes with it, indeed! If there were a genuine plot to put me on the throne, I could never forget that—willing or unwilling, successful or unsuccessful—Jurt would be a step or two behind me all the way.

"I may have to kill him," I said. "I don't want to. But he's not giving me a whole lot of choice. Sooner or later, he's going to force us into a position where it has to be one or the other."

"Why do you tell me this?"

"So you'll know how I feel about it, and so that you might use whatever influence you may still have to persuade him to find a different hobby."

He shook his head.

"Jurt moved beyond my influence a long time ago," he said. "Dara's about the only one he'll listen to—though I suspect he's still afraid of Suhuy. You might speak to her concerning this matter, soon."

"It's the one thing neither of us can discuss with her—the other."

"Why not?"

"It's just the way it is. She always misunderstands."

"I'm certain she's not going to want her sons killing each other."

"Of course not, but I don't know how to put the matter to her."

"I suggest you make an effort to find a way. In the meantime, I would contrive not to be alone with Jurt, should your paths cross. And if it were me, in the presence of witnesses, I would make certain that the first blow was not mine."

"Well taken, Mandor," I said.

We sat for a time in silence. Then, "You will think about my proposal," he said.

"As I understand it," I replied.

He frowned.

"If you have any questions. . . ."

"No. I'll be thinking."

He rose. I got to my feet, also. With a gesture, he cleared the table. Then he turned away and I followed him out of the gazebo and across its yard to the trail.

We emerged after a stroll in his external study cum receiving room. He squeezed my shoulder as we headed for the exit.

"I'll see you at the funeral then," he remarked.

"Yes," I said. "Thanks for the breakfast."

"By the way, how well do you like that lady, Coral?" he asked.

"Oh, pretty well," I said. "She's quite—nice. Why?"

He shrugged.

"Just curious. I was concerned about her, having been present at the time of her misadventure, and I wondered how much she meant to you."

"Enough that it bothers me a lot," I said.

"I see. Well, give her my good wishes if you should talk to her."

"Thanks, I will."

"We'll talk again later."

"Yes."

I strode into the way, making no haste. I still had

considerable time before I was due by the Ways of Sawall.

I paused when I came to a gibbet-shaped tree. A moment's reflection and I turned left, following an ascend-
ing trail among dark rocks. Near its top, I walked
directly into a mossy boulder, emerging from a sandbank
into a light rain. I ran across the field before me, till I
came to the fairy circle beneath the ancient tree. I
stepped to its middle, made up a couplet with my name
for the rhyme, and sank into the ground. When I was
halted and the moment's darkness went away, I found
myself beside a damp stone wall, looking downhill
across a prospect of headstones and monuments. The sky
was fully overcast and a cool breeze wandered by. It felt
to be one of the ends of a day, but whether morning or
twilight lay near, I could not tell. The place looked exactly as I remembered it—cracked mausoleums hung
with ivy, falling stone fences, wandering paths beneath
high, dark trees. I moved down familiar trails.

As a child, this had been a favored playground of
mine, for a time. I met here almost daily, for dozens of
cycles, with a little shadow girl named Rhanda. Kicking
through boneheaps, brushing by damp shrubbery, I came
at length to the damaged mausoleum where we had
played house. Pushing aside the sagging gate, I entered.

Nothing had changed, and I found myself chuckling.
The cracked cups and saucers, tarnished utensils, were
still stacked in the corner, heavy with dust, stained with
seepage. I brushed off the catafalque we'd used as a
table, seated myself upon it. One day Rhanda had simply
stopped coming, and after a time I had, too. I'd often
wondered what sort of woman she had become. I'd left
her a note in our hiding place, beneath a loose floor
stone, I recalled. I wondered whether she'd ever found
it.

I raised the stone. My filthy envelope still lay there,

unsealed. I took it out, shook it off, slid out my folded sheet.

I unfolded it, read my faded childish scrawl: *What happened Rhanda? I waited and you didn't come.* Beneath it, in a far neater hand, was written: *I can't come anymore because my folks say you are a demon or a vampire. I'm sorry because you are the nicest demon or vampire I know.* I'd never thought of that possibility. Amazing, the ways one can be misunderstood.

I sat there for a time, remembering growing up. I'd taught Rhanda the bonedance game in here. I snapped my fingers then, and our old ensorcelled heap of them across the way made a sound like stirring leaves. My juvenile spell was still in place; the bones rolled forward, arranged themselves into a pair of manikins, began their small, awkward dance. They circled each other, barely holding their shapes, pieces flaking away, cobwebs trailing; loose ones—spares—began to bounce about them. They made tiny clicking sounds as they touched. I moved them faster.

A shadow crossed the doorway, and I heard a chuckle.

"I'll be damned! All you need's a tin roof. So this is how they spend their time in Chaos."

"Luke!" I exclaimed as he stepped inside, my manikins collapsing as my attention left them, into little gray, sticklike heaps. "What are you doing here?"

"Could say I was selling cemetery lots," he observed. "You interested in one?"

He had on a red shirt and brown khakis tucked into his brown suede boots. A tan cloak hung about his shoulders. He was grinning.

"Why aren't you off ruling?"

His smile went away, to be replaced by a moment of puzzlement, returned almost instantly.

"Oh, felt I needed a break. What about you? There's a funeral soon, isn't there?"

I nodded.

"Later on," I said. "I'm just taking a break myself. How'd you get here, anyway?"

"Followed my nose," he said. "Needed some intelligent conversation."

"Be serious. Nobody knew I was coming here. I didn't even know it till the last minute. I—"

I groped about in my pockets.

"You didn't plant another of those blue stones on me, did you?"

"No, nothing that simple," he replied. "I seem to have some sort of message for you."

I got to my feet, approached him, studying his face.

"Are you okay, Luke?"

"Sure. As okay as I ever am, that is."

"It's no mean stunt, finding your way this near to the Courts. Especially if you've never been here before. How'd you manage it?"

"Well, the Courts and I go back a long ways, old buddy. You might say it's in my—blood."

He moved aside from the doorway and I stepped outside. Almost automatically, we began walking.

"I don't understand what you're saying," I told him.

"Well, my dad spent some time here, back in his plotting days," he said. "It's where he met my mother."

"I didn't know that."

"It never came up. We never talked family, remember?"

"Yeah," I said, "and no one I asked seemed to know where Jasra came from. Still, the Courts. . . . She's a long way from home."

"Actually, she was recruited from a nearby shadow," he explained, "like this one."

"Recruited?"

"Yes, she worked as a servant for a number of

years—I think she was fairly young when she started—at the Ways of Helgram.''

"Helgram? That's my mother's House!''

"Right. She was a maid-companion to the lady Dara. That's where she learned the Arts.''

"Jasra got her instruction in sorcery from my mother? And she met Brand at Helgram? That would make it seem Helgram had something to do with Brand's plot, the Black Road, the war—''

"—and the Lady Dara going looking for your father? I guess so.''

"Because she wanted to be a Pattern initiate as well as one of the Logrus?''

"Maybe," he said. "I wasn't present.''

We moved down a gravelly trail, turned at a huge cluster of dark shrubbery, passing through a forest of stone and over a bridge that crossed a slow black stream that reflected high branches and sky, monochrome. A few leaves rustled in a stray breeze.

"How come you never mentioned any of this later?'' I asked.

"I intended to, but it never seemed urgent," he said, "whereas a lot of other things did.''

"True," I said. "The pace did seem to keep picking up each time our trails crossed. But now— Are you saying it's urgent now, that I suddenly need to know this?''

"Oh, not exactly.'' He halted. He reached out and leaned upon a headstone. His hand began to grip it, growing white about the knuckles, across the back. The stone at his fingertips was ground to powder, fell snow-like to the earth. "Not exactly," he repeated. "That part was my idea, just because I wanted you to know. Maybe it'll do you some good, maybe it won't. Information is like that. You never know.'' With a crunching, cracking sound, the top of the headstone suddenly gave way. Luke hardly seemed to notice this, and his hand kept on squeezing. Small pieces fell from the larger one he now held.

"So you came all this way to tell me that?"

"No," he answered, as we turned and began walking back the way we had come. "I was sent to tell you something else, and it's been pretty hard holding off. But I figured if I talked about this first, it couldn't let me go, would keep feeding me till I got around to the message."

There came a huge crunch, and the stone he held turned to gravel, falling to mix with that on the trail.

"Let me see your hand."

He brushed it off and held it out. A tiny flame flickered near the base of his index finger. He ran his thumb over it and it went out. I increased my pace, and he matched it.

"Luke, you know what you are?"

"Something in me seems to, but *I* don't, man. I just feel—I'm not right. I'd probably better tell you what I feel I should pretty quick now."

"No. Hold off," I said, hurrying even more.

Something dark passed overhead, too quick for me to make out its shape, vanishing among the trees. We were buffeted by a sudden gust of wind.

"You know what's going on, Merle?" he asked.

"I think so," I said, "and I want you to do exactly what I tell you, no matter how weird it might seem. Okay?"

"Sure thing. If I can't trust a Lord of Chaos, who can I trust, eh?"

We hurried past the clump of shrubs. My mausoleum was just up ahead.

"You know, there really is something I feel obliged to tell you right now, though," he said.

"Hold it. Please."

"It *is* important, though."

I ran on ahead of him. He began running, too, to keep up.

"It's about your being here at the Courts, just now."

I extended my hands, used them to brake myself when I came up against the wall of the stone building. I swung myself through the doorway and inside. Three big steps, and I was kneeling in the corner, snatching up an old cup, using the corner of my cloak to wipe it out.

"Merle, what the hell are you doing?" Luke asked, entering behind me.

"Just a minute and I'll show you," I told him, drawing my dagger.

Placing the cup upon the stone where I had been seated earlier, I held my hand above it and used the dagger to cut my wrist.

Instead of blood, flame came forth from the incision.

"No! Damn it!" I cried.

And I reached into the spikard, located the proper line, and found the flowing channel of a cooling spell that I laid upon the wound. Immediately, the flames died and it was blood that flowed from me. However, as it fell into the cup it began to smoke. Cursing, I extended the spell to control its liquidity there, also.

"Yeah, it's weird, Merle. I'll give you that," Luke observed.

I laid the dagger aside and used my right hand to squeeze my arm above the wound. The blood flowed faster. The spikard throbbed. I glanced at Luke. There was a look of strain upon his face. I pumped my fist. The cup was more than half-full.

"You said you trust me," I stated.

"Afraid so," he answered.

Three-quarters. . . .

"You've got to drink this, Luke," I said. "I mean it."

"Somehow, I suspected you were leading up to this,"

he said, "and, really, it doesn't sound like such a bad idea. I've a feeling I need a lot of help just now."

He reached out and took the cup, raised it to his lips. I pressed the palm of my hand against the wound. Outside, the winds were gusting regularly.

"When you've finished, put it back," I said. "You're going to need more."

I could hear the sounds of his swallowing.

"Better than a slug of Jameson," he said then. "Don't know why." He replaced the cup on the stone. "A little salty, though," he added.

I removed my hand from the incision, held the wrist above it again, pumped my fist.

"Hey, man. You're losing a lot of blood there. I feel okay now. Was just a little dizzy, that's all. I don't need any more."

"Yes, you do," I said. "Believe me. I gave a lot more than this in a blood drive once and ran in a meet the next day. It's okay."

The wind rose to a gale, moaning past us now.

"Mind telling me what's going on?" he asked.

"Luke, you're a Pattern ghost," I told him.

"What do you mean?"

"The Pattern can duplicate anybody who ever walked it. You've got all the signs. I know them."

"Hey, I feel real. I didn't even do the Pattern in Amber. I did it in Tir-na Nog'th."

"Apparently, it controls the two images as well, since they're true copies. Do you remember your coronation in Kashfa?"

"Coronation? Hell no! You mean I made it to the throne?"

"Yep. Rinaldo the First."

"God damn! Bet Mom's happy."

"I'm sure."

"This is kind of awkward then, there being two of

me. You seem familiar with the phenomenon. How does the Pattern handle it?''

''You guys tend not to last very long. It seems the closer you are to the Pattern itself the stronger you are, too. It must have taken a lot of juice to project you this far. Here, drink this.''

''Sure.''

He tossed off a half cupful and handed the cup back.

''So what's with the precious bodily fluids?'' he asked.

''The blood of Amber seems to have a sustaining effect on Pattern ghosts.''

''You mean I'm some kind of vampire?''

''I suppose you could put it that way, in a sort of technical sense.''

''I'm not sure I like that—especially such a specialized one.''

''It does seem to have certain drawbacks. But one thing at a time. Let's get you stabilized before we start looking for angles.''

''All right. You've got a captive audience.''

There came a rattle, as of a rolled stone, from outside, followed by a small clanking noise.

Luke turned his head.

''I don't think that's just the wind,'' he stated.

''Take the last sip,'' I said, moving away from the cup and groping after my handkerchief. ''It'll have to hold you.''

He tossed it off as I wrapped my wrist. He knotted it in place for me.

''Let's get out of here,'' I said. ''The vibes are getting bad.''

''Fine with me,'' he replied as a figure appeared at the doorway. It was backlighted, its features lost in shadow.

"You're not going anywhere, Pattern ghost," came an almost-familiar voice.

I willed the spikard to about 150 watts illumination.

It was Borel, showing his teeth in an unfriendly fashion.

"You are about to become a very large candle, Patterner," he said to Luke.

"You're wrong, Borel," I said, raising the spikard.

Suddenly, the Sign of the Logrus swam between us.

"Borel? The master swordsman?" Luke inquired.

"The same," I answered.

"Oh, shit!" Luke said.

V

As I probed forward with two of the more lethal energies of the spikard the Logrus image intercepted them and turned them off.

"I didn't save him for you to take him out this easily," I said, and just then something like the image of the Pattern but not really the same flashed into existence nearby.

The Sign of the Logrus slid to my left. The new thing—whatever it was—kept pace with it, both of them passing silently through the wall. Almost immediately, there followed a thunderclap that shook the building. Even Borel, who was reaching for his blade, paused in mid-gesture, then moved his hand to catch hold of the doorway. As he did this, another figure appeared at his back and a familiar voice addressed him: "Please excuse me. You're blocking my way."

"Corwin!" I cried. "Dad!"

Borel turned his head.

"Corwin, Prince of Amber?" he said.

"Indeed," came the reply, "though I'm afraid I haven't had the pleasure."

"I am Borel, Duke of Hendrake, Master of Arms of the Ways of Hendrake."

"You speak with a lot of capitals, sir, and I'm pleased to make your acquaintance," Corwin said. "Now, if you don't mind, I'd like to get through here to see my son."

Borel's hand moved to the hilt of his blade as he turned. I was already moving forward by then, and so was Luke. But there was a movement beyond Borel—a kick, it seemed, low—causing him to expel a lot of air and double forward. Then a fist descended upon the back of his neck and he fell.

"Come on," Corwin called, gesturing. "I think we'd better get out of here."

Luke and I emerged, stepping over the fallen Master of Arms of the Ways of Hendrake. The ground off to the left was blackened, as if from a recent brushfire, and a light rain had begun to fall. There were other human figures in the distance now, moving toward us.

"I don't know whether the force that brought me here can get me out again," Corwin said, looking about. "It may be otherwise occupied." Several moments passed, then, "I guess it is," he said. "Okay, it's up to you. How do we flee?"

"This way," I told him, turning and breaking into a run.

They followed me up the trails that had brought me to this place. I looked back and saw that six dark figures pursued us.

I headed uphill, past the markers and monuments, coming at last to the place beside the old stone wall. By then, there were shouts from behind us. Ignoring them, I drew my companions to me and came up with an impromptu couplet that described the situation and my desire in somewhat less than perfect meter. Still, the charm held, and a hurled cobble only missed me because we were already sinking into the earth.

We emerged from the fairy ring, coming up like mushrooms, and I led my companions across the field, jogging, to the sandbank. As we entered there I heard another shout. We exited the boulder and descended the rocky trail to the gibbet tree. Turning left on the trail, I began to run.

"Hold up!" Corwin called. "I feel it around here somewhere. There!"

He left the trail to the right and began running toward the base of a small hill. Luke and I followed. From behind us came the sounds of our pursuers' emergence from the way at the boulder.

Ahead, I saw something flickering between two trees. We seemed to be heading toward it. As we drew nearer, its outline became clearer, and I realized that it possessed the contours of that Pattern-like image I had beheld back in the mausoleum.

Dad did not break stride as he approached, but charged right into the thing. And vanished. Another cry rose up behind us. Luke was next through the shimmering screen, and I was close on his heels.

We were running through a straight, glowing, pearly tunnel now, and when I glanced back I saw that it seemed to be closing in behind me.

"They can't follow," Corwin shouted. "That end's already closed."

"Then why are we running?" I asked.

"We're still not safe," he replied. "We're cutting through the Logrus's domain. If we're spotted there could still be trouble."

We raced on through that strange tunnel, and, "We're running through Shadow?" I asked.

"Yes."

"Then it would seem that the farther we go, the better—"

The whole thing shook, and I had to put out a hand to keep from being thrown down.

"Oh-oh," Luke said.

"Yes," I agreed as the tunnel began to come apart. Big chunks seemed to be torn out of the walls, the floor. There was only murk behind these rents. We kept going, leaping the openings. Then something struck again, soundlessly, completely shattering the entire passage— around us, behind us, before us.

We fell.

Well, we didn't exactly fall. We sort of drifted in a twilit fog. There didn't seem to be anything underfoot, or in any other direction either. It was a free-fall sensation, with nothing to measure possible movement against.

"Damn!" I heard Corwin say.

We hovered, fell, drifted—whatever—for a time, and, "So close," I heard him mutter.

"Something that way," Luke suddenly announced, gesturing to his right.

A big shape loomed grayly. I moved my mind into the spikard and probed in that direction. Whatever it was, it was inanimate, and I commanded the spike that had touched it to guide us to it.

I did not feel myself moving, but the thing loomed larger, took on familiar outlines, began to show a reddish complexion. When the fins became apparent, I knew for certain.

"Looks like that Polly Jackson you have," Luke remarked. "Even has the snow on it."

Yes, it was my red and white '57 Chevy that we were approaching, there in Limbo.

"It's a construct. It's been pulled from my mind before," I told him. "Probably because it's vivid, I've studied it so often. Also, it seems very appropriate just now.''

I reached toward the door handle. We were coming up on the driver's side. I caught hold and pushed the button. It was, of course, unlocked. The others touched the vehicle in various places and drew themselves along to the other side. I opened the door, slid in behind the wheel, closed the door. Luke and Corwin were entering by then. The keys were in the ignition, as I'd expected.

When everyone was aboard I tried starting it. The engine caught immediately. I stared out across the bright hood into nothingness. I switched on the headlights and that didn't help.

''What now?'' Luke asked.

I shifted into first, released the emergency brake, and let out the clutch. As I gave it the gas, it seemed the wheels were turning. After a few moments I shifted into second. A bit later I put it into third.

Was there the tiniest feeling of traction, or was it only the power of suggestion?

I fed it more gas. The foggy prospect seemed to brighten slightly, far ahead, though I supposed this could simply be some effect of my staring in that direction. There was no particular feedback from the steering wheel. I pushed harder on the accelerator.

Luke reached out suddenly and turned on the radio.

''—hazardous driving conditions,'' came an announcer's voice. ''So keep your speed to a minimum.'' There immediately followed Wynton Marsalis playing ''Caravan.''

Taking it as a personal message, I eased up on the gas. This produced a definite feeling of light traction, as if, perhaps, we were gliding on ice.

A sensation of forward movement followed, and there did seem a brightening in the distance. Also, it seemed as if I had acquired some weight, was settling more deeply into the seat. Moments later the sensation of a real surface beneath the car became more pronounced. I wondered what would happen if I turned the wheel. I decided not to try it.

The sound from beneath the tires became more gritty. Dim outlines occurred at either hand, increasing the feeling of movement and direction as we passed them. Far ahead, the world was indeed brighter now.

I slowed even more because it began feeling as if I were negotiating a real road, with very poor visibility. Shortly thereafter, the headlights did seem to be operating with some effect, as they struck a few of the passing shapes, giving them the momentary appearance of trees and embankments, shrub clusters, rocks. The rearview mirror continued to reflect nothingness, however.

"Just like old times," Luke said. "Goin' out for pizza on a bad evening."

"Yeah," I agreed.

"I hope the other me has someone open a pizza parlor in Kashfa. Could use one there, you know?"

"I'll come by and try it, if he does."

"Where do you think this whole business is going to leave me, anyway?"

"I don't know, Luke."

"I mean, I can't keep drinking your blood. And what about the other me?"

"I think I can offer you a job that will take care of the problem," Corwin said to him. "For a while, anyway."

The trees were definitely trees now, the fog real fog— moving about a bit. Beads of moisture began to form on the windshield.

"What do you mean?" Luke asked.

"In a minute."

There were breaks in the fog now, real landscape visible through them. Abruptly, I became aware that it was not a real road surface on which I was driving, but rather a fairly level piece of ground. I slowed even more to accommodate this.

A big section of haze dissolved or blew away then, revealing the presence of an enormous tree. Also, a section of the ground seemed to be glowing. There was a familiar feeling to this partial tableau. . . .

"This is the place of *your* Pattern, isn't it?" I asked, as our way grew even clearer. "Fiona brought me here once."

"Yes," came the reply.

"And its image— That's the thing I saw confronting the Sign of the Logrus back in the graveyard—the same thing that led us into the tunnel."

"Yes."

"Then— It's sentient, too. Like Amber's, like the Logrus—"

"True. Park it over there, in that clear area by the tree."

I turned the wheel and headed toward the level spot he had indicated. Fog still hung about the place, but nowhere near as heavy and all-encompassing as on the trail we had taken. It might have been twilight, from the shading of the mist, but the glow from that eccentric Pattern brightened our cup-shaped world beyond a day's end dimness.

As we climbed out Corwin said to Luke, "Pattern ghosts tend not to last long."

"So I understand," Luke replied. "You know any tricks for someone in this position?"

"I know them all, sir. It takes one to know, as they say."

"Oh?"

"Dad . . .?" I said. "You mean . . ."

"Yes," he replied. "I do not know where the first version of myself might be."

"You are the one I encountered a while back? The one who might have been present in Amber recently, also?"

"Yes."

"I—see. Yet, you don't seem exactly like others I've encountered."

He reached out and clasped my shoulder.

"I'm not," he said, and he glanced toward the Pattern. "I drew that thing," he went on, a little later, "and I'm the only person ever to have walked it. Consequently, I'm the only ghost it can summon. Also, it seems to regard me with something other than utilitarian attention. We can communicate, in a way, and it seems to have been willing to devote the energy needed to keep me stable—for a long while now. We have our own plans, and our relationship seems almost symbiotic. I gather that those of Amber's Pattern and those of the Logrus are more in the nature of ephemera."

"That's been my experience," I said.

"—except for one, to whom you ministered, for which I am grateful. She is under my protection now, for so long as it shall last."

He released my shoulder.

"I haven't been properly introduced to your friend yet," he said then.

"Excuse me. A bit of extenuation there," I said. "Luke, I'd like you to meet my father, Corwin of Amber. Sir, Luke is properly known as Rinaldo, son of your brother Brand."

Corwin's eyes widened for an instant, then narrowed as he extended his hand, studying Luke's face.

"Good to meet a friend of my son's, as well as a relative," he said.

"Glad to know you, too, sir."

"I'd wondered what it was that seemed so familiar about you."

"It kind of slows down with appearances, if that's what you're getting at. Maybe even stops there."

Dad laughed.

"Where'd you two meet?"

"In school," Luke replied. "Berkeley."

"Where else might a pair of us come together? Not in Amber, of course," he said, turning away then to face his Pattern fully. "I'll get your story yet. But come with me now. I want to do an introduction myself."

He headed off toward the shining design and we followed him, a few wisps of fog drifting past us. Save for our short footfalls, the place was silent.

When we came up to the edge of his Pattern we halted and stared out across it. It was a graceful design, too big to take in at a glance; and a feeling of power seemed to pulse outward from it.

"Hi," he said. "I want you to meet my son and my nephew, Merlin and Rinaldo—though I believe you met Merlin once before. Rinaldo has a problem." There followed a long silence. Then he said, "Yes, that's right," and after a time, "You really think so?" and, "Okay. Sure, I'll tell them."

He stretched and sighed and took a few paces away from the Pattern's edge. Then he extended his arms and put them around both our shoulders.

"Men," he said then, "I've got an answer of sorts. But it means we're all going to have to walk this Pattern, for different reasons."

"I'm game," Luke said. "But what's the reason?"

"It's going to adopt you," Corwin said, "and sustain you as it does me. There's a price, though. The time's getting nearer when it will want to be guarded full-time. We can spell each other."

"Sounds fine," Luke said. "This place is kind of peaceful. And I didn't really want to go back to Kashfa and try to depose myself."

"Okay. I'll lead, and you hold on to my shoulder in case there are any funny vibes to deal with. Merlin, you come last and maintain contact with Luke, for the same reason. All right?"

"Sure," I said. "Let's go."

He released us and moved to the place where the line of the design began. We followed, and Luke's hand was on his shoulder as he took the first step. Soon we were all of us on the Pattern, struggling the familiar struggle. Even when the sparks began to rise, though, this one seemed a little easier than I recalled from Pattern walks in the past, possibly because someone else was leading the way.

Images of avenues lined with ancient chestnut trees filled my mind as we trudged along and fought our way through the First Veil. By then, the sparks came higher about us and I felt the forces of the Pattern beating about me, penetrating me, body and mind. I recalled my days in school, remembered my greatest efforts on the athletic field. The resistance continued to rise, and we leaned into it. Moving my feet became a great effort, and I realized that—somehow—the effort was more important than the movement. I felt my hair beginning to rise as a current passed entirely through my body. Still, this had not to it the maddening quality of the Logrus the time I had negotiated it, nor the adversarial feeling I had felt upon Amber's Pattern. It was almost as if I traversed the interior of a mind, one not unkindly disposed toward me. There was a feeling—of encouragement, almost— as I struggled along a curve, executed a turn. The resistance was as strong, the sparks came as high as on the other at about this point, yet I somehow knew that this Pattern held me in a different fashion. We pushed our way along the lines. We turned, we burned. . . . Penetrating the Second Veil was a slow-motion exercise in stamina and will. Our way eased for a time after that, and images from all over my life came to frighten and console me.

Walking. One, two. . . . Three. I felt that if I were able to take ten more steps I would have a chance to win through. Four. . . . I was drenched with perspiration. Five. The resistance was awful. It took all the effort of running a hundred meters just to inch my foot ahead. My lungs were working like a bellows. Six. The sparks reached my face, passed my eyes, enveloped me completely. I felt as if I had been transformed into an immortal blue flame and that I must, somehow, burn my way through a block of marble. I burned and I burned and the stone remained unchanged. I could spend all of eternity this way. Perhaps I already had. Seven. And the images were gone. All of memory had fled. Even my identity was on vacation. I was stripped to a thing of pure will. I was an act, an act of striving against resistance. Eight. . . . I no longer felt my body. Time was an alien concept. The striving was no longer striving, but a form of elemental movement now, beside which glaciers rushed. Nine. Now I was only movement—infinitesimal, constant. . . .

Ten.

There came an easing. It would become difficult again at the center end, but I knew that the rest of the walk was anticlimax. Something like a slow, low music buoyed me as I trudged ahead, turned, trudged. It was with me through the Final Veil, and as I passed the midpoint of that final stride, it became something like "Caravan."

We stood there at the center, silent for a long while, breathing deeply. Exactly what I had achieved, I was uncertain. I did feel, though, that, in some way, I knew my father better as a result. Strands of mist still drifted, across the Pattern, across the valley.

"I feel—stronger," Luke announced later. "Yes, I'll

help guard this place. It seems a good way to spend some time."

"By the way, Luke, what *was* your message for me?" I asked.

"Oh, to tell you to clear out of the Courts," he replied, "that things were getting dangerous."

"I already knew the danger part," I said. "But there are still things I must do."

He shrugged. "Well, that's the message," he said. "No place really seems safe just now."

"There won't be any problems here yet," Corwin said. "Neither Power knows exactly how to approach this place or what to do with it. It's too strong for Amber's Pattern to absorb, and the Logrus doesn't know how to destroy it."

"Sounds pretty easy, then."

"There will probably come a time later, though, when they will try to move against it."

"Until then, we wait and watch. Okay. If some things do come, what might they be?"

"Probably ghosts—like ourselves—seeking to learn more about it, to test. You any good with that blade?"

"In all modesty, yes. If that's not good enough, I've studied the Arts, as well."

"They'll fall to steel, though it's fire they'll bleed— not blood. You can have the Pattern transport you outside now, if you wish. I'll join you in a few moments to show you where the weapons are cached, and the other supplies. I'd like to take a little trip and leave you in charge for a while."

"Sure thing," Luke said. "What about you, Merle?"

"I've got to get back to the Courts. I've a luncheon engagement with my mother, and then Swayvill's funeral to attend."

"It may not be able to send you all the way to the Courts," Corwin said. "That's getting awfully near the

Logrus. But you'll work something out with it, or vice versa. How *is* Dara?''

"It's been a long time since I've seen her for more than a few moments," I answered. "She is still peremptory, arrogant, and over-solicitous when it comes to me. I get the impression, too, that she may be involved in local political scheming as well as aspects of the larger relationship between the Courts and Amber.''

Luke closed his eyes for a moment and vanished. Shortly afterward, I saw him beside the Polly Jackson car. He opened the door, slid onto the passenger seat, leaned and fiddled with something inside. A little later I could hear the radio playing music across the distance.

"It's likely," Corwin said. "I never understood her, you know. She came to me out of nowhere at a strange time in my life, she lied to me, we became lovers, she walked the Pattern in Amber, and she vanished. It was like a bizarre dream. It was obvious that she used me. For years I thought that it was only to get knowledge of the Pattern and access to it. But I've had a lot of time for reflection recently, and I'm no longer certain that that was the case.''

"Oh?" I said. "What, then?"

"You," he replied. "More and more I'm coming to think, what she really wanted was to bear a son or daughter of Amber.''

I felt myself grow cold. Could the reason for my own existence have been such a calculated thing? Had there been no affection there at all? Had I been intentionally conceived to serve some special purpose? I did not at all like the notion. It made me feel the way Ghostwheel must, carefully structured product of my imagination and intellect, built to test design ideas only an Amberite could have come up with. Yet he called me "Dad." He actually seemed to care about me. Oddly, I had begun feeling an irrational affection for him myself. Was it partly because we were even more alike than I had consciously realized?

"Why?" I asked. "Why would it have been so important to her that I be born?"

"I can only remember her final words when she had completed the Pattern, turning into a demon in the process. 'Amber,' she said, 'will be destroyed.' Then she was gone."

I was shaking now. The implications were so unsettling that I wanted to cry, sleep, or get drunk. Anything, for a moment's respite.

"You think that my existence might be part of a long-term plan for the destruction of Amber?" I asked.

" 'Might,' " he said. "I could be wrong, kid. I could be very wrong, and if that's the case I apologize for troubling you this much. On the other hand, it would also be wrong of me not to let you know what the possibility is."

I massaged my temples, my brow, my eyes.

"What should I do?" I said then. "I don't want to help destroy Amber."

He clasped me to his breast for a moment and said, "No matter what you are and no matter what's been done to you, there will have to be some element of choice for you, sooner or later. You are greater than the sum of your parts, Merlin. No matter what went into your birth and your life up to now, you've got eyes and a brain and a set of values. Don't let anybody bullshit you, not even me. And when the time comes, if it comes, make damn sure the choice is your own. Nothing that's gone before will matter then."

His words, general as they had to be, drew me back from the place in my spirit where I had retreated.

"Thanks," I said.

He nodded. Then, "While your first impulse may be to force a confrontation on this matter," he said, "I would advise against it. It would achieve nothing other than making her aware of your suspicions. It would be prudent to play a more careful game and see what you can learn.''

I sighed.

''You're right, of course,'' I said. ''You came after me as much to tell me this as to help me escape, didn't you?''

He smiled.

''Only worry about important things,'' he said. ''We'll meet again.'' And then he was gone.

I saw him, suddenly, over near the car, talking to Luke. I watched as he showed him where the caches were located. I wondered what time it was back in the Courts. After a while, they both waved to me. Then Corwin shook hands with Luke and turned and walked off into the fog. I could hear the radio playing ''Lili Marlene.''

I focused my mind on the Pattern's transporting me to the Ways of Sawall. There was a momentary swirling of blackness. When it cleared I was still standing at the center of the Pattern. I tried again, this time for Suhuy's castle. Again, it refused to punch my ticket.

''How close can you send me?'' I finally asked.

There was another swirling, but this one was bright. It delivered me to a high promontory of white stone beneath a black sky, beside a black sea. Two semicircles of pale flame parenthesized my position. Okay, I could live with that. I was at Fire Gate, a way-exchange in Shadow near to the Courts. I faced the sea and counted. When I'd located the fourteenth flickering tower on my left, I walked toward it.

I emerged before a fallen tower beneath a pink sky. Walking toward it, I was transported to a glassy cavern through which a green river flowed. I paced beside the river till I found the stepping-stones that took me to a trail through an autumn wood. I followed this for almost a mile till I felt the presence of a way near the base of an evergreen. This took me to the side of a mountain, whence three more ways and two filmies had me on the trail to lunch with my mother. According to the sky, I had no time to change clothes.

I halted near a crossroads to dust myself off, straighten my apparel, comb my hair. I wondered, as I was about the business, who might receive my calling were I to try to reach Luke via his Trump—Luke himself, his ghost, both? Could the ghosts receive Trump calls? I found myself wondering what was going on back in Amber, too. And I thought of Coral, and Nayda. . . .

Hell.

I wanted to be somewhere else. I wanted to be far away. The Pattern's warning, via Luke, was well taken. Corwin had given me too much to think about, and I hadn't had time to sort it through properly. I did not want to be involved in whatever was going on here in the Courts. I did not like all of the implications involving my mother. I did not feel like attending a funeral. I felt somehow, also, uninformed. You'd think that if somebody wanted something from me—something very important—they'd at least take the time to explain the situation and ask for my cooperation. If it were a relative, there was a strong possibility I'd go along with it. Getting my cooperation would seem a lot less dicey than any trickery intended to control my actions. I wanted to be away from those who would control me, as well as the games they were playing.

I could turn and head back into Shadow, probably lose myself there. I could head back to Amber, tell Random everything I knew, everything I suspected, and he would protect me against the Courts. I could go back to the Shadow Earth, come up with a new identity, get back into computer design. . . .

Then, of course, I would never know what was going on and what had gone before. As for my father's real whereabouts—I'd been able to reach him from the Courts, never from anywhere else. In this sense, he was nearby. And there was no one else around here likely to help him.

I walked ahead and turned right. I made my way toward a purpling sky. I would be on time.

And so I came, again, into the Ways of Sawall. I had emerged from the red and yellow starburst design painted high upon the gateside wall of the front courtyard, descended the Invisible Stair, and peered for long moments down into the great central pit, with its view of black turbulence beyond the Rim. A falling star burned its way down the purple sky as I turned away, headed for the copper-chased door and the low Maze of Art beyond it.

Within, I recalled the many times I had been lost in that maze as a child. The House of Sawall had been a serious collector of art for ages, and the collection was so vast that there were several ways into which one was cast within the maze itself, leading one through tunnels, a huge spiral, and what seemed an old train station before being shunted back to miss the next turn. I had been lost in it for days on one occasion, and was finally found crying before an assemblage of blue shoes nailed to a board. I walked it now, slowly, looking at old monstrosities, and some newer ones. There were also strikingly lovely pieces mixed in, such as the huge vase that looked as if it had been carved from a single fire opal, and a set of odd enameled tablets from a distant shadow whose meaning and function no one in the family could be found to recall. I had to stop and see both again, rather than shortcutting the gallery, the tablets being a particular favorite of mine.

I was humming an old tune Gryll had taught me as I came up to the fiery vase and regarded it. I seemed to hear a small chafing noise, but glances up and down the corridor revealed no one else in the vicinity. The almost sensual curves of the vase begged to be touched. I could remember all of the times I had been forbidden to do so as a child. I put my left hand forward slowly, rested it upon it. It was warmer than I'd thought it might be. I slid my hand along its side. It was like a frozen flame.

"Hello," I muttered, remembering an adventure we'd shared. "It's been a long time. . . ."

"Merlin?" came a small voice.

I withdrew my hand immediately. It was as if the vase had spoken.

"Yes," I said then. "Yes."

Again, the chafing sound, and a bit of shadow stirred within the creamy opening, above the fire.

"Ss," said the shadow, rising.

"Glait?" I asked.

"Yess."

"It can't be. You've been dead for years."

"Not dead. Ssleeping."

"I haven't seen you since I was a kid. You were injured. You disappeared. I thought you'd died."

"I ssleep. I ssleep to heal. I ssleep to forget. I ssleep to renew mysself."

I extended my arm. The shaggy snake head rose higher, extended itself, fell upon my forearm, climbed, wrapped itself.

"You certainly chose elegant sleeping quarters."

"I knew the jug to be a favorite of yourss. If I waited long enough I knew you would come by again, sstop to admire it. And I would know and rise up in my ssplendor to greet you. My, you have grown!"

"You look pretty much the same. A little thin, perhaps. . . ."

I stroked her head gently.

"It is good to know you are with us still, like some honored family spirit. You and Gryll and Kergma made my childhood a better thing than it might have been."

She raised her head high, stroked my cheek with her nose.

"It warmss my cold blood to ssee you again, dear boy. You've traveled far?"

"I have. Very."

"One night we shall eat mice and lie besside a fire. You will warm me a ssaucer of milk and tell me of your adventuress ssince you left the Wayss of Ssawall. We will find ssome marrow boness for Gryll, if he be sstill about—"

"He seems to serve my uncle Suhuy these days. What of Kergma?"

"I do not know. It hass been sso long."

I held her close to warm her.

"Thank you for waiting here for me in your great drowse, to greet me—"

"Iss more than friendliess, helloss."

"More? What then, Glait? What is it?"

"A thing to show. Walk that way."

She gestured with her head. I moved in the direction she indicated—the way I had been heading anyhow, to where the corridors widened. I could feel her vibrating against my arm with the barely audible purring sound she sometimes made.

Suddenly, she stiffened and her head rose, swaying slightly.

"What is it?" I asked.

"Mi-ice," she said. "Mi-ice nearby. I musst go hunting—after I show you—the thing. Breakfasst. . . ."

"If you would dine first, I will wait."

"No, Merlin. You musst not be late for whatever—

brought you here. There is importance in the air. Later—
feasst—vermin. . . .''

We came into a wide, high, skylighted section of the
gallery. Four large pieces of metal statuary—bronze and
copper, mostly—stood in an asymmetrical arrangement
about us.

"Onward," Glait said. "Not here."

I turned right at the next corner and plunged ahead.
Shortly, we came to another display—this one resembling a metal forest.

"Sslow now. Sslow, dear demon child."

I halted and studied the trees, bright, dark, shiny, dull.
Iron, aluminum, brass, it was most impressive. It was
also a display that had not been present the last time I
had passed this way, years before. Nothing odd about
that, of course. There had also been changes in other
areas I had passed through.

"Now. Here. Turn in. Go back."

I moved on into the forest.

"Bear right. The tall one."

I halted when I came to the curved trunk of the tallest
tree to my right.

"This one?"

"Yess. Negotiate it—upward—pleasse."

"You mean climb it?"

"Yess."

"Right."

One nice thing about a stylized tree—or, at least, *this*
stylized tree—was that it spiraled, swelled, and twisted
in such a fashion as to provide better handholds and
footholds than at first seemed apparent. I caught hold,
drew myself up, found a place for my foot, pulled again,
pushed.

Higher. Higher, still. When I was perhaps ten feet
above the floor I halted.

"Uh, what do I do now that I'm here?" I asked.

"Climb higher."

"Why?"

"Ssoon. Ssoon. You'll know."

I drew myself about a foot higher, and then I felt it. It is not so much a tingling as it is a kind of pressure. I only feel a tingling, too, sometimes, if they lead someplace risky.

"There's a way up there," I said.

"Yess. I wass coiled about a branch of the blue tree when a shadowmasster opened it. They sslew him afterwardss."

"It must lead to something very important."

"I ssuppose. I am not a good judge—of people thingss."

"You have been through?"

"Yess."

"Then it *is* safe?"

"Yess."

"All right."

I climbed higher, resisting the force of the way until I'd brought both feet to the same level. Then I relaxed into the tugging and let it take me through.

I extended both hands, too, in case the surface was uneven. But it wasn't. The floor was beautifully tiled in black, silver, gray, and white. To the right was a geometric design, to the left a representation of the Pit of Chaos.

My eyes were directed downward for only a few moments, though.

"Good Lord!" I said.

"Wass I right? It iss important?" Glait said.

"It is important," I replied.

VI

There were candles all about the chapel, many of them as tall as I am, and nearly as big around. Some were silver, some were gray; a few were white, a few black. They stood at various heights, in artful disposition, on banks, ledges, pattern points on the floor. They did not provide the main illumination, however. This obtained from overhead, and I first assumed it to proceed from a skylight. When I glanced upward to gauge the height of the vault, though, I saw that the light emanated from a large blue-white globe confined behind a dark metal grate.

I took a step forward. The nearest candle flame flickered.

I faced a stone altar that filled a niche across the way. Black candles burned at either hand before it, smaller silver ones upon it. For a moment, I simply regarded it.

"Lookss like you," Glait remarked.

"I thought your eyes didn't register two-dimensional representations."

"I've lived a long time in a musseum. Why hide your picture up a ssecret way?"

I moved forward, my gaze on the painting.

"It's not me," I said. "It's my father, Corwin of Amber."

A silver rose stood within a bud vase before the portrait. Whether it was a real rose or the product of art or magic, I could not tell.

And Grayswandir lay there before it, drawn a few inches from the scabbard. I'd a feeling this was the real thing, that the version worn by the Pattern ghost of my father was itself a reconstruction.

I reached forward, raised it, drew it.

There was a feeling of power as I held it, swung it, struck an *en garde*, lunged, advanced. The spikard came alive, center of a web of forces. I looked down, suddenly self-conscious.

". . . And this is my father's blade," I said, returning to the altar, where I sheathed it. Reluctantly, I left it there.

As I backed away, Glait asked, "Thiss iss important?"

"Very," I said as the way caught hold of me and sent me back to the treetop.

"What now, Masster Merlin?"

"I must get on to lunch with my mother."

"In that case, you'd besst drop me here."

"I could return you to the vase."

"No. I haven't lurked in a tree for a time. Thiss will be fine."

I extended my arm. She unwound herself and flowed away across gleaming branches.

"Good luck, Merlin. Vissit me."

And I was down the tree, snagging my trousers only once, and off up the corridor at a quick pace.

Two turns later I came to a way to the main hall and

decided I'd better take it. I popped through beside the massive fireplace—high flames braiding themselves within it—and turned slowly to survey the huge chamber, trying to seem as if I had been there a long while, waiting.

I seemed the only person present. Which, on reflection, struck me as a bit odd, with the fire roaring that way. I adjusted my shirtfront, brushed myself off, ran my comb through my hair. I was inspecting my fingernails when I became aware of a flash of movement at the head of the great staircase to my left.

She was a blizzard within a ten-foot tower. Lightnings danced at its center, crackling; particles of ice clicked and rattled upon the stair; the banister grew frosted where she passed. My mother. She seemed to see me at about the same time I saw her, for she halted. Then she made the turn onto the stair and began her descent.

As she descended, she shifted smoothly, her appearance changing almost from step to step. As soon as I realized what was occurring I relaxed my own efforts and reversed their small effects. I had commenced changing the moment I had seen her, and presumably she had done the same on viewing me. I hadn't thought she'd go to that extent to humor me, a second time, here on her own turf.

The shift was completed just as she reached the bottommost stair, becoming a lovely woman in black trousers and red shirt with flared sleeves. She looked at me again and smiled, moved toward me, embraced me.

It would have been gauche to say that I'd intended shifting but had forgotten. Or any other remark on the matter.

She pushed me out to arm's distance, lowered her gaze and raised it, shook her head.

"Do you sleep in your clothes before or after violent exercise?" she asked me.

"That's unkind," I said. "I stopped to sightsee on the way over and ran into a few problems."

"That is why you are late?"

"No. I'm late because I stopped in our gallery and took longer than I'd intended. And I'm not very late."

She took hold of my arm and turned me.

"I will forgive you," she said, steering me toward the rose and green and gold-flecked pillar of ways, set in the mirrored alcove across the room to the right.

I didn't feel that called for a response, so I didn't make one. I watched with interest as we entered the alcove, to see whether she would conduct me in a clockwise direction or its opposite about the pillar.

The opposite, it turned out. Interesting.

We were reflected and re-reflected from the three sides. So was the room we had quitted. And with each circuit we made of the pillar it became a different room. I watched it change, kaleidoscopically, until she halted me before the crystal grotto beside the underground sea.

"It's been a long time since I thought of this place," I said, stepping forth upon the pure white sand into the crystal-cast light, variously reminiscent of bonfires, solar reflections, candelabra, and LED displays, functions of size and distancing perhaps, laying occasional pieces of rainbow upon the shore, the walls, the black water.

She took my hand and led me toward a raised and railed platform some small distance off to the right. A table stood full set upon it. A collection of covered trays occupied a larger serving table inland of it. We mounted a small stair, and I seated her and moved to check out the goodies next door.

"Do sit down, Merlin," she said. "I'll serve you."

"That's all right," I answered, raising a lid. "I'm already here. I'll do the first round."

She was on her feet.

"Buffet style then," she said.

"Sure."

We filled our plates and moved to the table. Seconds after we had seated ourselves a brilliant flash of light came to us across the water, illuminating the arching dome of the cavern vault like the ribbed interior of some massive beast that was digesting us.

"You needn't look so apprehensive. You know they can't come in this far."

"Waiting for a thunderclap puts my appetite on hold," I said.

She laughed just as a distant roll of thunder reached us.

"And that makes everything all right?" she asked.

"Yes," I replied, raising my fork.

"Strange, the relatives life gives us," she said.

I looked at her, tried to read her expression, couldn't. So, "Yes," I said.

She studied me for a moment, but I wasn't giving anything away either. So, "When you were a child you went monosyllabic as a sign of petulance," she said.

"Yes," I said.

We began eating. There were more flashes out over the still, dark sea. By light of the last one I thought I caught sight of a distant ship, black sails full-rigged and bellied.

"You kept your engagement with Mandor earlier?"

"Yes."

"How is he?"

"Fine."

"Something bothering you, Merlin?"

"Many things."

"Tell Mother?"

"What if she's a part of it?"

"I would be disappointed if I were not. Still, how long will you hold the business of the *ty'iga* against me? I did what I thought was right. I still think it was."

I nodded and continued chewing. After a time, "You made that clear last cycle," I said.

The waters gave a small sloshing sound. A spectrum drifted across our table, her face.

"Is there something else?" she asked.

"Why don't *you* tell *me*?" I said.

I felt her gaze. I met it.

"I don't know what you mean," she answered.

"Are you aware that the Logrus is sentient? And the Pattern?" I said.

"Did Mandor tell you that?" she asked.

"Yes. But I already knew it before he did."

"How?"

"We've been in touch."

"You and the Pattern? You and the Logrus?"

"Both."

"To what end?"

"Manipulation, I'd say. They're engaged in a power struggle. They were asking me to choose sides."

"Which did you choose?"

"Neither. Why?"

"You should have told me."

"Why?"

"For counsel. Possibly for assistance."

"Against the Powers of the universe? How well connected are you, Mother?"

She smiled.

"It is possible that one such as myself may possess special knowledge of their workings."

"One such as yourself. . . ?"

"A sorceress of my skills."

"Just how good are you, Mother?"

"I don't think they come much better, Merlin."

"Family is always the last to know, I guess. So why didn't you train me yourself, instead of sending me off to Suhuy?"

"I'm not a good teacher. I dislike training people."

"You trained Jasra."

She tilted her head to the right and narrowed her eyes.

"Did Mandor tell you that, also?" she asked.

"No."

"Who, then?"

"What difference does it make?"

"Considerable," she replied. "Because I don't believe you knew it the last time we met."

I recalled suddenly that she had said something about Jasra back at Suhuy's, something implying her familiarity with her, something to which I would ordinarily have risen save that I was driving a load of animus in a different direction at the time and heading downhill in a thunderstorm with the brakes making funny noises. I was about to ask her why it mattered *when* I learned it, when I realized that she was really asking from whom I'd learned it, because she was concerned with whom I might have been speaking on such matters since last we'd met. Mentioning Luke's Pattern ghost did not seem politic, so, "Okay, Mandor let it slip," I said, "and then asked me to forget it."

"In other words," she said, "he expected it to get back to me. Why did he do it just that way? I wonder. The man is damnably subtle."

"Maybe he did just let it slip."

"Mandor lets nothing slip. Never make him an enemy, son."

"Are we talking about the same person?"

She snapped her fingers.

"Of course," she said. "It was only as a child that you knew him. You went away after that. You have seen him but a few times since. Yes, he is subtle, insidious, dangerous."

"We've always gotten along well."

"Of course. He never antagonizes without a good reason."

I shrugged and went on eating.

After a time she said, "I daresay he has made similar comments about me."

"I am unable to recall any," I answered.

"Has he been giving you lessons in circumspection, too?"

"No, though I've felt a need to teach myself, of late."

"Surely, you obtained a few in Amber."

"If I did, they were so subtle I didn't notice."

"Well, well. Can it be I need despair of you no more?"

"I doubt it."

"So, what might the Pattern or the Logrus want of you?"

"I already told you—a choice of sides."

"It is that difficult to decide which you prefer?"

"It is that difficult to decide which I dislike less."

"Because they are, as you say, manipulative of people in their struggle for power?"

"Just so."

She laughed. Then, "While it shows the gods as no better than the rest of us," she said, "at least, it shows them as no worse. See here the sources of human morality. It is still better than none at all. If these grounds be insufficient for the choosing of sides, then let other considerations rule. You are, after all, a son of Chaos."

"And Amber," I said.

"You grew up in the Courts."

"And I have dwelled in Amber. My relatives are as numerous there as they are here."

"It is really that close, then?"

"If it were not, it might have simplified matters."

"In that case," she said, "you must turn it around."

"What do you mean?"

"Ask not which appeals the most to you, but which can do the most for you."

I sipped a fine green tea as the storm rolled nearer. Something splashed within the waters of our inlet.

"All right," I said, "I'm asking."

She leaned forward and smiled and her eyes darkened. She has always had perfect control of her face and form, shifting them to suit her moods. She is obviously the same person, but at times she may choose to appear as little more than a girl, at other times becoming a mature and handsome woman. Generally, she seems somewhere in between. But now, a certain timeless quality came into her features—not age so much as the essence of Time— and I realized suddenly that I had never known her true age. I watched as something like a veil of ancient power came across it.

"The Logrus," she said, "will lead you to greatness."

I continued to stare.

"What sort of greatness?" I asked.

"What sort do you desire?"

"I don't know that I ever wanted greatness, on its own. It seems rather like wanting to be an engineer, rather than wanting to design something—or wanting to be a writer, rather than wanting to write. It should be a by-product, not a thing in itself. Otherwise, it's just an ego trip."

"But if you earn it—if you deserve it—shouldn't you have it?"

"I suppose. But so far I've done nothing"—my eyes fell to a bright circle of light beneath the dark waters, moving as if running before a storm—"except perhaps for an odd piece of equipment, which might fall into that category."

"You are young, of course," she said, "and the times for which you were meant to be uniquely qualified have come sooner than I'd anticipated.''

If I were to use magic to summon a cup of coffee,
would she resent that? Yes, I believed. She would. So I
decided on a glass of wine. As I poured it and took a
sip, I said, ''I'm afraid I don't understand what you're
talking about.''

She nodded.

''It is hardly something you could learn from intro-
spection,'' she said slowly, ''and no one would be so
rash as to mention the possibility to you.''

''What are you talking about, Mother?''

''The throne. To reign in the Courts of Chaos.''

''Mandor had sort of suggested I think about it,'' I
said.

''All right. No one, excepting Mandor, would be so
rash as to mention it.''

''I gather mothers get a certain kick out of seeing their
sons do well, but unfortunately you've named a job for
which I lack not only skill, aptitude, and training but
also any desire.''

She steepled her fingers and regarded me from just
above them.

''You are better qualified than you think, and your
desires have nothing to do with the matter.''

''As an interested party, I must beg to differ with
you.''

''Even if it were the only way to protect friends and
relatives both here and in Amber?''

I took another sip of wine.

''Protect them? Against what?''

''The Pattern is about to try redefining the middle
regions of Shadow in its own image. It is probably
strong enough to do it now.''

''You were talking of Amber and the Courts, not of
Shadow.''

''The Logrus will have to resist this incursion. Since

it would probably lose in a direct confrontation with its opposite, it will be forced to employ agents strategically, in a strike against Amber. The most effective agents would, of course, be champions of the Courts—''

"This is mad!'' I said. ''There must be a better way!''

"Possibly,'' she replied. ''Accept the throne and you'll be giving the orders.''

"I don't know enough.''

"You will be briefed, of course.''

"What about the proper order of succession?''

"That's not your problem.''

"I rather think I'd have an interest in how it's achieved—say, whether I'd owe you or Mandor for the majority of deaths.''

"In that we're both Sawall, the question becomes academic.''

"You mean you're cooperating on this?''

"We have our differences,'' she said, ''and I draw the line at any discussion of methods.''

I sighed and took another drink. The storm had grown worse over the dark waters. If that strange light effect beneath their surface were indeed Ghostwheel, I wondered what he was up to. The lightnings were becoming a steady backdrop, the thunder a continuing soundtrack.

"What did you mean,'' I said, ''when you spoke of the times for which I was meant to be uniquely qualified?''

"The present and the immediate future,'' she said, ''with the conflict that will come.''

"No,'' I responded. ''I was referring to the business about my being 'meant to be uniquely qualified.' How so?''

It must have been the lightning, for I had never seen her blush before.

"You combine two great bloodlines,'' she said. ''Technically, your father was King of Amber—

briefly—between the reign of Oberon and that of Eric.''

"Since Oberon was still alive at the time and had not abdicated, neither reign should be considered valid," I responded. "Random is Oberon's proper successor."

"A case can be made for an implied abdication," she said.

"You prefer that reading, don't you?"

"Of course."

I watched the storm. I swallowed some wine.

"That is why you wished to bear Corwin's child?" I asked.

"The Logrus assured me that such a child would be uniquely qualified to reign here."

"But Dad never really meant that much to you, did he?"

She looked away, out to where the circle of light was now racing toward us, lightnings falling behind it.

"You have no right to ask that question," she said.

"I know that. But it's true, isn't it?"

"You are mistaken. He meant a great deal to me."

"But not in any conventional sense."

"I am not a conventional person."

"I was the result of a breeding experiment. The Logrus selected the mate who would give you—what?"

The circle of light swam nearer. The storm followed it, coming closer in to the shore than I'd ever seen one reach here before.

"An ideal Lord of Chaos," she said, "fit to rule."

"Somehow I feel there's more to it than that," I said.

Dodging lightning bolts, the bright circle came up out of the water and flashed across the sand toward us. If she responded to my last remark, I couldn't hear it. The ensuing thunders were deafening.

The light came onto the decking, paused near to my foot.

"Dad, can you protect me?" Ghost asked in a lull between thunderclaps.

"Rise to my left wrist," I bade.

Dara stared as he found his place, taking on the appearance of Frakir. In the meantime, the final flash of lightning did not depart, but stood for a time like a sizzling stalk at the water's edge. Then it collapsed into a ball that hovered in the middle air for several moments before drifting in our direction. As it came on, its structure began to change.

When it drifted to a position beside our table it had become a bright, pulsing Sign of the Logrus.

"Princess Dara, Prince Merlin," came that awful voice I had last heard on the day of the confrontation at Amber Castle, "I did not wish to disturb your repast, but that thing you harbor makes it necessary." A jagged branch of the image was flipped in the direction of my left wrist.

"It's blocking my ability to shift away," Ghost said.

"Give it to me!"

"Why?" I asked.

"That thing has traversed the Logrus," came the words, differing at seeming random in pitch, volume, accent.

It occurred to me that I might defy it now if I were really as valuable to the Logrus as Dara had indicated. So, "It's theoretically open to all comers," I responded.

"I am my own law, Merlin, and your Ghostwheel has crossed me before. I'll have it now."

"No," I said, moving my awareness into the spikard, seeking and locating a means of instant transport to an area where the Pattern ruled. "I'll not surrender my creation so readily."

The brightness of the Sign increased.

At this, Dara was on her feet, moving to interpose herself between it and myself.

"Stay," she said. "We've more important matters to deal with than vengeance upon a toy. I have dispatched my cousins Hendrake for the bride of Chaos. If you wish this plan to succeed, I suggest you assist them."

"I recall your plan for Prince Brand, setting the lady Jasra to snare him. It could not fail, you told me."

"It brought you closer than you ever came, old Serpent, to the power you desire."

"That is true," it acknowledged.

"And the bearer of the Eye is a simpler being than Jasra."

The Sign slid past her, a tiny sun turning itself into a succession of ideograms.

"Merlin, you will take the throne and serve me when the time comes?"

"I will do what is necessary to redress the balance of power," I replied.

"That is not what I asked! Will you take the throne under the terms I set?"

"If that is what is needed to set things right," I answered.

"This pleases me," it said. "Keep your toy."

Dara moved aside, and it passed near to her before fading.

"Ask him of Luke and Corwin and the new Pattern," it said, and then it was gone.

She turned toward me and stared.

"Pour me a glass of wine," she said.

I did this. She raised it and took a swallow.

"So tell me of Luke and Corwin and the new Pattern," she said.

"Tell me of Jasra and Brand," I countered.

"No. You will go first in this," she said.

"Very well," I said. "It neglected to mention that they were Pattern ghosts. Luke's appeared to me on the way over here, sent by the Pattern to persuade me to depart this realm. The Logrus sent Lord Borel's to dispose of Luke.''

"Luke being Rinaldo, the son of Jasra and Brand, husband of Coral and King of Kashfa?"

"Very good. Now tell me of all that business at the end. You set Jasra to snare Brand, to guide him down the path he took?"

"He would have taken it anyhow. He came to the Courts seeking power to further his ends. She merely made things a little easier for him."

"That's not how it sounded to me. But does that mean my father's curse was not really a factor?"

"No, it helped—in a metaphysical way—making it easier to extend the Black Road to Amber. Why is it you are still here, when King Rinaldo bade you depart? Is it loyalty to the Courts?"

"I had a date with you for lunch, and it's been a while. Hated to miss it."

She smiled, very slightly, and took a small sip of wine.

"You change the subject well," she stated. "Let us return to it now. The ghost of Borel dispatched that of Rinaldo, I take it?"

"Not exactly."

"What do you mean?"

"My father's ghost showed up about then and dealt with Borel, permitting us to depart."

"Again? Corwin bested Borel again?"

I nodded.

"Neither remembered their first encounter, of course. Their memories only go back to the time of their recording, and—"

"I understand the principle. Then what happened?"

"We fled," I answered, "and I subsequently came here."

"What did the Logrus mean in referring to the new Pattern?"

"My father's ghost was apparently generated there, rather than by the old one."

She sat upright, eyes suddenly wide.

"How do you know this?" she demanded.

"He told me," I answered.

She stared past me then at the now-silent sea. "So the third power is actually taking a part in things," she mused. "This is fascinating, as well as disconcerting. Damn the man for having drawn it!"

"You really hate him, don't you?" I said.

Her eyes focused again upon my own.

"Let that subject be!" she ordered. "Save for this," she amended a moment later. "Did he give you any indication as to the new Pattern's allegiance—or its plans? The fact that it sent him to protect Luke might be seen as a seconding of the old Pattern's action. On the other hand—either because it was created by your father, or because it has its own uses for you—I can see it simply as an effort at your protection. What did he say?"

"That he wanted to get me away from where I was."

She nodded.

"Which he obviously did," she said. "Did he say anything else? Did anything else happen that might be important?"

"He asked after you."

"Really? And that was all?"

"He had no special message, if that's what you mean."

"I see."

She looked away, was silent for a time. Then, "Those ghosts don't last very long, do they?" she said.

"No," I replied.

"It's infuriating," she said at last, "to think that, despite everything, he is still able to play a hand in this."

"He's alive, isn't he, Mother?" I said. "And you know where he is."

"I'm not his keeper, Merlin."

"I think you are."

"It is impertinent to contradict me this way."

"Yet I must," I responded. "I saw him off on his way to the Courts. Certainly, he wanted to be here with the others for the peace settlement. Even more, though, he must have wanted to see you. There were so many unanswered questions in his mind—where you came from, why you came to him, why you parted as you did—"

"Enough!" she cried. "Let it be!"

I ignored her.

"And I know he was here in the Courts. He was seen here. He must have looked you up. What happened then? What sort of answers did you give him?"

She rose to her feet, glaring at me now.

"That will be all, Merlin," she said. "It seems impossible to conduct a civilized conversation with you."

"Is he your prisoner, Mother? Do you have him locked away somewhere, someplace where he can't bother you, can't interfere with your plans?"

She stepped quickly away from the table, almost stumbling.

"Wretched child!" she said. "You're just like him! Why did you have to resemble him so?"

"You're afraid of him, aren't you?" I said, suddenly realizing this could well be the case. "You're afraid to kill a Prince of Amber, even with the Logrus on your side. You've got him locked away somewhere, and you're afraid he'll come loose and blow your latest plans. You've been scared for a long time now because of what you've had to do to keep him out of action."

"Preposterous!" she said, backing away as I rounded

the table. There was a look of genuine fear on her face now. "You're just guessing!" she went on. "He's dead, Merlin! Give up! Leave me alone! Never mention his name in my presence again! Yes, I hate him! He would have destroyed us all! He still would, if he could!"

"He is not dead," I stated.

"How can you say that?"

I bit down on the desire to tell her I'd spoken with him, held it back.

"Only the guilty protest so strongly," I said. "He's alive. Where is he?"

She raised her hands, palms inward, and crossed them upon her breast, elbows low. The fear was gone, the anger was gone. When she spoke again, something like mockery seemed her main humor: "Then seek him, Merlin. By all means, seek him."

"Where?" I demanded.

"Look for him in the Pit of Chaos."

A flame appeared near her left foot and began orbiting her body in a counterclockwise direction, spiraling upward, leaving a line of fire to blaze redly behind it. By the time it reached the crown of her head she was entirely concealed. It went out with a faint whooshing sound then, taking her along with it.

I moved forward and knelt, feeling the area on which she'd stood. It was a little warm, that's all. Nice spell. Nobody'd ever taught me that one. Thinking back on it then, I realized that Mom had always had a flair when it came to entrances and exits.

"Ghost?"

He danced away from my wrist to hover in the air before me.

"Yes?"

"Are you still barred from transporting yourself through Shadow?"

"No," he replied. "That was lifted when the Sign of

the Logrus departed. I can travel—in or out of Shadow. I can provide transportation for you. Would you like me to?''

"Yes. Take me into the gallery upstairs."

"Gallery? I plunged directly from the place of the Logrus into the dark sea, Dad. I'm not quite sure as to the lay of the land here."

"Never mind," I said. "I'll manage it myself."

I activated the spikard. Energies spiraled from six of its tines, encaging Ghost and myself, swirling us upward to the place of my desire in the Maze of Art. I tried for a flash of fire as we went, but had no way of knowing whether I'd achieved it. Makes you wonder how the really good ones get their practice.

VII

I delivered us into that eerie hall that had always been old Sawall's chief delight in the maze. It was a sculpture garden, with no outside light sources and small base lighting only about the huge pieces, making it several times darker than my favorite lounge. The floor was uneven—concave, convex, stepped, ridged—with concavity being the dominant curve. It was difficult to guess at its dimensions, for it seemed of different size and contour depending upon where one stood. Gramble, Lord Sawall, had caused it to be constructed without any plane surfaces—and I believe the job involved some unique shadowmastery.

I stood beside what appeared to be a complicated rigging in the absence of its ship—that, or an elaborate musical instrument fit to be strummed by Titans—and the light turned the lines to silver, running like life from darkness to darkness within some half-seen frame. Other pieces jutted from walls and hung like stalactites. As I strolled, what had seemed walls became floor to me. The pieces that had seemed floored now jutted or depended.

The room changed shape as I went, and a breeze blew through it, causing sighs, hums, buzzes, chimes. Gramble, my stepfather, had taken a certain delight in this hall, whereas for me it had long represented an exercise in intrepidity to venture beyond its threshold. As I grew older, however, I, too, came to enjoy it, partly for the occasional *frisson* it provided my adolescence. Now, though— Now I just wanted to wander it a few moments, for old times' sake, as I sorted through my thoughts. There were so damned many of them. Things that had tantalized me for much of my adult life seemed near to explanation now. I was not happy with all of the possibilities that tumbled through my mind. Still, no matter which ones came out on top, it would beat ignorance.

"Dad?"

"Yes?"

"What is this place, anyway?" Ghost asked.

"It's a part of the big art collection here at the Ways of Sawall," I explained. "People come from all over the Courts and nearby Shadow to see it. It was a passion with my stepfather. I spent a lot of time wandering these halls when I was a kid. There are many hidden ways in this place."

"And this particular room? There's something wrong with it."

"Yes and no," I said. "I guess it depends on what you mean by 'wrong.'"

"My perceptions are strangely affected just now."

"That is because the space itself is folded in here, like some odd origami figure. The hall is much larger than it seems. You can wander through many times and witness a different array of displays on each occasion. There may even be some internal movement involved. I was never sure. Only Sawall knew for certain."

"I was right. Something's wrong with it."

"I rather like it this way."

I seated myself on a silver stump beside a sprawled silver tree.

"I want to see how it folds," he said at last.

"Go ahead."

As he drifted off, I thought of my recent interview with my mother. I was reminded of everything Mandor had said or implied, of the conflict between the Pattern and the Logrus, of my father as the champion of the Pattern and intended king in Amber. Had she known this, known it as fact rather than speculation? I imagined she could have, for she seemed to enjoy a special relationship with the Logrus, and it would surely have been aware of its adversary's more prominent decisions. She'd admitted that she did not love the man. It seemed as if she had sought him for whatever genetic material had so impressed the Pattern. Had she really been trying to breed a champion for the Logrus?

I chuckled as I considered the result. She had seen me trained well in arms, but I was nowhere near Dad's league. I'd preferred sorcery, but sorcerers were a dime a dozen in the Courts. Finally, she'd shipped me off to college on that Shadow Earth the Amberites favor. But a degree in Computer Science from Berkeley didn't much qualify me to uphold the banner of Chaos against the forces of Order either. I must have been a disappointment to her.

I thought back to my childhood, to some of the strange adventures for which this place had served as a point of departure. Gryll and I would come here, Glait slithering at our feet, coiled about a limb or riding somewhere amid my garments. I would give that odd ululant cry I had learned in a dream, and sometimes Kergma would join us, come skittering down the folds of darkness, out some frayed area of twisted space. I was never sure exactly what Kergma was, or even of what gender, for Kergma was a shapeshifter and flew, crawled, hopped, or ran in a succession of interesting forms.

On an impulse, I voiced that ancient call. Nothing, of course, happened, and I saw it moments later for what it was: a cry after a vanished childhood, when I had at least felt wanted. Now, now I was nothing—neither Amberite nor Chaosite, and certainly a disappointment to my relatives on both sides. I was a failed experiment. I'd never been wanted for myself, but as something that might come to pass. Suddenly my eyes were moist, and I held back a sob. And I'll never know what sort of mood I might have worked myself into because I was distracted then.

There came a flare of red light from a point high on the wall to my left. It was in the form of a small circle about the feet of a human figure.

"Merlin!" called a voice from that direction, and the flames leapt higher. By their light, I saw that familiar face, reminding me a bit of my own, and I was pleased with the meaning it had just given to my life, even if that meaning was death.

I raised my left hand above my head and willed a flash of blue light from the spikard.

"Over here, Jurt!" I called, rising to my feet. I began forming the ball of light that was to be his distraction while I readied the strike that would electrocute him. On reflection, it had seemed the surest way of taking him out. I'd lost count of the number of attempts he'd made on my life, and I'd resolved to take the initiative the next time he came calling. Frying his nervous system seemed the surest way to ice him, despite what the Fountain had done for him. "Over here, Jurt!"

"Merlin! I want to talk!"

"I don't. I've tried it too often, and I've nothing left to say. Come on over and let's get this done—weapons, hands, magic. I don't care."

He raised both hands, palms outward.

"Truce!" he cried. "It wouldn't be right to do it here in Sawall."

"Don't give me that scruples shit, brother!" I cried, but even as I said it I realized there might be something to it. I could remember how much the old man's approval had meant to him, and I realized that he'd hate to do anything to antagonize Dara here on the premises. "What do you want, anyway?"

"To talk. I mean it," he said. "What do I have to do?"

"Meet me over there," I said, casting my ball of light to shine above a familiar object that looked like a giant house of cards made of glass and aluminum, bouncing light from hundreds of planes.

"All right," came the reply.

I began walking in that direction. I saw him approaching from his, and I angled my course so that our paths would not intersect. Also, I increased my pace so as to arrive ahead of him.

"No tricks," he called out. "And if we do decide we can only take it to the end, let's go outside."

"Okay."

I entered the structure at a point around the corner from his approach. Immediately, I encountered six images of myself.

"Why here?" came his voice from somewhere near at hand.

"I don't suppose you ever saw a movie called *Lady from Shanghai*?"

"No."

"It occurred to me that we could wander around in here and talk, and the place would do a lot to keep us from hurting each other."

I turned a corner. There were more of me in different places. A few moments later, I heard a sharp intake of breath from somewhere near at hand. It was followed almost immediately by a chuckle.

"I begin to understand," I heard him say.

Three steps and another turn. I halted. There were two of him and two of me. He was not looking at me, though. I reached out slowly toward one of the images. He turned, he saw me. His mouth opened as he stepped back and vanished.

"What did you want to talk about?" I asked, halting.

"It's hard to know where to begin."

"That's life."

"You upset Dara quite a bit. . . ."

"That was quick. I only left her ten, fifteen minutes ago. You're staying here at Sawall?"

"Yes. And I knew she was having lunch with you. I just saw her briefly a little while ago."

"Well, she didn't make me feel too good either."

I turned another corner and passed through a doorway in time to see him smile faintly.

"She's that way sometimes. I know," he said. "She tells me the Logrus came by for dessert."

"Yes."

"She said it seems to have chosen you for the throne."

I hoped he saw my shrug.

"It seemed that way. I don't want it, though."

"But you said you'd do it."

"Only if there's no other way to restore a certain balance of forces. It's a last resort sort of thing. It won't come to that, I'm sure."

"But it chose you."

Another shrug.

"Tmer and Tubble precede me."

"That doesn't matter. I'd wanted it, you know."

"I know. Seems a pretty dumb career choice."

Suddenly, he surrounded me.

"It does now," he admitted. "It was getting that way for some time, though, before you got designated. I thought I had the edge each time we met, and each time you came a little closer to killing me."

"It did keep getting messier."

"That last time—in the church—in Kashfa, I was certain I could finally take you out. Instead, you damn near did me in."

"Say that Dara or Mandor removed Tmer and Tubble. You knew you'd have to take care of me yourself, but what about Despil?"

"He'd step aside for me."

"You asked him?"

"No. But I'm sure."

I moved on.

"You always assumed too much, Jurt."

"Maybe you're right," he said, appearing and vanishing again. "Either way, it doesn't matter."

"Why not?"

"I quit. I'm out of the running. The hell with it."

"How come?"

"Even if the Logrus hadn't made its intentions clear, I was beginning to feel nervous. It was not just that I was afraid you'd kill me either. I got to thinking about myself, and the succession. What if I made it to the throne? I'm not so sure as I once was that I'm competent to hold it." I turned again, caught a glimpse of him licking his lips, brows knotted. "I could mess up the realm severely," he went on, "unless I had good advice. And you know that, ultimately, it would come from Mandor or Dara. I'd wind up a puppet, wouldn't I?"

"Probably. But you've gotten me very curious. When did you start thinking this way? Might it coincide with your treatment in the Fountain? What if my interruption made yours closer to the correct course there?"

"It's possible there's something to that," he said.

"I'm glad now I didn't go the full route. I suspect it might have driven me mad, as it did Brand. But it may not have been that at all. Or—I don't know."

There was silence as I sidled along a passageway, my puzzled images keeping pace in the mirrors at either hand.

"She didn't want me to kill you," he finally blurted from somewhere off to my right.

"Julia?"

"Yes."

"How is she?"

"Recovering. Pretty rapidly, actually."

"Is she here at Sawall?"

"Yes."

"Look, I'd like to see her. But if she doesn't want to, I understand. I didn't know it was her when I stabbed Mask, and I'm sorry."

"She never really wanted to hurt you. Her quarrel was with Jasra. With you, it was an elaborate game. She wanted to prove she was as good as—maybe better than—you. She wanted to show you what you'd thrown away."

"Sorry," I muttered.

"Tell me one thing, please," he said. "Did you love her? Did you ever really love her?"

I didn't answer him immediately. After all, I'd asked myself that question many times, and I'd had to wait for the answer, too.

"Yes," I finally said. "I didn't realize it till it was too late, though. Bad timing on my part."

A little later I asked, "What about you?"

"I'm not going to make the same mistake you did," he replied. "She's what got me to thinking about all these things. . . ."

"I understand. If she won't see me, tell her that I said I'm sorry—about everything."

There was no reply. I stood still for a time, hoping he'd catch up with me, but he didn't.

Then, "Okay," I called out. "Our duel's ended, so far as I'm concerned."

I began moving again. After a time, I came to an exit and I stepped through it.

He was standing outside, looking up at a massive porcelain face.

"Good," he said.

I drew near.

"There's more," he said, still not looking at me.

"Oh?"

"I think they're stacking the deck," he stated.

"Who? How? What for?"

"Mom and the Logrus," he told me. "To put you on the throne. Who's the bride of the Jewel?"

"I guess that would be Coral. It seems I did hear Dara use that term at some point. Why?"

"I overheard her giving orders last cycle, to some of her Hendrake kin. She's sending a special team to kidnap this woman and bring her here. I got the impression she's intended as your queen."

"That's ridiculous," I said. "She's married to my friend Luke. She's Queen of Kashfa—"

He shrugged.

"Just telling you what I heard," he said. "It had to do with this balancing of forces thing."

Indeed. I hadn't thought of that possibility, but it made perfect sense. With Coral, the Courts would automatically obtain the Jewel of Judgment, or the Eye of the Serpent as it was known hereabout, and that balance would certainly be affected. A loss for Amber, a gain for the Courts. It could be sufficient to achieve what I wanted, the harmony that might postpone catastrophe indefinitely.

Too bad I couldn't let it occur. The poor girl had been

jerked around too much, because she happened to be in Amber at the wrong time, because she happened to take a liking to me. I can recall once feeling philosophical in the abstract and deciding, yes, it would be okay to sacrifice one innocent for the good of the many. That was back in college, and had something to do with principles. But Coral was my friend, my cousin, and technically my lover—though under a set of circumstances that should hardly count; and a quick check of my feelings, so as not to be caught up short again, indicated that I could fall in love with her. All of which meant that philosophy had lost yet another round in the real world.

"How long ago did she send these people off, Jurt?"

"I don't know when they left—or even *if* they've left yet," he replied. "And with the time differential, they could be gone and back already for that matter."

"True," I said, and, "Shit!"

He turned and looked at me.

"It's important in all sorts of other ways, too, I suppose?" he said.

"It is to her, and she is to me," I answered.

His expression changed to one of puzzlement.

"In that case," he said, "why don't you just let them bring her to you? If you have to take the throne, it will sweeten things. If you don't, you'll have her with you, anyhow."

"Feelings are hard enough to keep secret, even around non-sorcerers," I said. "She could be used as a hostage against my behavior."

"Oh. I hate to say this pleases me. What I mean is . . . I'm pleased you care about someone else."

I lowered my head. I wanted to reach out and touch him, but I didn't.

Jurt made a little humming noise, as he sometimes had when pondering things as a kid. Then, "We've got to get her before they do, and move her to someplace safe,'' he said. ''Or take her away from them if they've already got her.''

'' 'We'?''

He smiled, a rare event.

''You know what I've become. I'm tough.''

''I hope so,'' I said. ''But you know what'll happen if there are any witnesses to say it was a couple of the Sawall brothers behind this? Most likely a vendetta with Hendrake.''

''Even if Dara talked them into it?''

''It'll look like she set them up.''

''Okay,'' he said. ''No witnesses.''

I could have said that averting vendetta would save a lot of other lives, but that would have sounded hypocritical even if I didn't mean it that way. Instead, ''That power you gained in the Fountain,'' I said, ''gives you something I've heard referred to as a 'living Trump' effect. Seems to me you were able to transport Julia as well as yourself with it.''

He nodded.

''Can it get us from here to Kashfa in a hurry?''

The distant sound of an enormous gong filled the air.

''I can do anything the cards can do,'' he said, ''and I can take someone along with me. The only problem is that the Trumps themselves don't have that range. I'd have to take us there in a series of jumps.''

The gong sounded again.

''What's going on?'' I asked.

''The noise?'' he said. ''That's notice that the funeral is about to begin. It can be heard throughout the Courts.''

''Bad timing.''

''Maybe, maybe not. It's giving me an idea.''

''Tell me about it.''

''It's our alibi if we have to take out some Hendrakes.''

"How so?"

"The time differential. We go to the funeral and get seen. We slip out, run our errand, come back, and attend the rest of the service."

"You think the flow will allow that?"

"I think there's a good chance, yes. I've done a lot of jumping around. I'm starting to get a real feel for flows."

"Then we'll give it a try. The more confusion the better."

Again, the gong.

Red, the color of the fire of life that fills us, is the color of mourning garments in the Courts. I used the spikard rather than the Sign of the Logrus to summon suitable clothing for myself. I'd a desire to avoid any commerce, even the most mundane, with that Power, for now.

Jurt then trumped us to his quarters, where he had suitable garments of his own from the last funeral he'd attended. I'd a small desire to see my old room, too. Sometime, perhaps, when I wasn't rushed. . . .

We washed up, combed, trimmed, dressed quickly. I took on a changed form then, as did Jurt, and we went through the ritual again at this level, before garbing ourselves for the occasion. Shirt, breeches, jacket, cloak, anklets, bracelets, scarf, and bandanna—we looked incendiary. Weapons had to be left behind. We planned to return for them on the way out.

"Ready?" Jurt asked me.

"Yes."

He caught hold of my arm and we were transported, arriving at the inward edge of the Plaza at the End of the World, where a blue sky darkened above a conflagration of mourners milling along the route the procession would take. We passed among them, in hope of being seen by as many as possible. I was greeted by a few old acquaintances. Unfortunately, most wanted to stop and talk, not having seen me for some time. Jurt had similar problems. Most also wondered why we were here, rather than back at the Thelbane, the massive, glassy needle of Chaos far to our rear. Periodically, the air would vibrate as the gong continued its slow sounding. I felt it in the ground, also, as we were very near to its home. We made our way slowly across the Plaza, toward the massive pile of black stone at the very edge of the Pit, its gate an archway of frozen flame, as was its downward stair, each tread and riser time-barred fire, each railing the same. The rough amphitheater below us was also fire-furnished, self-illumed, facing the black block at the end of everything, no wall behind it, but the open emptiness of the Pit and its singularity whence all things came.

No one was entering it yet, and we stood near the gates of fire and looked back along the route the procession would follow. We nodded to friendly demonic faces, quivered to the note of the gong, watched the sky darken a little further. Suddenly, my head was filled with a powerful presence.

"Merlin!"

I immediately had an image of Mandor in a changed form, looking down his red-clothed arm, hand invisible, presumably regarding me through my Trump, wearing the closest thing I'd seen in a long while to an irritated expression.

"Yes?" I said.

His gaze moved past me. His expression suddenly changed, eyebrows rising, lips parting.

"That's Jurt you're with?" he asked.

"That's right."

"I'd thought you not on the best of terms," he said slowly, "as of our last conversation."

"We agreed to put aside our differences for the funeral."

"While it seems very civilized, I'm not certain how wise it is," he said.

I smiled.

"I know what I'm doing," I told him.

"Really?" he said. "Then why are you at the cathedral rather than here at Thelbane?"

"Nobody told me I was supposed to be at Thelbane."

"Odd," he responded. "Your mother was supposed to have informed both you and Jurt that you were to be part of the procession."

I shook my head and turned away.

"Jurt, did you know we were to be in the procession?" I asked.

"No," he said. "On the one hand, it makes sense. On the other, there's the black watch, which might recommend we maintain a low profile. Who's telling you this?"

"Mandor. He says Dara was supposed to let us know."

"She didn't tell me."

"You catch that?" I said to Mandor.

"Yes. It doesn't matter now. Come on through, both of you."

He extended his other hand.

"He wants us now," I said to Jurt.

"Damn!" Jurt mouthed, and came forward.

I reached out and clasped Mandor's hand just as Jurt came up and caught hold of my shoulder. We both moved forward then—

—into the slick and gleaming interior of Thelbane's main hall at ground level, a study in black, gray, mossy green, deep red, chandeliers like stalactites, fire sculptures about the walls, scaly hides hung behind them, drifting globes of water in the middle air, creatures swimming within them. The place was filled with nobles, relatives, courtiers, stirring like a field of flame about the catafalque at the hall's center. The gong sounded again just as Mandor said something to us.

He waited till the vibrations subsided, then spoke again: "I said Dara hasn't arrived yet. Go pay your respects, and let Bances assign you places in the procession."

Glancing toward the catafalque, I caught sight of both Tmer and Tubble in the vicinity. Tmer was talking to Bances, Tubble to someone who had his back turned this way. A horrible thought suddenly struck me.

"What," I asked, "is the security situation for the procession?"

Mandor smiled.

"There are quite a few guardsmen mixed in with the group here," he said, "and more spotted along the way. Someone will be watching you every second."

I glanced at Jurt to see whether he'd heard that. He nodded.

"Thanks."

Keeping my litany of obscenities subvocal, I moved toward the casket, Jurt at my back. The only way I could think to produce a double would be to talk the Pattern into sending in a ghost of myself to take my place. But the Logrus would detect the ringer's projected energies in no time. And if I just left, not only would my absence be noticed, but I'd probably be tracked—possibly by the Logrus itself once Dara called a conference. Then it would be learned that I'd gone off to thwart the Logrus's attempt to rebalance order, and the headwaters of Shit Creek are a cruel and treacherous expanse. I would not make the mistake of fancying myself indispensable.

"How are we going to do this, Merlin?" Jurt said softly as we found our way to the end of the slow-moving line.

The gong sounded again, causing the chandeliers to vibrate.

"I don't see how we can," I answered. "I think the best I can hope for is to try getting a message through as I walk along."

"It can't be done by Trump from here," he answered. "Well, maybe under perfect conditions," he amended, "but not with all these distractions."

I tried to think of some spell, some sending, some agent to serve me in this. Ghost would have been ideal. Of course, he'd drifted off to explore the spatial asymmetries of the Sculpture Hall. That could keep him occupied for a long while.

"I could get there pretty quickly," Jurt volunteered, "and with the time differential I might make it back before anyone noticed."

"And you know exactly two people in Kashfa you might tell," I said. "Luke and Coral. They both met you in church, when we were trying to kill each other— and you stole Luke's father's sword. Offhand, I'd say he'd try to kill you on sight and she'd scream for help."

The line advanced somewhat.

"So I don't ask for help," he said.

"Un-uh," I told him. "I know you're tough, but Hendrakes are pros. Also, you'd be faced with a very uncooperative rescuee in Coral."

"You're a sorcerer," Jurt said. "If we find out who the guards are, couldn't you lay a spell on them so that they *think* they see us for this whole affair? Then we disappear and no one's the wiser."

"I've a hunch either Mom or our big brother has laid protective spells on the guards. At such an ideal time for an assassination, I would. I wouldn't want anyone able to mess with my people's heads if I were running security here."

We shuffled a little farther along. By leaning to one

side and stretching my neck I was able to get a few glimpses of the wasted demonic form of old Swayvill, resplendently garbed, serpent of red-gold laid upon his breast, there in the flame-formed coffin, Oberon's ancient nemesis, going to join him at last.

As I moved nearer, it occurred to me that there was more than one approach to the problem. Perhaps I'd dwelled too long among the magically naive. I'd gotten out of the habit of thinking of magic against magic, of multiple mixed spells. So what if the guards were protected from any fiddling with their perceptions? Let it be. Find a way to work around it.

The gong sounded again. When the echoes died, Jurt leaned near.

"There's more to it than everything I said," he whispered.

"What do you mean?" I asked.

"Another reason I came to you back at Sawall was because I was scared," he replied.

"Of what?"

"At least one of them—Mandor or Dara—wants more than a balance, wants a total victory for the Logrus, for Chaos. I really believe that. It's not just that I don't want to be party to it. I don't want it to happen. Now that I can visit Shadow I don't want to see it destroyed. I don't want a victory for either side. Total control by the Pattern would probably be just as bad."

"How can you be sure one of them really wants this?"

"They tried it before with Brand, didn't they? He was out to destroy all order."

"No," I said. "He planned to destroy the old order, then replace it with his own. He was a revolutionary, not an anarchist. He was going to create a new Pattern within the Chaos he brought forth—his own, but still the real thing."

"He was duped. He couldn't have managed a thing like that."

"No way of knowing till he tried, and he didn't get the chance."

"Either way, I'm afraid someone's going to pull the plug on reality. If this kidnapping takes place, it'll be a big step in that direction. If you can't manage something to cover our absence, I think we should just go anyway and take our chances."

"Not yet," I said. "Hang on. I'm working something out. How's this sound? I don't locate the guards and hallucinate them. Instead, I do a transformation. I cause a couple of other people to look like us. You trump us out as soon as I do. That won't be a hallucination for anyone. Everyone will see them as us; we can go about our business—and check back if we have to."

"You do it and I'll get us out of here."

"Okay, I'll do it to the two guys in front of us. As soon as I've finished I'll gesture like this," I said, lowering my left hand from shoulder-height to waist-level, "and we both stoop as if one of us had dropped something. Then you take us away."

"I'll be ready."

The spikard made it easier than working out a transform spell. It was like a spell processor. I fed it the two end products, and it ran thousands of variations in a trice and handed me the finished products—a pair of spells it would have taken me a long while to work out along classical lines. I raised my hand as I hung them and accessed one of the many power sources the thing commanded off in Shadow. I fed juice into the constructs, watched the change commence, dropped my hand, and leaned forward.

There followed a moment's vertigo, and when I straightened we were back in Jurt's apartment. I laughed and he slapped my shoulder.

Immediately then, we were changing back into our human forms and garments. As soon as that was done, he caught hold of my arm again and trumped us to Fire Gate. A moment later, and he'd jumped us again, this time to a mountaintop overlooking a blue valley beneath a green sky. Then again, to the middle of a high bridge above a deep gorge, the sky putting away stars or taking them on.

"Okay, now," he said, and we stood atop a gray stone wall damp with dew, possibly even the remains of a storm. Clouds were taking fire in the east. There was a light breeze out of the south.

This was the wall that surrounded the innermost zone of Jidrash, Luke's capital in Kashfa. There were four huge buildings below us—including the palace and the Temple of the Unicorn directly across the Plaza from it—as well as a number of smaller buildings. Diagonally across the way from where we stood was the wing of the palace from which Gryll had fetched me (how long ago?) from my rendezvous with the queen. I could even make out the broken shutter of our window amid an expanse of ivy.

"Over there," I said, gesturing. "That's where I last saw her."

An eyeblink later we stood within the chamber, its only inhabitants. The place had been straightened, the bed made up. I withdrew my Trumps and shuffled out Coral's. Staring then till it grew cold, I felt her presence and reached for it.

She was there yet she wasn't. It was the disjointed sense of presence one encounters in dream or stupor. I passed my hand over the card and ended our tenuous contact.

"What happened?" Jurt asked.

"I think she's drugged," I replied.

"Then it would seem they've already got her," he

said. "Any way you can trace her in that state?"

"She could also be in the next building, on medication," I said. "She wasn't well when I left."

"What now?"

"Either way, we've got to talk to Luke," I said, searching for his card.

I reached him in an instant on uncovering it.

"Merlin! Where the hell are you?" he asked.

"If you're in the palace, I'm next door," I said.

He rose to his feet from what I now realized to be the edge of a bedstead, and he picked up a long-sleeved green shirt and drew it on, covering his collection of scars. I thought that I glimpsed someone in the bed behind him. He muttered something in that direction, but I could not overhear it.

"We've got to talk," he said, running his hand through his rusty hair. "Bring me through."

"Okay," I said. "But first, you'd better know that my brother Jurt is here."

"Has he got my dad's sword?"

"Uh—No."

"Guess I won't kill him right now," he said, tucking his shirt into his waistband.

Abruptly, he extended his hand. I clasped it. He stepped forward and joined us.

VIII

Luke grinned at me, scowled at Jurt.

"Where've you been, anyway?" he asked.

"The Courts of Chaos," I replied. "I was summoned from here at the death of Swayvill. The funeral's in progress right now. We sneaked away when I learned that Coral was in danger."

"I know that—now," Luke said. "She's gone. Kidnapped, I think."

"When did it happen?"

"Night before last, I'd judge. What do you know of it?"

I glanced at Jurt. "Time differential," he said.

"She represented a chance to pick up a few points," I explained, "in the ongoing game between the Pattern and the Logrus. So agents of Chaos were sent for her. They wanted her intact, though. She should be okay."

"What do they want her for?"

"Seems they feel she's specially suited to be queen in Thelbane, what with the Jewel of Judgment as a piece of her anatomy and all."

140

"Who's going to be the new king?"

My face felt warm of a sudden.

"Well, the people who came for her had me in mind for the job," I replied.

"Hey, congratulations!" he said. "Now I don't have to be the only one having all this fun."

"What do you mean?"

"This king business ain't worth shit, man. I wish I'd never gotten sucked into the deal in the first place. Everybody's got a piece of your time, and when they don't someone still has to know where you are."

"Hell, you were just crowned. Give it a chance to shake down."

" 'Just'? It's been over a month!"

"Time differential," Jurt repeated.

"Come on. I'll buy you a cup of coffee," Luke said.

"You've got coffee here?"

"I require it, man. This way." He led us out the door, turned left, headed down a stair.

"I had a funny thought," he said, "while you were talking back there—about you reigning, and Coral a desirable queen. I could get the marriage annulled pretty damn quick, since I'm in charge here. Now, you want her for your queen and I want that Golden Circle Treaty with Amber. I think I see a way to make everybody happy."

"It's a lot more complicated than that, Luke. I don't want the job, and it would be very bad for us if my kinsmen back in the Courts got custody of Coral. I've learned a lot of things recently."

"Such as?" Luke said, opening a postern that let upon a walkway to the rear of the palace.

I glanced back at Jurt.

"He's scared, too," I said. "That's why we're a little more cordial these days."

Jurt nodded.

"It's possible Brand could have been partly victim of a plan originated in the Courts," he said, "part of an idea that's still alive there."

"We'd better go for the whole breakfast," Luke said. "Let's swing around back and take it in the kitchen."

We followed him down a garden path.

And so we ate and talked as the day brightened about us. Luke insisted I try Coral's Trump again, which I did with the same result. Then he cursed, nodded, and said, "Your timing's actually pretty good. The guys who grabbed her were reported to have taken off along a black trail into the west."

"It figures," I said.

"I've reason to believe they didn't make it back to the Courts with her."

"Oh?"

"I understand these black thoroughfares you guys use are dangerous to outsiders," he observed. "But I can show you what's left of this one—it's a black pathway now, actually. I'd like to follow it, but I don't know that I can get away for long. Also, is there a way to protect me from the trail itself?"

"Just being in our company would keep you from harm as we traveled it," Jurt said.

I stood. The cook and two dishwashers glanced in our direction.

"There is somebody you have to meet, Luke," I told him. "Right now."

"Why not?" he said, rising. "Where is he?"

"Let's take a walk," I said.

"Sure."

We got to our feet, headed back to the servants' door.

"So, whether she was a willing accomplice or a magical time bomb, Mom might have conned Dad into his efforts to take over in Amber—and, ultimately, to change the world,'' Luke said.

"Well, I gather he didn't exactly come to her with clean hands,'' I said.

"True, but I wonder how elaborate his plans really were, to begin with,'' Luke mused. "This is the most cheerful thing I've heard all month.''

We exited into the little covered walkway that ran along the side of the palace. Luke halted and looked around.

"Where is he?'' he asked.

"Not here,'' I said. "I just needed a point of departure with no witnesses to say I'd kidnapped the king.''

"Where *are* we going, Merlin?'' Jurt asked, as I swirled a spiral from the center of the spikard, drawing upon sixteen different power sources.

"Good idea. Kidnap away,'' Luke was saying as he was caught up along with Jurt.

I used it as I had when I'd transported myself from Amber to Kashfa, forming the target from memory rather than discovered vision. Only this time there were three of us and a long, long way to go.

"Have I got a deal for you,'' I said.

It was like stepping into a kaleidoscope, and passing through about 120 degrees of cubist fragmentation and reassembly, before emerging on the other side beneath a towering tree, its top lost in the fog, in the vicinity of a red and white '57 Chevy, its radio playing Renbourn's "Nine Maidens.''

Luke's ghost emerged from the front seat and stared at the original. Luke stared back.

"Hi,'' I said. "Meet each other. You hardly need an introduction, though. You have so much in common.''

Jurt stared at the Pattern.

"That's my dad's edition,'' I said.

"I could have guessed that,'' Jurt told me. "But what are we doing here?''

"An idea I had. But I thought Corwin would be here, and I might discuss it with him."

"He came back, and he left again," said the resident Luke, overhearing me.

"Did he leave a forwarding address, or say when he might return?"

"Nope."

"Damn! Look, something that got said just a little while ago gave me the idea that you Lukes might want to change places for a time—if this Pattern could be persuaded to approve some leave."

Luke, whom I decided to continue calling Luke when his ghost was around, brightened suddenly. I resolved to think of his double as Rinaldo, to keep things sorted.

"It's an experience no man should do without," he said.

"Then why are you so anxious to get away from it?" Rinaldo replied.

"To help Merle find Coral," Luke said. "She's been kidnapped."

"Really? By whom?"

"Agents of Chaos."

"Hm." Rinaldo began to pace. "Okay, you know more about it than I do," he finally said. "If Corwin gets back soon and the Pattern excuses me, I'll help you any way I can."

"The trail will be getting colder while we wait," Luke observed.

"You don't understand," Rinaldo said. "I've got a job to do here, and I can't just take off—even if it's to go and be a king somewhere. What I do is more important."

Luke glanced at me.

"He's right," I said. "He's a guardian of the Pattern. On the other hand, nobody's about to hurt Coral. Why don't Jurt and I pop on back to the Courts for a few minutes, to check on the progress of the funeral? Corwin might show up while we're about it. I'm sure you two will find something to talk about.''

''Go ahead,'' Luke told me.

''Yeah,'' said Rinaldo. ''I'd like to know what we've been doing.''

I looked at Jurt, who nodded. I went and stood beside him.

''Your turn to drive,'' I said.

''Back soon,'' I remarked as we faded into the first jump.

. . . And so again to the Ways of Sawall, and back into our ruddy garb over demonform. I also changed our facial appearance to the nondescript before Jurt returned us to the funeral party, not wanting a matching set marching along.

The Thelbane proved deserted. A quick check outside, however, showed us the procession, perhaps a quarter way across the Plaza, halted and in a state of confusion.

''Uh-oh,'' Jurt remarked. ''What should I do?''

''Take us down there,'' I told him.

Moments later, we were at the outer edge of the crowd. Swayvill's blazing casket had been lowered to the ground, a guard posted about it. My attention was immediately attracted to a knot of figures perhaps twenty feet off to the right of it. There was some shouting going on, something lay upon the ground, and two demonic forms were being held tightly by several others. My stomach tightened as I saw that the two were the pair I had ensorcelled to resemble Jurt and myself. Both were protesting something.

As I pushed my way forward, I withdrew my spells, causing the two to revert to their own appearance. There were more shouts as this occurred, including an ''I told you!'' from the nearest. The response to this was a ''Yes, they are!'' from someone I suddenly realized to be Mandor. He stood between them and the thing on the ground.

"It was a trick!" Mandor said. "A distraction! Release them!"

I decided the moment was propitious for dropping the spells that masked Jurt and myself. Glorious confusion!

Moments later, Mandor saw me and signaled for me to approach. Jurt, I saw, off to my right, had stopped to talk to someone he knew.

"Merlin!" he said as soon as I was near. "What do you know of this?"

"Nothing," I said. "I was way to the rear, with Jurt. I don't even know what happened."

"Someone gave two of the security guards your appearance and Jurt's. This was obviously intended to create confusion when the assassin struck. They rushed forward insisting they were guards. Obviously, they weren't. Clever—especially with you and Jurt on their black watch list."

"I see," I agreed, wondering whether I had helped an assassin to escape. "Who got hit?"

"Tmer, with a very professional dagger stroke," he explained, left eyelid twitching. A faint wink? Meaning? "And he was gone in an instant."

Four mourners, having made a stretcher of cloaks, raised the fallen body. After they'd moved only a few paces with it, I saw another knot of people beyond them.

Seeing my puzzled expression, Mandor glanced back.

"More security," he said. "They're surrounding Tubble. I think I'll order him out of here for now. You and Jurt, too. You can come to the temple later. I'll see that security's even heavier there."

"Okay," I said. "Is Dara here?"

He glanced about.

"I haven't seen her. Don't now, either. You'd better go."

I nodded. As I turned away, I saw a half-familiar face off to my right. She was tall and dark-eyed, shifting from a swirl of multicolored jewels to a swaying flowerlike form, and she had been staring at me. I had been trying to recall her name earlier, and had failed. Seeing her brought it back, though. I approached her.

"I have to leave for a time," I said. "But I wanted to say hello, Gilva."

"You do remember. I was wondering."

"Of course."

"How are you, Merlin?"

I sighed. She smiled her way into furry, half-human solidity.

"Me, too," she said. "I'll be so glad when this is all settled."

"Yes. Listen, I want to see you—for several reasons. When would be a good time?"

"Why, anytime after the funeral, I guess. What about?"

"No time now. Mandor's giving me angry looks. See you later."

"Yes. Later, Merlin."

I hurried back to Jurt and caught him by the elbow.

"We're ordered to leave," I said. "Security reasons."

"All right." He turned to the man he'd been talking with. "Thanks. I'll see you later," he told him.

The world slipped away. A new one dawned: Jurt's apartment, our clothes strewn about it.

"Good timing for us. Bad for Tmer," he remarked.

"True."

"How's it feel to be number two?" he asked as we changed again—both clothing and form.

"It advances your case, too," I said.

"I've a feeling he died on your account, brother, not mine."

"I hope not," I said.

He laughed.

"It's between Tubble and you."

"If it were, I'd be dead already," I said. "If you're right, it's really between Sawall and Chanicut."

"Wouldn't it be funny, Merlin, if I were sticking with you because it's the safest place to be just now?" he asked. "I'm sure our guards and assassins are better than Chanicut's. Supposing I'm just waiting, saving my final effort till Tubble's out of the way? Then, trusting me and all, you turn your back—Coronation!"

I looked at him. He was smiling, but he also seemed to be studying me.

I was about to say, "You can have it, without the trouble," in a joking way. But I wondered just then: Even in jest, if it were a choice between the two of us ... It occurred to me that if we were the only options, this was a circumstance under which I'd agree to take the throne. I'd resolved to give him the benefit of the doubt, to meet him more than halfway. But I couldn't help it. For all his conciliatory talk and apparent cooperation, a lifelong habit is a hard thing to break. I couldn't bring myself to trust him anymore than I had to.

"Tell it to the Logrus," I said.

A look of fear—the widening of the eyes, the shifting of the gaze downward, a small forward tightening of the shoulders—then, "You really do have an understanding with it, don't you?" he asked.

"There seems to be an understanding, but it only works one way," I said.

"What do you mean?"

"I'm not about to help either side wreck our world."

"Sounds like you're prepared to double-cross the Logrus."

I raised a finger to my lips.

"It must be your Amber blood," he said then. "I've

been told they're all a little crazy."

"Maybe so," I said.

"Sounds like something your father would do."

"What do you know of him?"

"You know, everybody has a favorite Amber story."

"Nobody around here ever told any to me."

"Of course not—considering."

"Me being a half-breed and all?" I said.

He shrugged. Then, "Well, yes."

I pulled on my boots.

"Whatever you're doing with that new Pattern," he said, "it probably won't make the old one too happy."

"Doubtless you're right," I agreed.

"So you won't be able to run to it for protection if the Logrus is after you."

"I guess not."

". . . And if they're both after you, the new one won't be able to stand against them."

"You think they'd really get together on anything?"

"Hard to say. You're playing a wild game. I hope you know what you're doing."

"Me, too," I said, rising. "My turn."

I unwound the spikard at a level I'd never attempted before, and I got us there in a single jump.

Luke and Rinaldo were still talking. I could tell them apart by their garments. Corwin was nowhere in sight.

Both waved as we made our appearance.

"How's everything in the Courts?" Luke asked.

"Chaotic," Jurt replied. "How long have we been away?"

"Six hours, I'd guess," Rinaldo replied.

"No sign of Corwin?" I asked.

"No," Luke said. "But in the meantime, we've worked out a deal with each other—and Rinaldo's been in touch with the Pattern here. It will release him and continue his maintenance as soon as Corwin returns."

"Regarding that . . ." Jurt said.

"Yes?" Rinaldo asked.

"I'll stay here and cover for Rinaldo while you go find the lady with the glass eye."

"Why?" Rinaldo asked.

"Because you'll do a better job together and I'll feel a lot safer here than I would most other places."

"I'd have to see whether that's acceptable," Rinaldo said.

"Do it," said Jurt.

He moved off toward the Pattern. I searched the fog in all directions, hoping to see my father returning. Jurt studied the car, its radio now playing a Bruce Dunlap number from "Los Animales."

"If your father comes back and relieves me," Jurt said, "I'll return to the funeral and make excuses for you if you're not there. If you get back and I'm not there, you do the same. All right?"

"Yes," I said, wisps of mist rising like smoke between us. "And whichever of us is free first and has something worth saying . . ."

"Yes," he agreed. "I'll come looking if you don't get to me."

"Didn't happen to pick up my sword while you were back in the Courts, did you?" Luke asked.

"Didn't have time," Jurt replied.

"Next time you're back, I wish you'd make time."

"I will, I will," Jurt said.

Rinaldo moved away from the Pattern, returned to us.

"You're hired," he said to Jurt. "Come with me. There's a spring I want to show you, and a store of food, some weapons."

Luke turned and watched them move off to our left.

"I'm sorry," he said softly, "but I still don't trust him."

"Don't be sorry. I don't either. I've known him too

long. But we have better reasons for trusting each other now than we've had for a long time.''

''I'm wondering whether it was wise to let him know where this Pattern is, and now to leave him alone with it.''

''I'm pretty sure the Pattern knows what it's doing, and that it can take care of itself.''

He raised a pair of crossed fingers.

''I'd've argued against it,'' he said, ''save that I need my double.''

When they returned, a deejay's baritone suddenly rolled forth, saying, ''It all goes to show, timing is everything. Road conditions are fine. It is a good day for travel.'' Immediately, there followed a drum solo I'd have sworn was something I once heard Random play.

''You're on duty as of now,'' Rinaldo said to Jurt. To us, he nodded. ''Anytime.''

I caught us up with the spikard and spun us back to Kashfa, bringing us into Jidrash near twilight, to the same walltop vantage I had enjoyed earlier with my brother.

''And so at last,'' Rinaldo said, looking out over the town.

''Yes,'' Luke replied. ''It's all yours—for a time.'' Then, ''Merle, how's about jumping us to my apartment?''

I turned to the west where clouds had gone orange, glanced upward to where several hung purple.

''Before we do that, Luke,'' I said, ''I'd like to use what daylight's left for a look at that black trail.''

He nodded.

''Good idea. Okay, take us over there.''

His gesture indicated a hilly area to the southwest. I caught us up and spikarded us to it, creating a verb for which I felt a need in the same act. Such is the power of Chaos.

Arriving on a small hilltop, we followed Luke down its far side.

"Over this way," he said.

Long shadows lay all about us, but there is a difference between their dimness and the blackness of a travel-thread from the Courts.

"It was right here," Luke finally said when we came to a place between a pair of boulders.

I moved forward into the area but I felt nothing special.

"You sure this is the place?" I asked.

"Yes."

I advanced another ten paces, twenty.

"If this is really where it was, it's gone now," I told him. "Of course . . . I wonder how long we've been away?"

Luke snapped his fingers.

"Timing," he observed. "Take us back to my apartments."

We kissed the day good-bye as I sent forth a lead and opened our way through the wall of dark. We stepped through into the room I had occupied earlier with Coral.

"Close enough?" I asked. "I'm not sure where your rooms are."

"Come on," he said, taking us out, to the left and down the stair. "Time to consult the resident expert. Merle, do something about this guy's appearance. Too much of a good thing might cause comment."

It was easy, and the first time I'd made anyone look like the big portrait of Oberon back home.

Luke knocked on a door before entering. Somewhere beyond it, a familiar voice spoke his name.

"I have some friends with me," he said.

"Bring them in," came her reply.

He opened the door and did so.

"Both of you know Nayda," Luke announced. "Nayda, this is my double. Let's call him Rinaldo and me Luke while we're together. He's going to run things for me here while Merle and I are off looking for your sister."

I changed Rinaldo back then, in response to her puzzled look.

She had on black trousers and an emerald blouse, her hair bound back by a matching green scarf. She smiled as she greeted us, and when she regarded me she touched her lips lightly, almost casually, with a fingertip. I nodded immediately.

"I trust you are recovered from any misadventures in Amber," I said. "You were, of course, there at a bad time."

"Of course," she responded. "Fully recovered, thank you. Kind of you to ask. Thanks, too, for the recent directions. It was you, I take it, who spirited Luke away these two days past?"

"It's really been that long?" I said.

"It has, sir."

"Sorry about that, my dear," Luke said, squeezing her hand and looking long into her eyes.

"That explains why the trail's faded," I said.

Rinaldo seized her hand and kissed it, while executing an elaborate bow.

"Amazing how much you've changed from the girl I knew," he stated.

"Oh?"

"I share Luke's memories as well as his appearance," he explained.

"I could tell there was something not quite human about you," she remarked. "I see you as a man whose very blood is fire."

"And how might you see that?" he inquired.

"She has her means," Luke said, "though I thought

it only a psychic bond with her sister. Apparently it goes somewhat further.''

She nodded.

''Speaking of which, I hope you can use it to help us track her,'' he continued. ''With the trail gone and a drug or a spell barring a Trump call, we'll be needing assistance.''

''Yes,'' she answered, ''though she is in no danger at the moment.''

''Good,'' he said. ''In that case, I'll order us all food and set to briefing this good-looking fellow on what's going on in Kashfa these days.''

''Luke,'' I said. ''It sounds like an ideal time for me to head back to the Courts for the rest of the funeral.''

''How long would you be gone, Merle?''

''I don't know,'' I replied.

''Back by morning, I trust?''

''Me, too. What if I'm not, though?''

''I've a feeling I should go looking without you.''

''Try reaching me first, though.''

''Sure. See you later.''

I drew my cloak of space about me, shrugging Kashfa away. When I opened it again I was back in Jurt's quarters at Sawall.

I stretched, I yawned. I did a quick turn about the room, making certain I was alone. I unfastened my cloak and tossed it upon the bed. I paced as I unbuttoned my shirt.

Halt. What was it? Also, where?

I retraced a few paces. I had never spent a great deal of time in my younger brother's rooms, but I would have recalled what I was feeling.

There was a chair and table in the corner formed by the wall and an armoire of dark, almost black wood. Kneeling on the chair and reaching over the table, I could feel it—the presence of a way, not quite strong enough for transport, though. Ergo. . . .

I moved off to my right, opened the armoire. It had to be inside, of course. I wondered how recently he had installed it. I also felt slightly funny about poking about in his quarters this way. Still, he owed me for a lot of misery and inconvenience. A few confidences and a little cooperation hardly cleaned the slate. I hadn't learned to trust him yet, and it was possible he was setting me up for something. Good manners, I decided, would have to be sacrificed to prudence.

I pushed garments aside, making a way clear to the back of the thing. I could feel it strongly. A final shove at the garments, a quick shuffle to the rear, and I was at the focus. I let it take me away.

Once there was a forward yielding, the pressure of the garments at my back gave me a small push. That, plus the fact that someone (Jurt, himself?) had done a sloppy shadowmastering job resulting in mismatched floor levels, sent me sprawling as I achieved destination.

At least, I didn't land in a pit full of sharpened stakes or acid. Or the lair of some half-starved beast. No, it was a green-tiled floor, and I caught myself as I fell. And from the flickering light all about me I guessed there was a mess of candles burning.

Even before I looked up I was sure they'd all be green.

Nor was I incorrect. About that or anything else.

The setup was similar to that of my father, with a groined vault containing a light source superior to the candles. Only there was no painting above this altar. This one featured a stained-glass window, lots of green in it, and a little red.

Its principal was Brand.

I rose and crossed to it. Lying upon it, drawn a few inches from its sheath, was Werewindle.

I reached out and took hold of it, my first impulse

being to bear it away with me for eventual restoration
to Luke. Then I hesitated. It wasn't something I could
wear to a funeral. If I took it now I'd have to hide it
somewhere, and it was already well-hidden right here. I
let my hand rest upon it, though, as I thought. It contained a similar feeling of power to that which Grayswandir bore, only somehow brighter, less tragedy-
touched and brooding. Ironic. It seemed an ideal blade
for a hero.

I looked about. There was a book on a reading stand
off to my left, a pentagram upon the floor behind me,
worked in different shades of green, a smell—as of a
recent wood fire—hung in the air. Idly, I wondered what
I might find if I were to knock a hole in the wall. Was
this chapel located upon a mountaintop? Beneath a lake?
Underground? Was it drifting somewhere in the heav-
ens?

What did it represent? It looked to be religious in
nature. And Benedict, Corwin, and Brand were the three
I knew about. Were they admired, respected—venerated—by certain of my countrymen and relatives? Or
were these hidden chapels somehow more sinister?

I removed my hand from Werewindle, stepped to the
vicinity of the pentagram.

My Logrus vision revealed nothing untoward, but an
intense scan with the spikard detected the residue of a
long-removed magical operation. The traces were too
faint to tell me anything of its nature, however. While
it seemed possible I might probe further after this and
come up with a clearer picture, I also realized I hadn't
the time such an operation would require.

Reluctantly, I retreated to the vicinity of the way.
Could these places have been used to try to influence
the individuals involved?

I shook my head. This was something I would have

to save for another day. I located the way and gave myself to it.

I stumbled on my return, also.

Catching hold of the frame with one hand, I seized a garment with another, kept myself upright, straightened, and stepped out. Then I shifted the clothing back into place and shut the doors.

I stripped quickly, altering my form as I was about it, and I donned my mourning garb once again. I felt some activity in the vicinity of the spikard, and for the first time I caught it drawing upon one of the many sources it commanded to alter its shape, accommodating the changing size of my finger. It had obviously done this several times before, though this was the first time I had noted the process. This was interesting, in that it showed the device capable of acting independent of my will.

I didn't really know what the thing was, what its origin might have been. I kept it because it represented a considerable source of power, an acceptable substitute for the use of the Logrus, which I now feared. But as I watched it change shape to remain snug upon my changing finger, I wondered. What if it were somehow booby-trapped to turn upon me at exactly the wrong moment?

I turned it a couple of times upon my finger. I moved into it with my mind, knowing this to be an exercise in futility. It would take ages for me to run down each line to its source, to check out hidden spells along the way. It was like taking a trip through a Swiss watch—custom-made. I was impressed both with the beauty of its design, and with the enormous amount of work that had gone into its creation. It could easily possess hidden imperatives that would only respond to special sets of circumstances. Yet—

It had done nothing untoward, yet. And the alternative was the Logrus. It struck me as a genuine instance of the preferability of the devil one didn't know.

Growling, I adjusted my apparel, focused my attention on the Temple of the Serpent, and bade the spikard deliver me near its entrance. It performed as smoothly and gently as if I had never doubted it, as if I had not discovered in it yet another cause for paranoia.

And for a time, I simply stood outside the doors of frozen flame, there at the great Cathedral of the Serpent at the outer edge of the Plaza at the End of the World, situated exactly at the Rim, opened to the Pit itself—where, on a good day, one can view the creation of the universe, or its ending—and I watched the stars swarm through space that folded and unfolded like the petals of flowers; and as if my life were about to change, my thoughts returned to California and school, of sailing the *Sunburst* with Luke and Gail and Julia, of sitting with my father near the end of the war, of riding with Vinta Bayle through the wine country to the east of Amber, of a long, brisk afternoon spent showing Coral about the town, of the strange encounters of that day; and I turned and raised my scaly hand, stared past it at the spire of Thelbane, and ''they cease not fighting, east and west, on the marches of my breast,'' I thought. How long, how long . . . ?—irony, as usual, a three-to-one favorite whenever sentimentality makes its move.

Turning again, I went in to see the last of the King of Chaos.

IX

Down, down into the pile, into the great slag heap, window onto the ends of time and space, where nothing is to be seen at the end, I went, between walls forever afire, never burnt down, walking in one of my bodies toward the sound of a voice reading from the Book of the Serpent Hung upon the Tree of Matter, and at length came into the grotto that backed upon blackness, widening semicircles of red-clad mourners facing the reader and the grand catafalque beside which he stood, Swayvill clearly in view within it, half-covered with red flowers dropped by mourners, red tapers flickering against the Pit, but a few paces behind them; across the rear of the chamber then, listening to Bances of Amblerash, High Priest of the Serpent, his words sounding as if spoken beside me, for the acoustics of Chaos are good; finding a seat in an otherwise empty arc, where anyone looking back would be certain to notice me; seeking familiar faces, finding Dara, Tubble, and Mandor seated in frontal positions that indicated they were to assist Bances in sliding the casket past the edge into forever when the time came; and in my divided heart I recalled the last funeral I had attended before this: Caine's, back in Amber, beside the sea, and I thought again of Bloom and the way the mind wanders on these occasions.

I sought about me. Jurt was nowhere in sight. Gilva of Hendrake was only a couple of rows below me. I shifted my gaze to the deep blackness beyond the Rim. It was almost as if I were looking down, rather than out—if such terms had any real meaning in that place. Occasionally, I would perceive darting points of light or rolling masses. It served me as a kind of Rorschach for a time, and I half-dozed before the prospect of dark butterflies, clouds, pairs of faces—

I sat upright with a small start, wondering what had broken my reverie.

The silence, it was. Bances had stopped reading.

I was about to lean forward and whisper something to Gilva when Bances began the Consignment. I was startled to discover that I recalled all of the appropriate responses.

As the chanting swelled and focused, I saw Mandor get to his feet, and Dara, and Tubble. They moved forward, joining Bances about the casket—Dara and Mandor at its foot, Tubble and Bances at its head. Service assistants rose from their section and began snuffing candles, until only the large one, at the Rim, behind Bances, still flickered. At this point we all stood.

The ever-eerie light of flame mosaics, worked into the walls at either hand, granted additional illumination to the extent that I could detect the movement below when the chanting ceased.

The four figures stooped slightly, presumably taking hold of the casket's handles. They straightened then and moved toward the Rim. An assistant advanced and stood beside the candle just as they passed it, ready to snuff

the final flame as Swayvill's remains were consigned to
Chaos.

A half-dozen paces remained. . . . Three. Two. . . .

Bances and Tubble knelt at the verge, positioning the
casket within a groove in the stone floor, Bances inton-
ing a final bit of ritual the while, Dara and Mandor re-
maining standing.

The prayer finished, I heard a curse. Mandor seemed
jerked forward. Dara stumbled away to the side. I heard
a *clunk* as the casket hit the floor. The assistant's hand
had already been moving, and the candle went out at
that moment. There followed a skidding sound as the
casket moved forward, more curses, a shadowy figure
retreating from the Rim. . . .

Then came a wail. A bulky outline fell and was gone.
The wail diminished, diminished, diminished. . . .

I raised my left fist, caused the spikard to create a
globe of white light as a bubble pipe does a bubble. It
was about three feet in diameter when I released it to
drift overhead. Suddenly, the place was filled with bab-
bling. Others of sorcerous background having exercised
their favorite illumination spells at about the same time
I had, the temple was now over-illuminated from dozens
of point-sources.

Squinting, I saw Bances, Mandor, and Dara in converse near the Rim. Tubble and the remains of Swayvill
were no longer with us.

My fellow mourners were already moving. I did, too,
realizing that my time here was now extremely limited.

I stepped down over the empty row, moved to the
right, touched Gilva's still humanized shoulder.

"Merlin!" she said, turning quickly. "Tubble—went
over—didn't he?"

"Sure looked that way," I said.

"What will happen now?"

"I've got to leave," I said, "fast!"

"Why?"

"Somebody's going to start thinking about the succession in a few moments, and I'm going to be smothered with protection," I told her. "I can't have that, not just now."

"Why not?"

"No time to go into that. But I'd wanted to talk to you. May I borrow you now?"

There were milling bodies all about us.

"Of course—sir," she said, apparently having just thought about the succession.

"Cut that out," I said, spikard spiraling the energies that caught us and took us away.

I brought us to the forest of metal trees, and Gilva kept hold of my arm and looked about her.

"Lord, what is this place?" she asked.

"I'd rather not say," I replied, "for reasons that will become apparent in a moment. I only had one question for you the last time I spoke with you. But now I have two, and this place figures in one of them, in a way, besides being fairly deserted most of the time."

"Ask," she said, moving to face me. "I'll try to help. If it's important, though, I may not be the best person—"

"Yes, it's important. But I haven't time to make an appointment with Belissa. It concerns my father, Corwin."

"Yes?"

"It was he who slew Borel of Hendrake in the war at Patternfall."

"So I understand," she said.

"After the war, he joined the royal party that came here to the Courts to work out the Treaty."

"Yes," she said. "I know that."

"He disappeared shortly thereafter, and no one

seemed to know where he'd gotten off to. For a time, I thought he might be dead. Later, however, I received indications that he was not, but rather was imprisoned somewhere. Can you tell me anything about this?''

She turned away suddenly.

"I am offended," she said, "by what I believe you imply."

"I'm sorry," I said, "but I had to ask."

"Ours is an honorable House," she said. "We accept the fortunes of war. When the fighting is ended, we put it all behind us."

"I apologize," I said. "We're even related, you know, on my mother's side."

"Yes, I know," she said, turning away. "Will that be all, Prince Merlin?"

"Yes," I answered. "Where shall I send you?"

She was silent for a moment, then, "You said there were two questions," she stated.

"Forget it. I changed my mind about the second one."

She turned back.

"Why? Why should I forget it? Because I maintain my family's honor?"

"No, because I believe you."

"And?"

"I'll trouble someone else for an opinion."

"Do you mean it's dangerous, and you've decided against asking me?"

"I don't understand it, so it could be dangerous."

"Do you want to offend me again?"

"Heaven forbid!"

"Ask me your question."

"I'll have to show you."

"Do it."

"Even if it means climbing a tree?"

"Whatever it means."

"Follow me."

So I led her to the tree and climbed it, an enormously simple feat in my present form. She was right behind me.

"There's a way up here," I said. "I'm about to let it take me. Give me a few seconds to move aside."

I moved a little farther upward and was transported. Stepping aside, I surveyed the chapel quickly. Nothing seemed changed.

Then Gilva was at my side. I heard a sharp intake of breath.

"Oh, my!" she said.

"I know what I'm looking at," I said, "but I don't know what I'm seeing, if you follow me."

"It is a shrine," she said, "dedicated to the spirit of a member of the royal house of Amber."

"Yes, it's my father Corwin," I agreed. "That's what I'm looking at. But what am I seeing? Why should there be such a thing here in the Courts, anyway?"

She moved forward slowly, studying Dad's altar.

"I might as well tell you," I added, "that this is not the only such shrine I've seen since my return."

She reached out and touched the hilt of Grayswandir. Searching beneath the altar, she found a supply of candles. Removing a silver one and screwing it into the socket of one of a number of holders, she lit it from one of the others and placed it near Grayswandir. She muttered something while she was about it, but I did not make out the words.

When she turned back to me again she was smiling.

"We both grew up here," I said. "How is it that you seem to know all about this when I don't?"

"The answer is fairly simple, Lord," she told me. "You departed right after the war, to seek an education in other lands. This is a sign of something that came to pass in your absence."

She reached out, took hold of my arm, led me to a bench.

"Nobody thought we would actually lose that war," she said, "though it had long been argued that Amber would be a formidable adversary." We seated ourselves. "Afterward, there was considerable unrest," she continued, "over the policies that had led to it and the treaty that followed it. No single house or grouping could hope for a deposition against the royal coalition, though. You know the conservatism of the Rim Lords. It would take much, much more to unite a majority against the Crown. Instead, their discontent took another form. There grew up a brisk trade in Amber memorabilia from the war. People became fascinated by our conquerors. Biographical studies of Amber's royal family sold very well. Something like a cult began to take shape. Private chapels such as this began to appear, dedicated to a particular Amberite whose virtues appealed to someone."

She paused, studying my face.

"It smacked too much of a religion," she went on then, "and for time out of mind the Way of the Serpent had been the only significant religion in the Courts. So Swayvill outlawed the Amber cult as heretical, for obvious political reasons. That proved a mistake. Had he done nothing it might have passed quickly. I don't really know, of course. But outlawing it drove it underground, made people take it more seriously as a rebellious thing. I've no idea how many cult chapels there are among the Houses, but that's obviously what this is."

"Fascinating sociological phenomenon," I said, "and your cult figure is Benedict."

She laughed.

"That wouldn't have been hard to guess," she said.

"Actually, I had the chapel described to me by my brother Mandor. He claimed to have wandered into it at a party at Hendrake, not knowing what it was."

She chuckled.

"He must have been testing you," she said. "The practice has been common knowledge for a long while. And I happen to know he's a cultist himself."

"Really? How do you know this?"

"He made no secret of it in the old days, before the general proscription."

"And who might his personal patron be?" I said.

"The Princess Fiona," she replied.

Curiouser and curiouser. . . .

"You've actually seen his chapel to her?" I asked.

"Yes. Before the ban it was not uncommon to have your friends over for a service whenever you were feeling particularly disgruntled with royal policy."

"And after the ban?"

"Everyone claimed publicly that their shrines had been destroyed. Many were simply relocated, I think, up hidden ways."

"And the business of having friends over for services?"

"I'd guess it would depend on how good a friend you're talking about. I don't really know how organized the Amber cult is." She gestured widely. "A place like this is illegal, though. Good thing I don't know where we are."

"I guess so," I said. "What about the relationship between the cult figure and the real thing? I'd say that Mandor really does have a thing about Fiona. He's met her, you know, and I've been present and seen it. Someone else I know stole something belonging to his—patron?—and keeps it in his shrine. And that"— I rose, crossed the altar, and picked up Corwin's sword—"is the real thing. I'd seen Grayswandir close-up, touched it, held it. This is it. But what I'm getting at is that my father is missing, and the last time I saw him he was wearing that blade. Would it be in keeping with the tenets of this cult to keep your patron prisoner?''

"I never heard of such a thing," she said. "But I don't see why not. It is really the spirit of the person that is being venerated. There is no reason the person could not be imprisoned.''

"Or dead?''

"Or dead," she agreed.

"Then fascinating as all this is," I said, turning away from the altar, "it doesn't really help me to find my father.''

I moved back to her, across what must have been a representation of Amber, stylized as the pattern on a Caucasian rug, there in the dark and light tile, the Chaotic one far off to my right.

"You would have to ask the person responsible for his blade's being there," she said, rising.

"I already asked the person I believed responsible. The response was not satisfactory.''

I took her arm to steer her back toward the way to the tree, and she was suddenly standing very close.

"I would like to serve our next king any way I might," she said. "Though I may not normally speak for our House, I am certain Hendrake would agree to help you bring pressure upon the person responsible.''

"Thanks," I said as we embraced. Her scales were cool. Her fangs would have shredded my human ear, but it was only a nibble in demonform. "I will talk to you again if I need help along those lines.''

"Talk to me again, anyway.''

It was good to hold and be held for a time, and that is what we did, till I saw a shadow move in the vicinity of the way.

"Masster Merlin.''

"Glait!''

"Yess. I ssaw you come thiss way. Manform, demonform, grown or ssmall, I know you.''

"Merlin, what is it?" Gilva asked.

"An old friend," I told her. "Glait, meet Gilva. And vice versa."

"Pleassed. I came to warn you that ssomeone approachess."

"Who?"

"Princess Dara."

"Oh, dear!" Gilva remarked.

"You suspect where we are," I said to her. "Keep it to yourself."

"I value my head, Lord. What do we do now?"

"Glait, to me," I said, kneeling and extending an arm.

She flowed up it and made herself comfortable. I rose and caught hold of Gilva with the other. I sent my will into the spikard.

Then I hesitated.

I didn't know where the hell we were—really, physically, in terms of geography. A way can deliver you next door, or somewhere thousands of miles distant from its point of origin, or somewhere off in Shadow. It would take a while to have the spikard figure where we were and then work out the way back, if we were going to bypass the way. Too long, I was certain.

I could simply use it to render us invisible. But I feared my mother's sorcerous sensitivity would be sufficient to detect our presence at levels beyond the visual.

I faced the nearest wall and extended my senses past it on a line of the spikard's force. We were not underwater or drifting on a sea of lava or quicksand. We seemed to be in a wooded spot.

So I walked toward the wall and passed us through it when we got there.

Several paces later, in the midst of a shaded glade, I looked back and beheld a grassy hillside, with no singing coming from beneath it. We stood under a blue sky, orange sun nearing its top. There were bird and insect sounds about us.

"Marrow!" Glait exclaimed, unwound herself from my arm and vanished into the grasses.

"Don't stay away long!" I hissed, trying to keep my voice low; and I led Gilva away from the hill.

"Merlin," she said, "I'm frightened at what I've learned."

"I won't tell anyone if you won't," I said. "If you'd like, I can even remove these memories before I send you back to the funeral."

"No, let me keep them. I can even wish there were more."

"I'll figure our location and get you back before you're missed."

"I'll wait with you while your friend hunts."

I half expected her to continue, ". . . in case I never see you again," what with the near skateboarding of Tmer and Tubble off this ever-mortal helix. But no, she was a demure and well-bred battle-maid—with over thirty notches on the haft of her broadsword, I later learned—and she was above stating the distasteful obvious in the presence of her possible future liege.

When Glait returned after an appropriate time, I said, "Thanks, Gilva. I'm going to send you back to the funeral now. If anyone saw us together and wants to know where I am, tell them I said I was going into hiding."

"If you do need a place to hide . . ."

"Talk to you sometime later perhaps," I said, and I sent her back to the temple at the edge of everything.

"Good vermin," Glait remarked, as I commenced my shift humanward. (It's always easier that way for me than the demon-shift.)

"I'd like to send you back to Sawall's sculpture garden," I said.

"Why there, Masster Merlin?"

"To wait for a time, to see whether you behold a sentient circle of light. And if you do, to address it as Ghostwheel and tell it to come to me."

"Where shall I tell it to sseek you?"

"That I do not know, but it is good at that sort of thing."

"Then ssend me. And if you are not eaten by ssomething bigger, come tell me your sstory one night."

"I shall."

It was the work of but a moment to hang the serpent back in her tree. I've never been sure when she's joking, reptilian humor being more than a little strange.

I summoned fresh garments and garbed myself in gray and purple. Fetched me blades long and short then, also.

I wondered what my mother might have been up to in her chapel, but decided against trying to spy on her. I raised the spikard and regarded it for a moment, then lowered it. It seemed possibly counterproductive to transport myself to Kashfa when I was uncertain how much time had passed and whether Luke was actually still there. I took out my Trumps, which I had had along in my mourning garb, uncased them.

I located Luke's, focused upon it. Before too long it went cold and I felt Luke's presence.

"Yes?" he said. "That you, Merle?" at about the same time as his image swam and altered, causing me to see him mounted and riding through a part-blasted, part-normal countryside.

"Yeah," I answered. "I gather you're no longer in Kashfa."

"Right," he said. "Where're you?"

"Somewhere in Shadow. How's about yourself?"

"Damned if I know for sure," he responded. "We've been following this black path for days—and I can only say 'somewhere in Shadow,' too."

"Oh, you located it?"

"Nayda did. I didn't see anything, but she just led me on. Eventually, the trail got clear to me. Hell of a tracker, that gal."

"She's with you now?"

"That's right. She says we're gaining on them, too."

"Better bring me through then."

"Come ahead."

He extended a hand. I reached forward, clasped it, took a step, released his hand, began walking beside him, a pack horse to the rear.

"Hi, Nayda!" I called, to where she rode at his other side. A grim figure was mounted upon a black horse ahead and to her right.

She smiled.

"Merlin," she said. "Hello."

"How about Merle?" I said.

"If you wish."

The figure on the dark horse turned and regarded me. I halted a death strike that ran from reflex to the spikard so fast that it scared me. The air between us was smudged and filled with a screeching note, as of a car grabbing pavement to avert collision.

He was a big, blond-haired son of a bitch, and he had on a yellow shirt and black trousers, black boots, lots of cutlery. The medallion of the Lion rending the Unicorn bounced upon his broad chest. Every time I'd seen or heard of the man, he'd been about something nasty, damn near killing Luke on one occasion. He was a mercenary, a Robin Hood figure out of Eregnor, and a sworn enemy of Amber—illegitimate son of her late liege Oberon. I believed there was a price on his head within the Golden Circle. On the other hand, he and Luke had been buddies for years, and Luke swore he wasn't all that bad. He was my uncle Dalt, and I'd a feeling that if he moved too quickly the flexing of his muscles would shred his shirt.

"... And you remember my military adviser, Dalt," Luke said.

"I remember," I stated.

Dalt stared at the black lines in the air that faded, smokelike, between us. He actually smiled then, a little.

"Merlin," he said, "son of Amber, Prince of Chaos, the man who dug my grave."

"What's this?" Luke asked.

"A little conversational gambit," I replied. "You've a good memory, Dalt—for faces."

He chuckled.

"Hard to forget something like a grave opening itself," he said. "But I've no quarrel with you, Merlin."

"Nor I you—now," I said.

He grunted then and I grunted back and considered us introduced. I turned back toward Luke.

"Is the path itself giving you any trouble?" I asked.

"No," he replied. "It's nothing at all like those stories I'd heard about the Black Road. It looks a little bleak at times, but nothing's really threatened us." He glanced downward and chuckled. "Of course it's only a few yards wide," he added, "and this is the broadest it's been, so far."

"Still," I said, opening my senses and studying its emanations with my Logrus sight, "I'd think something might have threatened."

"I guess we've been lucky," he said.

Again, Nayda laughed, and I felt foolish. The presence of a *ty'iga* would count as surely as my own in offsetting the dire effects of a Chaos roadway in the realm of Order.

"Guess you had a little luck coming," I said.

"You're going to need a horse, Merle," he said then.

"I suppose you're right," I agreed.

I was afraid to use Logrus magic and call attention to my location. Still, I had already learned that the spikard could be used in a similar fashion, and I entered it with my will, extended, extended, made contact, summoned. . . .

"It'll be along any minute," I said. "Did you say something about our gaining on them?"

"That's what Nayda tells me," he explained. "She has an amazing rapport with her sister—not to mention a high sensitivity to this pathway itself.

"Knows a lot about demons, too," he added.

"Oh, are we likely to encounter any?" I asked her.

"It was demonformed warriors from the Courts who abducted Coral," she said. "They seem headed toward a tower up ahead."

"How far ahead?" I asked.

"Hard to say, since we're cutting through Shadow," she answered.

The trail, which consisted of blackened grasses and which produced the same effect on any tree or shrub that so much as overhung it, wound its way through a hilly area now; and as I stepped onto and off of it I noted that it seemed brighter and warmer each time I departed. It had reached this point now after having been virtually undetectable in the vicinity of Kashfa—an index of how far we were into the realm of the Logrus.

A little past the next bending of the trail, I heard a whinny from off to the right.

"Excuse me," I said. "Delivery time," and I departed the trail and entered a grove of oval-leafed trees.

Snorting and stamping sounds reached me from ahead, and I followed them down shaded ways.

"Wait up!" Luke called. "We shouldn't separate."

But the wood was fairly dense, not at all easy going for someone on horseback, so I hollered back, "Don't worry!" and plunged ahead.

. . . And that, of course, was why he was there.

Fully saddled and bridled, his reins tangled in the

dense foliage, he was cursing in horse-talk, shaking his
head from side to side, pawing at the earth. I halted,
stared.

I may have given the impression that I would rather
pull on a pair of Adidas and jog through Shadow than
plunge through on the back of a beast driven half-mad
by the changes going on about it. Or ride a bicycle. Or
hop through on a pogo stick.

Nor would this impression be incorrect. It is not that
I don't know how to drive the things. It is just that I'd
never been particularly fond of them. Admitted, I never
had the use of one of those wonder horses, such as Julian's Morgenstern, Dad's Star, or Benedict's Glemdenning, which stood to mortal horses in terms of life span,
strength, and endurance as did Amberites to the inhabitants of most shadows.

I looked all about, but could detect no injured
rider. . . .

"Merlin!" I heard Luke call, but my attention was
nearer at hand. I advanced slowly, not wanting to upset
him further. "Are you all right?"

I had simply put in an order for a horse. Any old hay
burner would have served, for purposes of keeping up
with my companions.

I found myself looking at an absolutely lovely animal—black and orange-striped like a tiger. In this, he
resembled Glemdenning with his red and black striping.
In that I didn't know where Benedict's mount came from
either, I was glad to let it be the place of magic.

I advanced slowly.

"Merle! Anything wrong?"

I didn't want to shout back a reply and frighten the
poor beast. I placed my hand gently upon his neck.

"It's okay," I said. "I like you. I'll undo it and we'll
be friends, all right?"

I took my time untangling the reins, using my other

hand to massage his neck and shoulders. When he was free he did not pull away, but seemed to study me.

"Come on," I said, taking up the reins, "this way."

I led him back the way I had come, talking the while. I realized by the time we emerged that I actually liked him. I met Luke about then, a blade in his hand.

"My God!" he said. "No wonder it took you so long! You stopped to paint it!"

"You like, huh?"

"You ever want to get rid of that one, I'll make you a good offer."

"I don't think I'll be getting rid of him," I said.

"What's his name?"

"Tiger," I said without premeditation, and then I mounted.

We headed back to the trail, where even Dalt eyed my mount with something like pleasure. Nayda reached out and stroked the black and orange mane.

"Now we may be able to make it in time," she said, "if we hurry."

I mounted, and I guided Tiger over onto the trail. I anticipated all manner of reactions to the trail, as I recalled from my father's story the possibly intimidating effects of the thing upon animals. It didn't seem to bother him, though, and I released the breath I hadn't realized I was holding.

"In time for what?" I asked as we found a formation—Luke in the lead, Dalt behind him and to the right, Nayda to the left of the trail, rear, me to her right and somewhat back.

"I cannot tell for certain," she said, "because she is still sedated. However, I do know that she is no longer being moved; and I have the impression that her abductors have taken refuge in the tower, where the trail is much wider."

"Hm," I said. "You wouldn't have happened to notice the rate of change in width per unit of distance traveled on this trail, would you?''

"I was in liberal arts," she said, smiling. "Remember?''

She turned suddenly then, glancing in Luke's direction. He was still an entire horse's length ahead, eyes front—though he had looked back moments before.

"Damn you!" she said softly. "Being with you both this way gets me to thinking about school. Then I start talking that way—''

"In English," I said.

"Did I say that in English?''

"Yes.''

"Shit! Help me if you catch me at it, will you?''

"Of course," I said. "It seems to show you'd enjoyed it somewhat, despite its being a job Dara'd laid on you. And you're probably the only *ty'iga* with a degree from Berkeley.''

"Yes, I enjoyed it—confused as I was over which of you was which. Those were the happiest days in my life, with you and Luke, back in school. For years I tried to learn your mothers' names so I'd know who I was supposed to be protecting. You were both so cagey, though.''

"It's in the genes, I guess," I observed. "I enjoyed your company as Vinta Bayle—appreciated your protection as others, too.''

"I suffered," she said, "when Luke began his yearly attempts on your life. If he were the son of Dara I was supposed to protect, it shouldn't have mattered. But it did. I was already very fond of both of you. All I could tell was that you were both of the blood of Amber. I didn't want either of you harmed. The hardest thing was when you went away, and I was sure Luke had lured you into the mountains of New Mexico to kill you. By then, I suspected very strongly that you were the one, but I was not certain. I was in love with Luke, I had taken over the body of Dan Martinez, and I was carrying a pistol. I followed you everywhere I could, knowing that if he tried to harm you the *geas* I was under would force me to shoot the man I loved.''

"You shot first, though. We were just standing talking, by the side of the road. He shot back in self-defense.''

"I know. But everything seemed to indicate that you were in peril. He'd taken you to a perfect spot for an execution, at an ideal time—''

"No,'' I said. "Your shot went wide, and you left yourself open for what followed.''

"I don't understand what you're saying.''

"You solved the problem of possibly having to shoot Luke by setting up a situation where he shot you.''

"I couldn't do that, under a *geas*.''

"Maybe not consciously,'' I said. "So something stronger than the *geas* found a way.''

"You really believe that?''

"Yes, and it's all right for you to admit it now. You're released from the *geas*. My mother told me. You told me—I think.''

She nodded. "I don't know exactly when it came undone, or how,'' she said. "But it's gone—though I'd still try to protect you if something threatened. It's good that you and Luke are really friends, and—''

"So why the secret?'' I interrupted. "Why not just tell him you were Gail? Surprise the hell out of him—pleasantly.''

"You don't understand,'' she said. "He broke up with me, remember? Now I've another chance. It's like it was, all over again. He—likes me a lot. I'm afraid to say, 'I'm really the girl you once broke up with.' It might get him to thinking of all the reasons why, and make him decide he was right the first time.''

"That's silly," I said. "I don't know what reasons he gave. He never told me about it. Just said there'd been an argument. But I'm sure they were specious. I know he liked you. I'm sure he really broke up with you because he was a son of Amber about to come home on some very nasty business, and there was no room for what he thought was a normal shadow girl in the picture. You'd played your part too well."

"Is that why you broke up with Julia?" she asked.

"No," I said.

"Sorry."

I noticed the black trail had widened about a foot since we'd begun talking. I was in the market for a mathematical problem just then.

X

And so we rode—six paces along a city street, amid the blare of horns, our black way edged by skid marks; a quarter mile along a black sand beach, beside a soft green sea, stirring palms to our left; across a tarnished snowfield; beneath a bridge of stone, our way a dead and blackened streambed; then to prairie; back to wooded way—and Tiger never flinched, even when Dalt put a booted foot through a windshield and broke off an antenna.

The way continued to widen, to perhaps twice its width when I had first come upon it. Stark trees were more common within it now, standing like photographic negatives of their bright mates but a few feet off the trail. While the leaves and branches of these latter were regularly stirred, we felt no wind at all. The sounds—of our voices, of our mounts' hooves—came somehow muted now, also. Our entire course had a constant, wavery twilight atmosphere to it, no matter that a few paces away—which brief excursion we essayed many times—it might be high noon or midnight. Dead-looking birds were perched within the blackened trees, though they seemed on occasion to move, and the raspy, croaking sounds that sometimes came to us may well have been theirs.

At one time, a fire raged to our right; at another, we seemed to be passing near the foot of a glacier on the left. Our trail continued to widen—nothing like the great Black Road Corwin had described to me from the days of the war, but big enough now for us all to ride abreast.

"Luke," I said, after a time.

"Yeah?" he answered, from my left. Nayda rode to my right now, and Dalt to her right. "What's up?"

"I don't want to be king."

"Me neither," he said. "How hard they pushing you?"

"I'm afraid they're going to grab me and crown me if I go back. Everybody in my way died suddenly. They really plan to stick me on the throne, to marry me to Coral—"

"Uh-huh," he said, "and I've two questions about it. First, will it work?"

"The Logrus seems to think it will, at least for a time—which is all politics is about, anyhow."

"Second," he said, "if you feel about the place the way I feel about Kashfa, you're not going to let it go to hell if you can help it—even if it means some personal misery. You don't want to take the throne, though, so you must have worked out some alternative remedy. What is it?"

I nodded as the trail turned sharply to the left and headed uphill. Something small and dark scuttled across our path.

"I've a notion—not even a full idea," I said, "which I want to discuss with my father."

"Tall order," he said. "You know for sure that he's even alive?"

"I talked to him not all that long ago—very briefly. He's a prisoner, somewhere. All I know for sure is that it's somewhere in the vicinity of the Courts—because I can reach him by Trump from there, but nowhere else."

"Tell me about this communication," he said.

And so I did, black bird and all.

"Sounds like busting him out's going to be tricky," he said. "And you think your mom's behind it?"

"Yep."

"I thought I was the only one with these maternal problems. But it figures, seeing as yours trained mine."

"How come we turned out so normal?" I said.

He just stared at me for several seconds. Then he started to laugh.

"Well, I *feel* normal," I said.

"Of course," he said quickly then, "and that's what counts. Tell me, if it came to an out-and-out crossing of powers, do you think you could beat Dara?"

"Hard to say," I told him. "I'm stronger now than I ever was before, because of the spikard. But I'm beginning to believe she's very good."

"What the hell's a spikard?"

So I told him that story, too.

"That's why you were so flashy back in the church when you were fighting with Jurt?" he said.

"That's right."

"Let's see it."

I tried to pull it off, but it wouldn't pass the knuckle. So I simply extended my hand. Luke reached for it. His fingers halted a couple of inches above it.

"It's holding me off, Merle. Protective little devil."

"Hell," I said, "I'm not a shapeshifter for nothing." I took hold of it then, slimmed my finger suddenly, and slid it off. "Here."

He held it in the palm of his left hand as we bounced along, regarding it through narrowed eyes. Suddenly, I felt dizzy. Withdrawal symptoms from the thing? I forced myself upright, reversed my breathing, refused to let it show.

"Heavy," Luke said at last. "I can feel the power there. Other things, too. It won't let me in, though."

I reached for it and he drew his hand away.

"I can feel it in the air all around us," he said. "Merle, this thing lays a spell on anybody who wears it."

I shrugged.

"Yes," I said. "A benign one, though. It's done nothing to harm me, and it's helped me a number of times."

"But can you trust anything that came to you in such an odd way—almost by trickery, caused you to abandon Frakir when she tried to warn you about it, and for all you know has been influencing your behavior ever since you put it on?"

"I admit to a kind of disorientation at first," I said, "but I think that was just in the way of accommodation to the levels of voltage it draws. I've been back to normal for some time now."

"How can you tell for sure? Maybe it's brainwashed you."

"Do I seem brainwashed to you?"

"No. I was just trying to say that I wouldn't completely trust anything with such questionable credentials."

"Well taken," I agreed, holding forth my hand. "But so far the benefits have outweighed any hypothetical dangers. Consider me warned, and I'll take my chances."

He handed it back.

"If I think it's making you act weird I'm going to hit you over the head and pull it off, though."

"Fair enough," I said, slipping it back on. Immediately, I felt a rush of energy throughout my system as the lines of control were reestablished.

"If you're not sure you can force the information out of your mother," he said, "how do you propose finding Corwin and freeing him?"

"Several things suggest themselves," I said. "The simplest way may be a foot in the door technique. That is, I'd open all of the channels on the spikard and go for another Trump contact. As soon as there's any sort of opening I'd just push ahead with full force, jamming any spells that try to stop me and burning them out."

"Sounds as if it could be dangerous."

"I can't think of any way to go about this that wouldn't be."

"Then why haven't you tried it?"

"It only occurred to me recently, and I haven't had the time since then."

"However you go about it, you're going to need some help," he said. "So count me in."

"Thanks, Luke. I—"

"Now, about the king business," he said. "What happens if you simply refuse to take the throne? Who's next in line?"

"It's a bit tangled when you come to Sawall," I said. "By rights, Mandor should be first in line of succession from our House. He'd removed himself from the line years ago, though."

"Why?"

"I believe he claimed he was unfit to rule."

"No offense, Merle. But he seems like the only one of you who *is* fit for the job."

"Oh, without a doubt," I responded. "Most of the Houses have someone like him, though. There's usually a nominal head and a de facto one, someone for show and someone for scheming. Mandor likes the climate behind the scenes."

"Sounds as if your House has two," he said.

"I'm not really clear on it," I said. "I don't know Dara's status right now in her father's House—Helgram—or her mother's—Hendrake. But it might be worth a power struggle within Sawall if that's where the next king is coming from. Still, the more I learn of Mandor the more intimidating such a struggle would seem. I'd guess they're cooperating."

"I take it you're next in line, and then Jurt?"

"Actually, our brother Despil is next after me. Jurt said that Despil would probably step aside for him, but I think that was wishful thinking. I'm not at all sure he would. Anyhow, Jurt says now that he isn't interested."

"Ha! I think he's just taking a different approach. You whipped him too many times, and he's trying to get in good with you. Hope that spikard can protect your back."

"I don't know," I said. "I'd like to believe him. He spent a lot of time making sure that it wouldn't be easy, though."

"Supposing you all decline. Who's next?"

"I'm not certain," I said, "but I think it would go to Hendrake then."

"Damn," Luke said. "It's as twisted a place as Amber, isn't it?"

"Neither one's twisted, exactly. Just a little complicated, till you've learned the ropes."

"What say I just listen, and you fill me in on everything that you haven't so far?"

"Good idea."

So I talked for a long while, breaking to summon food and water. We halted twice during that time, causing me to realize just how tired I had become. And briefing Luke reminded me yet again that I should be telling all of this to Random. But if I got in touch and tried it I was certain he would order me back to Amber. And I couldn't disobey a direct order from the king, even if

I was almost his opposite number.

"We're getting nearer," Nayda announced somewhat later, and I noted that our roadway had widened even more, almost to the point she'd described. I drew a jolt of energy into my system, digested it, and kept going.

Shortly thereafter, she remarked, "Much nearer."

"Like just around the corner?" Luke asked.

"Could be," she answered. "I can't be more precise, the condition she's in."

But a little later, we heard distant shouts.

Luke drew rein.

"Something about a tower," he said.

She nodded.

"Were they heading for it, holing up in it, or defending themselves there?"

"All of the above," she said. "I understand now. Her captors were pursued, headed for a place of refuge, reached it, are there now."

"How come you're suddenly that precise?"

She gave me a quick look that I took as a request for an explanation other than *ty'iga* powers.

"I was using the spikard," I offered, "trying to see whether I could give her a clearer vision."

"Good," Luke said. "Can you boost it even more, so we can see what we're up against?"

"I can try," I said, narrowing my eyes at her in inquiry. She responded with a very slight nod.

I wasn't certain how to go about it, so I just fed her energy in the way of that jolt I'd given myself a while back.

"Yes," she said after a few moments, "Coral and her captors—six of them, I believe—have taken refuge in a tower near here. They are under attack."

"How large is the party of attackers?" Luke asked.

"Small," she said. "Quite small. I can't give you a number."

"Let's go and see," Luke said, and he led the way, Dalt behind him.

"Three or four," Nayda whispered to me, "but they're Pattern ghosts. That's probably all it can maintain this far from home, on a Black Road."

"Ouch," I said. "This makes it tricky."

"How so?"

"It means I have relatives on both sides."

"It also looks as if Amber's ghosts and the Court's demons are only agents, and that it's really a confrontation between the Logrus and the Pattern."

"Damn! Of course!" I said. "It could easily escalate into another of those. I'm going to have to warn Luke what we're riding into."

"You can't! Not without telling him what I am!"

"I'll tell him I learned it myself—that I had a sudden insight into a new spell."

"But what then? Which side are you on? What do we do?"

"Neither," I said. "We're on our own, and against both of them."

"You're crazy! There's no place you can hide, Merle! The Powers divide the universe between them!"

"Luke!" I cried. "I just probed ahead, learned the attackers are Pattern ghosts!"

"You don't say?" he called back. "Think we should be taking their side? It's probably better for the Pattern to take her back than for the Courts to get her, wouldn't you think?"

"She shouldn't be used that way," I said. "Let's take her away from both of them."

"I agree with your feelings," he stated. "But what if we succeed? I don't really care to be struck by a meteor or transported to the bottom of the nearest ocean."

"As near as I can tell, the spikard doesn't draw its

power from the Pattern or the Logrus. Its sources are scattered through Shadow.''

''So? I'm sure it's not a match for either one, let alone both.''

''No, but I can use it to start an evasion course. They'll be getting in each other's way if they decide to pursue us.''

''But eventually they'd find us, wouldn't they?''

''Maybe, maybe not,'' I said. ''I have some ideas, but we're running out of time.''

''Dalt, did you hear all that?'' Luke asked.

''I did,'' Dalt replied.

''If you want out, now's your chance.''

''And miss an opportunity to twist the Unicorn's tail?'' he said. ''Keep riding!''

We did, and the shouts grew louder as we raced ahead. There was a certain timeless feeling to it, though—with the muffled sounds and the dimness—as if we had always been riding here and always would be. . . .

Then we rounded a bend and I saw the top of the tower in the distance, heard more shouts. We slowed as we came to the next turn, advancing more cautiously, working our way through a small stand of black saplings.

Finally, we halted, dismounted, worked our way forward on foot. We pushed aside the final screening branches and looked down a slight slope to a blackened, sandy plain beside a three-story gray tower with slit windows and a narrow entranceway. It took a while to sort out the tableau at its base.

There were two demonformed individuals standing to either side of the tower's entrance. They were armed and their attention seemed focused upon the contest taking place on the sands before them. Familiar figures stood at the far end of this impromptu arena and at either side:

Benedict stroked his chin, expressionless; Eric hunkered and smiled; Caine juggled, flipped, palmed, and passed a dagger, reflexively, through some private routine, an expression of amused fascination on his face. From the tower's top, I suddenly noted, two horned demons leaned forward, their gazes as intent as those of Amber's Pattern ghosts.

At the circle's center Gérard faced a demonformed son of Hendrake, of his own height and greater girth. It looked to be Chinaway himself, who was said to have a collection of over two hundred skulls of those he'd dispatched. I preferred Gérard's collection of a thousand or so mugs, steins, and drinking horns, but your ghost will walk, you lover of trees, in an English lane, if you know what I mean.

Both were stripped to the waist, and from the scuffed-up condition of the sands about them I guessed they had been at it for some time. Chinaway tried to trip Gérard just then, who caught his arm and head as he stepped behind him, and sent him cartwheeling away. The demon lord came up on his feet, however, and immediately advanced once again, arms extended, hands weaving a sinuous pattern before him. Gérard simply waited in a ready position. Chinaway stabbed taloned fingers toward Gérard's eyes and hooked a blow against his rib cage. Gérard caught hold of his shoulder, however, as Chinaway dropped and caught him about the thigh.

"Let's wait," Dalt said softly. "I want to watch."

Luke and I both nodded as Gérard locked Chinaway's head and Chinaway wrapped his other arm about Gérard's waist. Then they simply stood there, muscles bulging beneath two hides, one pale and smooth, the other red and scaly. Their lungs worked like bellows.

"I assume the thing's been dragging out," Luke whispered, "and they decided to settle it champion against champion."

"Looks that way," I said.

"Coral must be inside then, wouldn't you think?"

"Wait a minute."

I ran a quick probe into the structure, locating two people within. I nodded then.

"Her and a single guard, I'd say."

Gérard and Chinaway still stood like statues.

"Now might be the best time to grab Coral," Luke said, "while everybody's watching the fight."

"You're probably right," I told him. "Let me see whether I can make myself invisible. That might simplify matters."

"Okay," he said about a quarter minute later. "Whatever you did just then worked. You're gone."

"Indeed I am," I said. "Back in a bit."

"How will you get her out?"

"I'll decide after I've reached her. Just be ready."

I moved slowly, careful not to scuff the sand. I skirted the circle, passing behind Caine. I approached the door to the tower, soundless, checking about me constantly. Gérard and Chinaway still stood exactly as they had been, locked, and applying enormous pressures to each other.

I passed between the guards, entering the dim interior of the tower. It consisted of a single round room with a bare earth floor, stone pedestals beneath each slit window. A ladder led up to the second floor through a hole in the ceiling. Coral lay upon a blanket to my left; the individual who was ostensibly guarding her stood upon a pedestal, watching the fight through the nearest window.

I moved nearer, knelt, caught up her left wrist and felt her pulse. It was strong and steady. I decided against trying to awaken her, though. Instead, I wrapped the blanket around her, raised her in my arms, and stood.

I was about to try extending the invisibility spell to

include her when the watcher at the window turned. I must have made some noise in moving her.

For a moment, the guard stared at the sight of his prisoner drifting below him. Then he opened his mouth, as if to give alarm—leaving me with small choice but to shock his nervous system into insensibility with a charge from my ring.

Unfortunately, there was a rattle of arms as he fell from his pedestal to the floor. Almost immediately, I heard a cry from overhead, followed by sounds of rapid movement.

Turning, I hurried to the door. I had to slow and turn because of its narrowness. I wasn't certain what the guards outside would think when a comatose Coral drifted by, but I didn't want to be trapped inside. Peering ahead, I saw that Gérard and Chinaway seemed in the same position as before. Seconds later, however, as I turned my body and took my first sidling step, there came a sudden, sharp twisting movement from Gérard, followed immediately by a sound like that of a snapping stick.

Gérard let his arms fall and stood erect. The body of Chinaway hit the ground at his side, neck at an unnatural angle. Eric and Caine applauded. The two guards beside the door moved forward. Behind me, within, the ladder rattled at the other side of the room. I heard a cry from that direction.

Two more steps and I turned, headed left. The outside guards were rushing toward their fallen champion. A half-dozen paces, and there were more cries at my back, as my pursuers exited the tower; and there were human cries as well, from the killing circle.

I knew that I couldn't outrun any of them, carrying my burden; and all that motor activity interfered with my concentration to the point where I was incapable of performing magical operations.

So I dropped to my knees, lowering Coral to the ground before me, turned without even rising, and extended my left fist, plunging my mind deep within the ring, calling for extreme measures to halt the pair of Hendrake commandos who were only a few paces away now, edged weapons ready to pierce and to slash.

. . . And then they were caught up in the midst of flames. I think they screamed, but there was a lot of noise just then. Two paces more, perhaps, and they fell, blackened and twitching, before me. My hand was shaking, from its proximity to the powers that caused this; and I hadn't time, even, to think or to feel as I swung toward the sandy place of the recent contest and whatever might be coming at me from that direction.

One of the two guards who had rushed forward lay smoldering on the ground at Eric's feet. Another—who had apparently attacked Caine—clutched at the knife in his gullet, fires spreading outward, downward, upward, from his throat, as he sank slowly, then toppled to the rear.

Immediately, Caine, Eric, and Benedict turned to stare at me. Gérard, having just drawn on a blue shirt, was buckling his swordbelt in place. He turned, too, just as Caine said, "And who, sir, are you?"

"Merlin," I replied, "son of Corwin."

Caine actually looked startled.

"Does Corwin have a son?" he asked the others.

Eric shrugged and Gérard said, "I don't know." But Benedict studied me.

"There is a resemblance," he said.

"True," Caine agreed. "All right, boy. Even if you are Corwin's son, that woman you're making off with belongs to us. We just won her fair and square off these well-done Chaosites."

With that, he began walking toward me. A moment later, Eric joined him. Then Gérard fell into step behind

them. I didn't want to harm them, even if they were only
ghosts, so I gestured and a line was drawn in the sand
before them. Immediately, it caught fire.

They halted.

Suddenly, a huge figure appeared at my left. It was
Dalt, a naked blade in his hand. A moment later, Luke
was there. Then Nayda. The four of us faced the four of
them, across the fire.

"She's ours now," Dalt said, and he took a single
step forward.

"You are mistaken," came the reply, and Eric crossed
the line, drawing his weapon.

Dalt was a couple of inches taller than Eric, and he
had a longer reach. He moved forward immediately. I
expected some kind of cut from that big blade he carried,
but he went in for a point-attack. Eric, using a lighter
weapon, sidestepped and came in under his arm. Dalt
dropped the point of his blade, moved to his left, and
parried it. The two weapons were suited for very different styles—Eric's being at the heaviest end of the rapier
class, Dalt's at the lighter end of broadsword. Dalt's
could be a single-handed weapon for a big-enough,
strong-enough guy. I'd have had to use it two-handed
myself. Dalt tried an upward cut just then, of the sort a
Japanese swordsman would refer to as *kiriage*. Eric simply stepped back and tried for a wrist cut as it passed
him. Dalt suddenly moved his left hand to the haft and
executed a blinding two-handed cut of the sort known
as *naname giri*. Eric continued to circle, trying for the
wrist yet again.

Suddenly, Dalt opened his right hand and let it drift
back, as his right foot performed a huge semicircular
step to his rear and his left arm moved forward, leaving
him in a left-handed European *en garde* position, from
which that massive arm and matching blade immediately
extended, performing an inside beat upon Eric's blade

followed by a lunge. Eric parried as his right foot crossed behind his left and he sprang backward. Even so, I saw a spark as his guard was creased. He feinted in *sixte,* however, dropped his point beneath the parry that followed, extended his arm in *quatre,* raised himself and his blade into something resembling a stop-thrust targeting the left shoulder as the parry crossed, turned his wrist, and slashed Dalt across the left forearm.

Caine applauded, but Dalt simply brought his hands together and separated them again, executing a little hop-step as he did so, leaving him in a right *en garde* position. Eric drew circles in the air with the point of his weapon and smiled.

"Cute little dance routine you have there," he said.

Then Eric lunged, was parried, retreated, sidestepped, threw a front kick at Dalt's kneecap, missed, then moved with perfect timing as Dalt attempted a head cut. Switching to the Japanese himself, he spun in to the larger man's right, a maneuver I'd seen in a *kumatchi* exercise, his own blade rising and falling as Dalt's cut swept past. Dalt's right forearm went suddenly wet, a thing I did not really notice until after Eric had rotated his weapon, blade pointing outward and upward, and, the guard covering his knuckles, had driven his fist against the right side of Dalt's jaw. He kicked him then behind the knee and struck him with his left shoulder. Dalt stumbled and fell. Eric immediately kicked him, kidney, elbow, thigh—the latter only because he missed the knee—set his boot upon Dalt's weapon and swung his own about to bring its point in line with the man's heart.

I had been hoping all along, I suddenly realized, that Dalt would kick Eric's ass—not just because he was on my side and Eric wasn't, but because of the rough time Eric had given my dad. On the other hand, I doubted there were too many people of such ass-kicking prowess about. Unfortunately, two of them stood on the other side of the line I had drawn. Gérard could have out-wrestled him. Benedict, Master of Arms at Amber, could have beaten him with any weapon. I just didn't see us as having much of a chance against them all, with Caine thrown in for good measure—not even with a *ty'iga* on our side. And if I were suddenly to tell Eric that Dalt was his half brother, it wouldn't slow his thrust by an instant, even if he believed me.

So I made the only decision I could make. They were, after all, only Pattern ghosts. The real Benedict and Gérard were somewhere else at this moment and would in no way be harmed by anything I did to their doubles here. Eric and Caine were, of course, long dead, Caine being the fratricidal hero of the Patternfall war and subject of a recent statue on the Grand Concourse, on the occasion of Luke's assassinating him for killing his father. And Eric, of course, had found a hero's death on the slopes of Kolvir, saving him, I suppose, from dying at the hands of my father. The bloody history of my family swam through my head as I raised the spikard to add a footnote to it, calling again for the wave of incineration that had taken out two of my Hendrake kin.

My arm felt as if someone had struck it with a baseball bat. A wisp of smoke rose from the spikard. For a moment, my four upright uncles stood unmoving. And my fifth remained supine.

Then, slowly, Eric raised his weapon. And he continued to raise it, as Benedict, Caine, and Gérard drew theirs. He straightened as he held it before his face. The others did the same. It looked strangely like a salute; and Eric's eyes met mine.

"I know you," he said.

Then they all completed the gesture, and faded, faded, turned to smoke, and blew away.

Dalt bled, my arm ached, and I figured out what was

going on just moments before Luke gasped and said, "Over there."

My line of fire had gone out some time ago, but beyond the mark it had left, where my faded kinsmen had just been standing, the air began to shimmer.

"That will be the Pattern," I said to Luke, "come calling."

A moment later the Sign of the Pattern hovered before us.

"Merlin," it said, "you certainly move around a lot."

"My life has become very busy of late," I said.

"You took my advice and left the Courts."

"Yes, that seemed prudent."

"But I do not understand your purposes here."

"What's to understand?"

"You took the lady Coral away from the agents of the Logrus."

"That's right."

"But then you attempted to keep her from my agents as well."

"That, too, is correct."

"You must realize by now that she bears something that contributes to our balance of power."

"Yes."

"So one of us must have her. Yet you would deny us both."

"Yes."

"Why?"

"It's her whom I care about. She has rights and feelings. You're treating her like a game piece."

"True. I recognize her personhood, but unfortunately she is become both."

"Then I would deny her to both of you. Nothing would be changed, in that neither of you has her now, anyway. But I would take her out of the game."

"Merlin, you are a more important piece than she is,

but you are still only a piece and you may not dictate to me. Do you understand?''

"I understand my value to you," I said.

"I think not," it responded.

I was wondering just then how strong it really was in this place. It seemed obvious that in terms of energy expenditure, it had been necessary for it to release its four ghosts to be able to manifest itself here. Dared I oppose it with every channel on the spikard opened? I had never tried accessing every Shadow source it controlled simultaneously. If I did this, and if I were to move very quickly, could I get us all out of here before the Pattern reacted? If I couldn't, could I punch through whatever it raised up to stop us? And if I succeeded— either way—to what place should we flee?

Finally, how might this affect the Pattern's attitude toward me?

(. . . if you are not eaten by something bigger, come tell me your story one night.)

What the hell, I decided. It is a good day to be listed à la carte.

I opened all the channels.

It felt as if I had been jogging along at a good clip and a brick wall had suddenly appeared six inches before me.

I felt the smash and I went away.

I lay upon a smooth, cool stone surface. There was a terrible rushing of energies in my mind and body. I reached into their source and took control of them, dampening them to something that didn't threaten to take the top of my head off. Then I opened one eye, slightly.

The sky was very blue. I saw a pair of boots, standing a few feet off, faced away from me. I recognized them as Nayda's, and turning my head slightly, I saw that she wore them. I also saw then that Dalt lay sprawled several yards off to my left.

Nayda was breathing heavily, and my Logrus vision showed a pale red light about her vibrating hands, menacing.

Propping myself upon my left elbow and peering about her, I saw that she stood between me and the Sign of the Pattern that hovered in the air perhaps ten feet away.

When it spoke again it was the first time I'd heard it express anything like amusement: "You would protect him, against me?"

"Yes," she replied.

"Why?"

"I did it for so long that it would be a shame to fail him when he really needs it."

"Creature of the Pit, do you know where you stand?" it asked.

"No," she said.

I looked beyond them both at a perfectly clear blue sky. The surface upon which I lay was a level area of rock, perhaps oval in shape, opening onto nothing. A quick turning of my head showed that it seemed bitten out of a mountainside, however, several dark recesses to the rear indicating the possibility of caves. I saw, too, that Coral lay behind me. Our stony shelf was several hundred meters wide. And there was movement beyond Nayda and the Sign of the Pattern. Luke had just hauled himself up into a kneeling position.

I could have answered the question put to Nayda, but there was no percentage in my doing so. Not when she was doing such a fine job of holding our captor's attention and providing a crucial respite.

To my left, I saw gold-pink swirls within the stone, and though I had never been here I recalled the description from my father's story and knew this to be the place of the primal Pattern, the deeper level of reality that underlay Amber itself.

I rolled onto all fours then, and crawled a few steps, seaward, Patternward.

"You are at the other end of the universe, *ty'iga*, in the place of my greatest power."

Dalt groaned and rolled over, sat up, massaged his eyes with the palms of his hands.

I could feel something like a vibration just at the edge of hearing coming from Nayda now, and her entire form had taken on that reddish glow. I knew that she would die if she attacked the Sign, and I realized that I would attack it myself if it killed her.

I heard a moan from Coral.

"You will not hurt my friends," Nayda said.

I wondered then at its slapping me down before I could use the spikard, and transporting us immediately to its stronghold. Did this mean I might actually have had a chance against it, out there in Logrus territory where it was weakened?

"Creature of the Pit," it told her, "such a doomed, pathetic gesture as yours verges on the heroic. I feel a certain fondness for you. Would that I had such a friend. No, I will not harm your companions. But I must detain Coral and Merlin here as power counters, and the rest of you for political reasons, until this dispute with my adversary is settled."

"Detain?" she said. "Here?"

"There are comfortable quarters within the rock," it said.

I rose carefully to my feet, fumbling at my belt for my dagger.

Luke got up and walked over to Coral, knelt beside her.

"Are you awake?" he asked.

"Sort of," she answered.

"Can you stand?"

"Maybe."

"Let me help you."

Dalt rose while Luke was assisting her. I continued to sidle toward the design. Where was Dworkin when I really needed him?

"You may enter the caves behind you and inspect your quarters," the Sign said. "But first you must remove that ring, Merlin."

"No, now's hardly a time to be unpacking and getting comfortable," I answered, slashing my left palm with the dagger and taking a final step. "We won't be staying long."

A sound like a small thunderclap emerged from the Sign of the Pattern, but there was no lightning, nor did I think there would be. Not when it realized what I was holding in my hand, and where I was holding it.

"A thing I learned from Luke's father," I explained. "Let's talk."

"Yes," said the Sign of the Pattern, "like the reasonable beings that we are. Would you care for some cushions?"

Immediately, three such objects appeared nearby.

"Thanks," I said, drawing up a green one. "I could sure use an iced tea."

"Do you take sugar?"

XI

Seated upon a cushion, dagger at my side, I held my left hand out over the Pattern, cupped palm filled with my blood. The Sign of the Pattern hovered in the air before me, seeming, of a sudden, to have forgotten Coral, Nayda, Dalt, and Luke. I sipped from the frosted glass in my right hand, a sprig of fresh mint visible amid the ice.

"Prince Merlin," inquired the Sign, "tell me what it is that you desire, and let us resolve this matter quickly. Are you sure I mightn't fetch you a napkin to place at the danger point? It would not minimize your bargaining ability, if you stop to think of it. But it would serve to prevent accidents."

"No, that's okay," I said, half-gesturing with the blood-filled hand, so that its contents were stirred, a small line of red trickling up my wrist. "Thanks, any-how."

The Sign of the Pattern vibrated, grew still.

"Prince Merlin, you have made your point," it said. "But I do not think you realize the full implications of

200

your threat. A few drops of your blood upon my physical design could disturb the functioning of the universe.''

I nodded.

''I know,'' I said.

''Very well,'' it answered. ''State your demands.''

''Our freedom,'' I said. ''Let us go, and you remain intact.''

''You give me small choice, but the same applies to your friends.''

''What do you mean?''

''You may send Dalt whenever you wish,'' it said. ''As for the demon lady, I relinquish her with regret, as I feel she would have provided good company—''

Luke regarded Nayda.

''What is this 'creature of the Pit,' 'demon lady' business, anyway?'' he asked.

''Well, there are a few things you don't know about me . . .'' she responded.

''Is it a long story?'' he asked.

''Yes.''

''Am I an assignment? Or do you really like me?''

''You're not an assignment, and I really like you.''

''Then we'll hear the story later,'' he said.

''As I said, send her,'' it went on. ''And Dalt. And Luke. I will be happy to send the three of them wherever you wish. But does it occur to you that you and Coral are probably safer here than anywhere else?''

''Maybe. Maybe not,'' I answered. ''Coral, how do you feel about it?''

''Get me out of here,'' she said.

''So much for that notion,'' I told it. ''Now—''

''Wait. You want to be fair to your friends, don't you?''

''Sure I do.''

''Then let me point some things out to them which they may not have considered.''

"Go ahead."

"Lady," it said, "they want your eye in the Courts of Chaos. Your feelings on the matter are immaterial. If this can only be achieved by making you a prisoner, then it will be done."

Coral laughed softly.

"The alternative being to remain your prisoner?" she asked.

"Think of yourself as a guest. I will provide for your every comfort. Of course, there is a positive gain for me in this state of affairs—apart from denying the adversary your presence. I acknowledge this. But you must choose one of us, else the other will grab you off."

I looked at Coral, who shook her head slightly.

"So what'll it be?" I asked.

Coral came over and placed her hand upon my shoulder.

"Get me out of here," she said.

"You heard 'em," I told it. "Everybody goes."

"I crave your indulgence a moment more," it said.

"For what?" I asked.

"Consider. Choosing between the Logrus and myself is not a mere matter of politics—of selecting this person or that to do a particular job. My adversary and I represent two fundamental principles by means of which the universe is organized. You may tag us with nouns and adjectives from most languages and dozens of disciplines, but we represent, basically, Order and Chaos—Apollonian and Dionysiac, if you like; reason and feeling, if you prefer; madness and sanity; light and dark; signal and noise. As much as this may seem to indicate it, however, neither of us seeks the other's extinction. Heat death or fireball, classicism or anarchy, each of us proceeds along a single track, and without the other it would lead to a dead end. Both of us know this, and the game we have played since the beginning is a far more subtle thing—ultimately, perhaps, to be judged only esthetically.

"Now, I have gained a significant edge over my ancient adversary, for the first time in ages. I am in a position now to produce a historian's dream throughout Shadow—an age of high civilization and culture such as shall never be forgotten. If the balance were tipped the other way we would be contemplating a period of upheaval at least on par with that of an ice age. When I spoke of you as game pieces it was not to minimize your roles in this. For this is a time of great fluidity, when the Jewel and the man who would be king will make a difference. Stay with me, and I will guarantee the Golden Age of which I spoke, and you a part in it. Leave, and you will be snatched away by the other. Darkness and disorder will follow. Which would you have?"

Luke smiled.

"I know a good sales pitch when I hear it," he said. "Narrow it down to a simple choice. Make them think it's their own."

Coral squeezed my shoulder.

"We're going," I said.

"Very well," said the Sign. "Tell me where you want to go, and I'll send you all there."

"Not all," Luke said suddenly. "Just them."

"I do not understand. What about you?"

He drew a dagger and slashed his palm. He advanced and stood beside me, extending his hand out over the Pattern, also.

"If we go, only three of us may arrive," he said, "if that. I'll stay here and keep you company while you deliver my friends."

"How will you know I've done it in a satisfactory fashion?"

"Good question," he said. "Merle, you got a set of Trumps on you?"

"Yes."

I removed them and showed them to him.

"Still got one of me in there?"

"Last time I looked I did."

"Then get it out and have it ready. Figure your next move before you take off. Stay in touch with me till you make it."

"What about yourself, Luke? You can't sit there forever as a bloody threat to Order. It's only a temporary stalemate. You have to surrender your position sooner or later, and when you do—"

"Do you still have some odd cards in that deck?"

"What do you mean?"

"The ones you once referred to as the Trumps of Doom."

I riffled through. They were mostly near the bottom.

"Yes," I said. "Beautifully executed. I wouldn't have tossed them."

"You really think so?"

"Yeah. Get together a bunch of stuff this good, and I'll get you an exhibit back in Amber."

"You serious? You're not just saying that because—"

The Sign of the Pattern emitted a growling sound.

"Everybody's a critic," Luke observed. "Okay. Pull all the Trumps of Doom."

I did this.

"Mix 'em up a little. Keep 'em face down, please."

"All right."

"Fan 'em."

He leaned forward, took a card.

"Okay," he said. "I'm in business. Whenever you're ready, tell it where to take you. Stay in touch. Hey, Pattern, I want an iced tea of my own."

A frosty glass appeared near his right foot. He stooped and took it up, sipped from it.

"Thanks."

"Luke," Nayda said, "I don't understand what's going on. What will happen to you?"

"Nothing much," he replied. "Don't cry for me, demon lady. I'll see you later."

He looked at me and quirked an eyebrow.

"Send us to Jidrash," I said, "in Kashfa—to the open area between the palace and the church."

I held Luke's Trump in my moist left hand, near to a humming spikard. I felt the card grow cold just as Luke said, "You heard him."

And the world swirled and unswirled, and it was a brisk, windy morning in Jidrash. I regarded Luke through his Trump. I opened channel after channel of the ring.

"Dalt, I might as well leave you here," I said. "You, too, Nayda."

"No," the big man said, just as Nayda said, "Hold on a minute."

"You're both out of the picture now," I explained. "Neither side wants you for anything. But I've got to get Coral someplace safe. Me, too."

"You're a focus of the action," Nayda said, "and I can help Luke by helping you. Take me along."

"I feel the same way about it," Dalt said. "I still owe Luke a big one."

"Okay," I said. "Hey, Luke! You hear all that?"

"Yeah," he said. "Better be about your business then. Shit! I spilled it—"

His Trump went black.

I didn't wait for avenging angels, tongues of fire, lightning bolts, or an opening of the earth. I got us out of jurisdiction real quick.

* * *

I sprawled on the green grass beneath the big tree. Wisps of fog drifted by. Dad's Pattern sparkled below me. Jurt was seated cross-legged on the hood of the car, blade across his knees. He hit the ground when we made our appearance. Corwin was nowhere in sight.

"What's going on?" Jurt asked me.

"I am beat, bushed, and whacked-out. I am going to lie here and stare at the fog till my mind goes away," I said. "Meet Coral, Nayda, and Dalt. Hear their story and tell them yours, Jurt. Don't wake me for the end of the world unless it has very good special effects."

I proceeded to do as I had promised, to the tune of a fading guitar and the distant voice of Sara K. The grass was wondrous soft. The fog swirled through my brain. Fade to black.

And then, and then. . . . And then, sir. . . .

Walking. I was walking, almost drifting, through a California shopping mall I used to frequent. Knots of kids, couples with infants, women with parcels, passed, words smothered by sounds from a music store speaker. Potted oases sheltered, deli smells drifted, sale signs promised.

Walking. Past the drugstore. Past the shoe store. Past the candy store. . . .

Narrow corridor to the left. I'd never noticed it. Must turn. . . .

Odd there should be a carpet—and candles in high holders, and sconces, and candelabra atop narrow chests. The walls glittered with their re—

I turned back.

There was no back. The mall was gone. The corridor ended in that direction at a wall. A small tapestry hung upon it, depicting nine figures who looked back at me. I shrugged and turned again.

"Still something left to your spell, Uncle," I remarked. "Let's be about it then."

Walking. In silence now. Ahead. To the place where the mirrors glittered. I had seen this place long ago, I recalled, though its disposition—I suddenly realized— was not peculiar to Amber Castle. It was right there, on the tip of memory—my younger self passing this way, not unaccompanied—but the price of that recollection would be loss of control here, I knew. Reluctantly, I released the image and turned my attention to the small oval mirror to my left.

I smiled. So did my image. I stuck out my tongue and was so saluted in return.

I moved on. Only after several paces did I realize that the image had been my demonformed self, while my person had not.

A soft throat-clearing sound occurred to my right. Turning in that direction, I beheld my brother Mandor within a black-framed lozenge.

"Dear boy," he stated, "the king is dead. Long live your august personage as soon as you have assumed the throne. You had best make haste to return for a crowning at the End of the World, with or without the bride of the Jewel."

"We ran into a few small problems," I said.

"Nothing worth resolving just now. Your presence in the Courts is far more important."

"No, my friends are," I said.

A momentary smile touched his lips.

"You will be in an ideal position to protect your friends," he said, "and to do as you would with your enemies."

"I will be back," I said, "soon. But not to be crowned."

"As you would, Merlin. It is your presence that is desired."

"I promise nothing," I said.

He chuckled, and the mirror was emptied.

I turned away. I walked on.

More laughter. From the left. My mother's.

From within a red frame of carved flowers, she stared at me, a look of vast amusement upon her features.

"Seek him in the Pit!" she said. "Seek him in the Pit!"

I passed, and her laughter continued at my back for a time.

"Hsst!"

To my right, a long, narrow mirror bordered in green.

"Masster Merlin," she said. "I have ssought, but the ghosst-light hass not passsed my way."

"Thanks, Glait. Keep looking, please."

"Yess. We musst ssit together in a warm place by night once again and drink milk and talk of the old dayss."

"That would be nice. Yes, we must. If we are not eaten by something bigger."

"S-s-s-s-s!"

Could that be laughter?

"Good hunting, Glait."

"Yess. S-s-s!"

. . . And on. Walking.

"Son of Amber. Wearer of the spikard"—this from within a shadowy niche to my left.

I halted and stared. The frame was white, the glass was gray. Within was a man I had never met. His shirt was black and opened at the neck. He wore a brown leather vest, his hair dark blond, eyes perhaps green.

"Yes?"

"A spikard was hidden in Amber," he stated, "for you to find. It conveys great powers. It also bears a series of spells that will cause its wearer to act in certain ways under certain circumstances."

"I suspected this," I said. "What is it set to do?"

"Formerly worn by Swayvill, King of Chaos, it will force the chosen successor to take the throne, behave in a certain fashion, and be amenable to the suggestions of certain persons."

"These being?"

"The woman who laughed and cried, 'Seek him in the Pit.' The man in black, who desires your return."

"Dara and Mandor. They laid these spells upon it?"

"Just so. And the man left it for you to find."

"I hate to surrender the thing just now," I said, "when it's proving so useful. Is there a way to lift these spells?"

"Of course. But it should not matter to you."

"Why not?"

"The ring you wear is not the one of which I speak."

"I do not understand."

"But you will. Never fear."

"Who are you, sir?"

"My name is Delwin, and we may never actually meet—unless certain ancient powers come loose."

He raised his hand, and I saw that he, too, wore a spikard. He moved it toward me.

"Touch your ring to mine," he commanded. "Then it can be ordered to bring you to me."

I raised mine and moved it toward the glass. At the moment they seemed to touch, there was a flash of light and Delwin was gone.

I let my arm fall. I walked on. On an impulse, I stopped before a chest and opened its drawer.

I stared. There was no way to one-up this place, it seemed. The drawer contained a miniature, scaled-down representation of my father's chapel—tiny colored tiles, diminutive burning tapers, even a doll-sized Grayswandir upon the altar.

"The answer lies before you, dear friend," came a throaty voice I knew yet did not know.

I raised my gaze to a lavender-bordered mirror I had not realized hung above the chest. The lady within had long, coal-black hair and eyes so dark I could not tell where the pupils left off and the irises began. Her complexion was very pale, emphasized perhaps by her pink eye shadow and lip coloring. Those eyes. . . .

"Rhanda!" I said.

"You remember! You do remember me!"

". . . And the days of our bonedance games," I said. "Grown and lovely. I thought of you but recently."

"And I felt the touch of your regard as I slept, my Merlin. I am sorry we parted so, but my parents—"

"I understand," I said. "They thought me demon or vampire."

"Yes." She extended her pale hand through the mirror, took hold of my own, drew it toward her. Within the looking glass, she pressed it to her lips. They were cold. "They would rather I cultivated the acquaintance of the sons and daughters of men and women, than of our own kind."

When she smiled, I beheld her fangs. They had not been apparent in her childhood.

"Gods! You look human!" she said. "Come visit me in Wildwood one day!"

Impulsively, I leaned forward. Our lips met within the mirror. Whatever she was, we had been friends.

"The answer," she repeated, "lies before you. Come see me!"

The mirror turned red and she was gone. The chapel stood unchanged within the drawer. I closed it and turned away.

Walking. Mirrors to the left. Mirrors to the right. Only myself within them.

Then—

"Well, well, nephew. Confused?"

"As usual."

"Can't say as I blame you."

His eyes were mocking and wise, his hair red as his sister Fiona's or his late brother Brand's. Or Luke's, for that matter.

"Bleys," I said, "what the hell is going on?"

"I've the rest of Delwin's message," he said, reaching into his pocket and extending his hand. "Here."

I reached into the mirror and accepted it. It was yet another spikard, like the one I wore.

"It is the one of which Delwin spoke," he said. "You must never wear it."

I studied it for several moments.

"What am I to do with it?" I asked.

"Put it in your pocket. A use may suggest itself at some point."

"How did you come by it?"

"I switched it after Mandor left it, for the one you wear now."

"How many are there, anyway?"

"Nine," he replied.

"I suppose you know all about them."

"More than most."

"That wouldn't be hard. I don't suppose you know where my father is?"

"No. But you do. Your lady friend with the sanguinary tastes told you."

"Riddles," I said.

"Always preferable to no answer at all," he responded.

Then he was gone and I walked again. After a while, this was gone, too.

Drifting. Black. Good. So good. . . .

A bit of light found its way through my eyelashes. I shut it out again. But the thunder rolled, and after a time the light leaked in once again.

Dark lines in brown, great horny ridges, ferny forests. . . .

A little later the faculty that evaluates perceptions awoke and pointed out that I was lying on my side staring at the cracked earth between a pair of roots from the tree, clumps of grass dotted here and there across the prospect.

. . . And I continued to stare, and there was a sudden brightness as of a lightning flash followed almost immediately by a crack of thunder. The earth seemed to shudder with it. I heard the pattering of drops upon the leaves of a tree, the hood of a car. I continued to stare at the largest crack that traversed the valley of my regard.

. . . And I realized that I knew.

It was the numb knowledge of awakening. The sources of emotion still dozed. In the distance, I could hear familiar voices in soft converse. I could also hear the sounds of cutlery against china. My stomach would awaken in a bit, I knew, and I would join them. For now, it was so very pleasant to lie here wrapped in my cloak, hearing the gentle rain and knowing. . . .

I returned to my micro-world and its dark canyon. . . .

The ground shook again, this time without benefit of lightning or thunder. And it kept on shaking. This irritated me, for it disturbed my friends and relatives, causing them to raise their voices in something like alarm. Also, it stirred a dormant California reflex at a time when I just wanted to loll and savor my fresh-acquired knowledge.

"Merlin, are you awake?"

"Yes," I said, sitting up suddenly, giving my eyes a quick rub, and running my hands through my hair.

It was the ghost of my father that knelt beside me, having just shaken my shoulder. "We seem to have a problem," he said, "with rather extreme ramifications."

Jurt, standing behind him, nodded several times. The ground shook once again, twigs and leaves fell about us, pebbles bounced, dust rose, the fogs were agitated. I heard a dish break in the vicinity of the heavy red and white cloth about which Luke, Dalt, Coral, and Nayda sat eating.

I untangled my cloak and rose to my feet, realizing then that someone had removed my boots while I slept. I drew them back on. There came another tremor, and I leaned against the tree for support.

"This is the problem?" I said. "Or is something bigger about to eat it?"

He gave me a puzzled look. Then, "Back when I drew the Pattern," he said, "I'd no way of knowing that this area was faulted, or that something like this would one day occur. If these shocks should crack the Pattern, we've had it—in more ways than one. As I understand it, that spikard you wear can draw upon enormous sources of energy. Is there some way you could use it to defuse this thing?"

"I don't know," I told him. "I never tried anything like it."

"Find out fast, okay?" he said.

But I was already spinning my mind about the circle of tines, touching each one to life. Then I seized upon the one possessed of the most juice, drew hard upon it, filled myself, body and mind, with its energy. Ignition completed and engine idling, with me in the driver's seat, I shifted into gear then, extending a line of force from the spikard down into the ground.

I reached for a long while, seeking a conversion metaphor to the subjective for anything I might discover.

... Wading out from the beach into the ocean—waves tickling my stomach, my chest—feeling with my toes the rocks, the strands of sea-weed. ... Sometimes a rock would turn, slip, bump against another, slide. ...

I couldn't see to the bottom with my eyes. But I saw the rocks, the wrack, in their disposition and movement, just the same, beheld them as clearly as if the bottom were fully illuminated.

Feeling, feeling my way now, down through the strata, single toe soft as a flashlight's beam running along rocky surfaces, testing the pressures of one upon another, isostatic kisses of mountains beneath the earth, orogenic erogenies of slow movement, flesh caressing mineral in the darkest of secret places—

Slip! The rock slides off. My body follows. . . .

I dive for it, following the sliding passage. I race ahead, pouring forth heat, cracking rock, splintering new pathways, outward, outward. . . . It was coming this way. I broke through a wall of stone, another. Another. I was not certain this was the way to divert it, but it was the only one I knew to try. Go that way! Damn it! That way! I accessed two more channels, a third, a fourth—

There was a slight vibration within the ground. I opened another channel. Within my metaphor the rocks grew stable beneath the waters. Shortly thereafter, the ground ceased its vibration.

I returned to the place where I had first felt the slide begin, stable now, yet still stressed. Feel it, feel it carefully. Describe a vector. Follow. Follow it to the point of original pressure. But no. This point is but a confluence of vectors. Trace them.

Yet again. More junctions. Trace them. Access more channels. The entire pressure structure, intricate as a nervous system, must be described. I must hold its tree within my mind.

Another layer. It may not be possible. I may be courting infinity in my topographic branchings. Freeze frame. Simplify the problem. Ignore everything beyond the tertiary. Trace to the next junction. There are some loops. Good. And a plate is now involved. Better.

Try another jump. No good. Too big a picture to contain. Discard tertiaries.

Yes.

Thus general lines sketched. Vectors of transmission simply drawn—back to plate, almost. Pressure exerted less than full pressure extended. Why? Additional point of input along second vector, redirecting shear forces this valley.

"Merlin? Are you all right?"

"Let me be," I hear my voice respond.

Extend then, input source, into, feeling, transmission signature. . . .

Is this a Logrus that I see before me?

I opened three more channels, focused on the area, began heating it.

Soon rocks were cracking, but a little later they melted. My newly created magma flowed down fault lines. A hollowed-out area occurred at the point whence the precipitating force had originated.

Back.

I withdrew my probes, shut down the spikard.

"What did you do?" he asked me.

"I found the place where the Logrus was messing with underground stresses," I said, "and I removed the place. There's a small grotto there now. If it collapses it may ease the pressure even more."

"So you've stabilized it?"

"At least for now. I don't know the limits of the Logrus, but it's going to have to figure a new route to reach this place. Then it's going to have to test it out. And if it's doing a lot of Pattern watching just now, that may slow it."

"So you've bought some time," he said. "Of course, the Pattern may move against us next."

"It could," I said. "I've brought everyone here because I thought they'd be safe from both Powers."

"Apparently you made the payoff worth the risk."

"Okay," I said. "I guess it's time to give them some other things to worry about."

"Such as?"

I looked at him, Pattern ghost of my father, guardian of this place.

"I know where your flesh-and-blood counterpart is," I said, "and I'm about to set him free."

There came a flash of lightning. A sudden gust of wind lofted the fallen leaves, stirred the fogs.

"I must accompany you," he said.

"Why?"

"I've a personal interest in him, of course."

"All right."

Thunder crashed about us, and the fogs were torn apart by a fresh onslaught of wind.

Jurt came up to us then.

"I think it's begun," he said.

"What?" I asked.

"The duel of Powers," he said. "For a long time the Pattern had an edge. But when Luke damaged it and you snatched away the bride of the Jewel, it must have weakened it more, relative to the Logrus, than it's been in ages. So the Logrus decided to attack, pausing only for a quick attempt to damage this Pattern."

"Unless the Logrus was just testing us," I said, "and this is simply a storm."

A light rain had begun while he was speaking.

"I came here because I thought it was the one place neither of them would touch in the event of a contest," he went on. "I'd assumed neither would care to divert energy from its own attack or defense for a swipe in this direction."

"That reasoning may still hold," I said.

"Just for once I'd like to be on the winning side," he stated. "I'm not sure I care about right or wrong.

They're very arguable quantities. I'd just like to be in with the guys who win for a change. What do you think, Merle? What are you going to do?"

"Corwin here and I are going to head for the Courts, and we're going to free my father," I said. "Then we're going to resolve whatever needs resolving and live happily ever after. You know how it goes."

He shook his head.

"I can never decide whether you're a fool or whether your confidence is warranted. Every time I decided you were a fool, though, it cost me." He looked up at the dark sky, wiped rain from his brow. "I'm really torn," he said, "but you could still be King of Chaos."

"No," I said.

". . . And you enjoy some special relationship with the Powers."

"If I do, I don't understand it myself."

"No matter," he said. "I'm still with you."

I crossed to the others, hugged Coral.

"I must return to the Courts," I said. "Guard the Pattern. We'll be back."

The sky was illuminated by three brilliant flashes. The wind shook the tree.

I turned away and created a door in the middle of the air. Corwin's ghost and I stepped through it.

XII

Thus did I return to the Courts of Chaos, coming through into Sawall's space-warped sculpture garden.

"Where are we?" my ghost-father asked.

"A museum of sorts," I replied, "in the house of my stepfather. I chose it because the lighting is tricky and there are many places to hide."

He studied some of the pieces, as well as their disposition upon the walls and ceiling.

"This would be a hell of a place to fight a skirmish," he observed.

"I suppose it would."

"You grew up hereabout, huh?"

"Yes."

"What was it like?"

"Oh, I don't know. I don't have anything to compare it to. I had some good times, alone, and with friends— and a few bad times. All a part of being a kid."

"This place . . . ?"

"The Ways of Sawall. I wish I had time to show you the whole thing, take you through all of the ways."

"One day, perhaps."

"Yes."

I began walking, hoping for the Ghostwheel or Kergma to appear. Neither did, however.

We finally passed into a corridor that took us to a hall of tapestries, whence there was a way to a room that I desired—for the room let upon the hallway that passed the gallery of metal trees. Before we could depart, however, I heard voices from that hallway. So we waited in the room—which contained the skeleton of a Jabberwock painted in orange, blue, and yellow, Early Psychedelic—as the speakers approached. One of them I recognized immediately as my brother Mandor; the other I could not identify by voice alone, but managing a glimpse as they passed, I saw it to be Lord Bances of Amblerash, High Priest of the Serpent Which Manifests the Logrus (to cite a full title just once). In a badly plotted story they'd have paused outside the doorway, and I'd have overheard a conversation telling me everything I needed to know about anything.

They slowed as they passed.

"That's the way it will be then?" Bances said.

"Yes," Mandor replied. "Soon."

And they were by, and I couldn't make out another word. I listened to their receding footsteps till they were gone. Then I waited a little longer. I would have sworn I heard a small voice saying, "Follow. Follow."

"Hear anything just then?" I whispered.

"Nope."

So we stepped out into the hallway and turned right, moving in the opposite direction from that which Mandor and Bances had taken. As we did, I felt a sensation of heat at a point somewhat below my left hip.

"You think he is somewhere near here?" the Corwin ghost asked. "Prisoner to Dara?"

"Yes and no," I said. "Ow!"

It felt like a hot coal pressed against my upper leg. I jammed my hand into my pocket as I slid into the nearest display niche, which I shared with a mummified lady in an amber casket.

Even as my hand closed about it, I knew what it was, raising all manner of philosophical speculations I had neither time nor desire to address at the moment and so treated in the time-honored fashion of dealing with such things: I shelved them.

It was a spikard that I withdrew, that lay warmly upon my palm. Almost immediately a small spark leapt between it and the one that I wore upon my finger.

There followed a wordless communication, a sequence of images, ideas, feelings, urging me to find Mandor and place myself in his hands for the preparations for my crowning as the next King of the Courts. I could see why Bleys had told me not to put the thing on. Unmediated by my own spikard, its injunctions would probably have been overpowering. I used mine to shut it off, to build a tiny insulating wall about it.

"You have *two* of the damned things!" Corwin's ghost observed.

I nodded.

"Know anything about them that I don't?" I asked. "That would include almost anything."

He shook his head.

"Only that they were said to be very early power objects, from the days when the universe was still a murky place and the Shadow realms less clearly defined. When the time came, their wielders slept or dissolved or whatever such figures do, and the spikards were withdrawn or stashed or transformed, or whatever becomes of such things when the story's over. There are many versions, of course. There always are. But bringing two of them to the Courts could conceivably draw a lot of attention to yourself, not to mention adding to the gen-

eral power of Chaos just by virtue of their presence at
this pole of existence.''

"Oh, my," I said. "I'll order the one I'm wearing to
conceal itself, also."

"I don't think that'll work," he said, "though I'm
not certain. I'd think they must maintain a constant flux-
pin with each source of power, and that would give some
indication of the thing's presence because of its broad-
cast nature.''

"I'll tell it to tune itself as low as it can then."

He nodded.

"It can't hurt to make it specific," he said, "though
I'd guess it probably does that anyhow, automatically.''

I placed the other ring back in my pocket, departed
the niche, and hurried on up the hallway.

I slowed when we neared what I thought to be the
area. But I seemed mistaken. The metal forest was not
there. We passed that section. Shortly, we came to a
familiar display—the one that had preceded the metal
forest, on approaching it from that direction.

Even as I turned back, I knew. I knew what had happened. When we reached what had been the area, I
stopped and studied it.

"What is it?" my ghostly father asked.

"It seems a display of every conceivable variety of
edged weapon and tool that Chaos has ever spewed
forth," I said, "all of them exhibited point up, you'll
note.''

"So?" he asked.

"This is the place," I answered, "the place where we
were going to climb a metal tree.''

"Merle," he said, "maybe this place does something
to my thought processes, or yours. I just don't understand.''

"It's up near the ceiling," I explained, gesturing. "I

know the approximate area—I think. Looks a little different now. . . ."

"What's there, son?"

"A way—a transport area, like the one we passed through to the place of the Jabberwock skeleton. Only this one would take us to your chapel."

"And that's where we're headed?"

"Right."

He rubbed his chin.

"Well, there were some fairly tall items in some of the displays we passed," he observed, "and not all of them were metal or stone. We could wrestle over that totem pole or whatever the hell it is, from back up the hall, clear away some of the sharp displays below that place, set the thing up—"

"No," I said. "Dara obviously caught on to the fact that someone had visited it—probably this last time around, when she almost surprised me. The display was changed because of this. There are only two obvious ways to get up there—transport something unwieldy, as you suggest, and clear away a lot of cutlery before we climb. Or rev up the spikard and levitate ourselves to the spot. The first would take too long and probably get us discovered. The second would employ so much power that it would doubtless set off any magical wards she's installed about the area."

He took hold of my arm and drew me on past the display.

"We've got to talk," he said, leading me into an alcove containing a small bench.

He seated himself and folded his arms.

"I've got to know what the hell's going on," he said. "I can't help properly unless I'm briefed. What's the connection between the man and the chapel?"

"I figured out something I think my mother really meant when she told me, 'Seek him in the Pit,' " I explained. "The floor of the chapel bears stylized representations of the Courts and of Amber worked out in tiles. At the extreme of the Courts' end is a representation of the Pit. I never set foot in that area when I visited the chapel. I'm willing to bet there's a way located there, and at the other end is the place of his imprisonment."

He'd begun nodding as I spoke, then, "So you were going to pass through and free him?" he asked.

"Right."

"Tell me, do these ways have to work both ways?" he said.

"Well, no. . . . Oh, I see what you're getting at."

"Give me a more complete description of the chapel," he said.

I proceeded to do so.

"That magic circle on the floor intrigues me," he said. "It might be a means of communicating with him without risking the dangers of presence. Some sort of image-exchange, perhaps."

"I might have to fool with it a long while to figure it out," I said, "unless I got lucky. What I propose doing is to levitate, enter, use the way at the Pit to reach him, free him, and get the hell out. No subtlety. No finesse. If anything fails to do what we expect, we force our way through it with the spikard. We'll have to move fast because they'll be after us once we start."

He stared past me for a long while, as if thinking hard.

At length, he asked, "Is there any way her wards might be set off accidentally?"

"Hm. The passage of a stray magical current from the real Pit, I suppose. It sometimes spews them forth."

"What would characterize its passage?"

"A magical deposit or transformation," I said.

"Could you fake such a phenomenon?"

"I suppose. But what would be the point? They'd still investigate, and with Corwin gone they'd realize it was just a trick. The effort would be wasted.''

He chuckled.

"But he won't be missing," he said. "I'm going to take his place."

"I can't let you do that!"

"My choice," he said. "But he's going to need the time if he's going to help stop Dara and Mandor from advancing the conflict between the Powers beyond anything at Patternfall."

I sighed.

"It's the only way," he said.

"I guess you're right."

He unfolded his arms, stretched, and rose to his feet.

"Let's go do it," he said.

I had to work out a spell, a thing I hadn't done recently—well, half of a spell, the effects half, as I had the spikard to juice it. Then I lay it in a swathe across the display, turning portions of blades into flowers, joined at the molecular level. As I did, I felt a tingling I was certain was the psychic alarm taking note of the enterprise and reporting it to central.

Then I summoned a lot of juice and lofted us. I felt the tug of the way as we neared it. I had been almost dead-on. I let it take us through.

He whistled softly on regarding the chapel.

"Enjoy," I said. "It's the treatment a god gets."

"Yeah. Prisoner in his own church."

He stalked across the room, unbuckling his belt as he went. He substituted it for the one upon the altar.

"Good copy," he said, "but not even the Pattern can duplicate Grayswandir."

"I thought a section of the Pattern was reproduced on the blade."

"Maybe it's the other way around," he said.

"What do you mean?"

"Ask the other Corwin sometime," he said. "It has to do with something we were talking about recently."

He approached and passed the lethal package to me—weapon, sheath, belt.

"Be nice if you take it to him," he said.

I buckled it and hung it over my head and shoulder.

"Okay," I told him. "We'd better move."

I headed toward the far corner of the chapel. As I neared the area where the Pit was represented I felt the unmistakable tug of a way.

"Eureka!" I said, activating channels on the spikard. "Follow me."

I stepped forward and it took me away.

We arrived in a chamber of perhaps fifteen feet square. There was a wooden post at its center and the floor was of stone with some straw strewn upon it. Several of the big candles, as from the chapel, were spotted about. The walls were of stone on two sides, wood on the others. The wooden walls contained unlatched wooden doors. One of the stone walls contained a windowless metal door, a keyhole at its left side. A key, which looked about the right size, hung from a nail in the post.

I took down the key and checked quickly beyond the wooden door to my right, discovering a large barrel of water, a dipper, and a variety of dishes, cups, utensils. Behind the other door were a few blankets and stacks of what were probably toilet tissues.

I crossed to the metal door then and knocked upon it with the key. There was no response. I inserted the key in the lock and felt my companion take hold of my arm.

"Better let me do that," he said. "I think like him, and I think I'll be safer."

I had to agree with the wisdom of this, and I stepped aside.

"Corwin!" he called out. "We're springing you! It's your son Merlin and me, your double. Don't jump me when I open the door, okay? We'll stand still and you can take a look."

"Open it," came a voice from within.

So he did, and we stood there.

"What do you know?" came the voice I remembered, finally. "You guys look for real."

"We are," said his ghost, "and as usual, at times such as this, you'd better hurry."

"Yeah." There came a slow tread from within, and when he emerged he was shielding his eyes with his left hand. "Either of you got a pair of shades? The light hurts."

"Damn!" I said, wishing I'd thought of it. "No, and if I send for them the Logrus might spot me."

"Later, later. I'll squint and stumble. Let's get the hell out."

His ghost entered the cell.

"Now make me bearded, thin, and grimy. Lengthen the hair and tatter the clothes," he said. "Then lock me in."

"What's going on?" my father asked.

"Your ghost will be impersonating you in your cell for a while."

"It's your plan," Corwin stated. "Do what the ghost says." And so I did. He turned and extended his hand back into the cell then. "Thanks, buddy."

"My pleasure," the other replied, clasping his hand and shaking it. "Good luck."

"So long."

I closed and locked the cell door. I hung the key on its nail and steered him to the way. It took us through.

He lowered his hand as we came into the chapel. The dimness must have been sufficient for him to handle now. He drew away from me and crossed to the altar.

"We'd better go, Dad."

He chuckled as he reached across the altar, raised a burning taper, and used it to light one of the others that had apparently gone out in some draft.

"I've pissed on my own grave," he announced. "Can't pass up the pleasure of lighting a candle to myself in my own church."

He extended his left hand in my direction without looking at me.

"Give me Grayswandir," he said.

I slipped it off and passed it to him. He unfastened it and buckled it about his waist, loosened it in its sheath.

"All right. What now?" he asked.

I thought fast. If Dara was aware that I had exited through the wall last time—a distinct possibility, considering—then the walls might well be booby-trapped in some fashion. On the other hand, if we went out the way I had come in we might encounter someone rushing this way in answer to the alarm.

Hell.

"Come on," I said, activating the spikard, ready to whisk us away at the glimpse of an intruder. "It's going to be tricky because it involves levitation on the way out."

I caught hold of him again and we approached the way. I wrapped us in energies as it took us, and I lofted us above the field of blades and flowers as we departed.

There were footfalls from up the corridor. I swirled us away to another place.

I took us to Jurt's apartment, which didn't seem a place anyone was likely to come looking for a man who was still in his cell; and I knew that Jurt had no need of it just then.

Corwin sprawled on the bed and squinted at me.

"By the way," he said, "thanks."

"Anytime," I told him.

"You know your way around this place pretty well?" he said.

"It doesn't seem to have changed that much," I told him.

"Then how's about raiding an icebox for me while I borrow your brother's scissors and razor for a quick shave and haircut."

"What would you like?"

"Meat, bread, cheese, wine, maybe a piece of pie," he said. "Just so it's fresh and there's lots of it. Then you're going to have a lot of story to tell me."

"I guess I am," I said.

And so I made my way to the kitchen, down familiar halls and ways I had traversed as a boy. The place was lit by just a few tapers, the fires banked. No one was about.

I proceeded to raid the larder, heaping a tray with the various viands requested, adding a few pieces of fruit I came across. I almost dropped the wine bottle when I heard a sharp intake of breath near the doorway I had entered.

It was Julia, in a blue silk wrap.

"Merlin!"

I crossed to her.

"I owe you several apologies," I said. "I'm ready to make them."

"I'd heard you were back. I heard you were to be king."

"Funny, I heard that, too."

"Then it would be unpatriotic of me to stay mad, wouldn't it?"

"I never meant to hurt you," I said. "Physically, or any other way."

Suddenly, we were holding each other. It lasted a long time before she told me, "Jurt says you're friends now."

"I guess we sort of are."

I kissed her.

"If we got back together again," she said, "he'd probably try to kill you again."

"I know. This time the consequences could really be cataclysmic, too."

"Where are you going right now?"

"I'm on an errand, and it's going to take me several hours."

"Why don't you stop by when you're finished? We've got a lot to talk about. I'm staying in a place called the Wisteria Room for now. Know where that is?"

"Yes," I said. "This is crazy."

"See you later?"

"Maybe."

The next day I traveled to the Rim, for I'd heard report that the Pit-divers—those who seek after artifacts of creation beyond the Rim—had suspended operations for the first time in a generation. When I questioned them they told me of dangerous activities in the depths—whirlwinds, wings of fire, blasts of new-minted matter.

Sitting in a secluded place and looking down, I used the spikard I wore to question the one I didn't. When I removed the shield in which I'd encased it, it commenced a steady litany, "Go to Mandor. Get crowned. See your brother. See your mother. Begin preparations." I wrapped it again and put it away. If I didn't do something soon he was going to suspect that I was beyond its control. Did I care?

I could just absent myself, perhaps going away with my father, helping him at whatever showdown might finally develop over his Pattern. I could even ditch both spikards there, enhancing the forces in that place. I could still rely on my own magic in a pinch. But—

My problem was right here. I had been bred and conditioned to be a perfect royal flunky, under the control of my mother, and possibly my brother Mandor. I loved Amber, but I loved the Courts as well. Fleeing to Amber, while assuring my safety, would no more solve my personal problem than running off with my dad—or returning to the Shadow Earth I also cared for, with or without Coral. No. The problem was here—and inside me.

I summoned a filmy to bear me to an elevated way to take me back to Sawall. As I traveled, I thought of what I must do, and I realized that I was afraid. If things got pushed as far as they well might, there was a strong possibility that I would die. Alternatively, I might have to kill someone I didn't really want to.

Either way, though, there had to be some resolution or I'd never know peace at this pole of my existence.

I walked beside a purple stream beneath a green sun atop a pearly sky. I summoned a purple and gray bird, which came and sat upon my wrist. I had thought to dispatch it to Amber with a message for Random. Try as I might, however, I could phrase no simple note. Too many things depended on other things. Laughing, I released it and leapt from the bank, where I struck another way above the water.

Returned to Sawall, I made my way to the sculpture hall. By then, I knew what I must try to do and how I must go about it. I stood where I had stood—how long ago?—regarding massive structures, simple figures, intricate ones.

"Ghost?" I said. "You in the neighborhood?"

There was no response.

"Ghost!" I repeated more loudly. "Can you hear me?"

Nothing.

I dug out my Trumps, located the one I had done for Ghostwheel, bright circle.

I regarded it with some intensity, but it was slow to grow cool. This was understandable, considering some of the odd areas of space to which this hall gave access. Also, it was irritating.

I raised the spikard. Using it here at the level I intended would be like setting off a burglar alarm. Amen.

I touched the Tarot with a line of subtle force, attempting to enhance the instrument's sensitivity. I maintained my concentration.

Again, nothing.

I backed it with more force. There followed a perceptible cooling. But there was no contact.

"Ghost," I said through clenched teeth. "This is important. Come to me."

No reply. So I sent power into the thing. The card began to glow and frost crystals formed upon it. Small crackling sounds occurred in its vicinity.

"Ghost," I repeated.

A weak sense of his presence occurred then, and I poured more juice into the card. It shattered in my hand, and I caught it in a web of forces and held all of the pieces together, looking like a small stained-glass window. I continued to reach through it.

"Dad! I'm in trouble!" came to me then.

"Where are you? What's the matter?" I asked.

"I followed this entity I met. Pursued her—it. Almost a mathematical abstraction. Called Kergma. Got caught here at an odd-even dimensional interface, where I'm spiraling. Was having a good time up until then—"

"I know Kergma well. Kergma is a trickster. I can feel your spatial situation. I am about to send bursts of energy to counter the rotation. Let me know if there are problems. As soon as you're able to Trump through, tell me and come ahead."

I pulsed it through the spikard and the braking effect began. Moments later, he informed me, "I think I can escape now."

"Come on, then."

Suddenly, Ghost was there, spinning about me like a magic circle.

"Thanks, Dad. I really appreciate this. Let me know if there's ever anything—"

"There is," I said.

"What?"

"Shrink yourself down and hide somewhere about my person."

"Wrist okay again?"

"Sure."

He did that thing. Then, "Why?" he asked.

"I may need a sudden ally," I replied.

"Against what?"

"Anything," I said. "It's showdown time."

"I don't like the sound of that."

"Then leave me now. I won't hold it against you."

"I couldn't do that."

"Listen, Ghost. This thing has escalated, and a line must be drawn now. I—"

The air began to shimmer, off to my right. I knew what it meant.

"Later," I said. "Be still."

. . . And there was a doorway, and it opened to admit a tower of green light: eyes, ears, nose, mouth, limbs cycling about its sea-like range—one of the more inspired demonic forms I'd beheld of late. And, of course, I knew the features.

"Merlin," he said. "I felt you ply the spikard here."

"I thought you might," I replied, "and I am at your service, Mandor."

"Really?"

"In all respects, brother."

"Including a certain matter of succession?"

"That in particular."

"Excellent! And what business were you about here?"

"I was but seeking something I had lost."

"That can wait upon another day, Merlin. We have much to do just now."

"Yes, that is true."

"So assume a more pleasing form and come with me. We must discuss the measures you are to take upon assuming the throne—which Houses are to be suppressed, who outlawed—"

"I must speak with Dara immediately."

"I would rather lay some groundwork first. Come! Shift, and let us be away!"

"Would you know where she is just now?"

"Gantu, I believe. But we will confer with her later."

"You wouldn't happen to have her Trump handy, would you?"

"I fear not. I thought you carried a deck of your own?"

"I do. But hers was inadvertently destroyed one night when I was drinking."

"No matter," he said. "We will see her later, as I explained."

I had been opening channels on the spikard as we spoke. I caught him at the center of a whirlwind of forces. I could see the transformation procedure within him, and it was a simple matter to reverse it, collapsing the green and spinning tower into the form of a white-haired man clad in black and white and looking very irritated.

"Merlin!" he cried. "Why have you changed me?"

"This thing fascinates me," I said, waving the spikard. "I just wanted to see whether I could do it."

"Now you've seen it," he said. "Kindly release me

to turn back, and find a more fitting form for yourself.''

"A moment," I said, as he attempted to melt and flow. "I require you just as you are.''

I held him against his effort, and I drew a fiery rectangle in the air. A series of quick movements filled it with a rough likeness of my mother.

"Merlin! What are you doing?" he cried.

I suppressed his effort to extricate himself by means of a transport spell.

"Conference time," I announced. "Bear with me.''

I didn't just meditate upon the impromptu Trump I had hung in the air before me, but practically attacked it with a charge of the energies I was cycling through my body and the space about me.

Suddenly, Dara stood within the frame I had created—tall, coal-black, eyes of green flame.

"Merlin! What's happening?" she cried.

I'd never heard of it being done quite this way before, but I held the contact, willed her presence, and blew away the frame. She stood before me then, perhaps seven feet tall, pulsing with indignation.

"What is the meaning of this?" she asked.

I caught her as I had Mandor and collapsed her down to human scale.

"Democracy," I said. "Let's all look alike for a minute.''

"This is not amusing," she responded, and she began to change back.

I canceled her effort.

"No, it isn't," I answered. "But I called this meeting, and it will be run on my terms.''

"Very well," she said, shrugging. "What has become so terribly urgent?''

"The succession.''

"The matter is settled. The throne is yours.''

"And whose creature am I to be?" I raised my left

hand, hoping they had no way of telling one spikard from another. "This thing confers great powers. It also charges for their use. It bore a spell for control of its wearer."

"It was Swayvill's," Mandor said. "I got it to you when I did to accustom you to the force of its presence. And yes, there is a price. Its wearer must come to terms with it."

"I have wrestled with it," I lied, "and I am its master. But the main problems were not cosmic. They were compulsions of your own installation."

"I do not deny it," he said. "But there was a very good reason for their presence. You were reluctant to take the throne. I felt it necessary to add an element of compulsion."

I shook my head.

"Not good enough," I said. "There was more to it than that. It was a thing designed to make me subservient to you."

"Necessary," he responded. "You've been away. You lack intimate knowledge of the local political scene. We could not simply let you take the reins and go off in your own direction—not in times such as these, when blunders could be very costly. The House needed some means to control you. But this was only to be until your education was complete."

"Permit me to doubt you, brother," I said.

He glanced at Dara, who nodded slightly.

"He is right," she said, "and I see nothing wrong with such temporary control until you learn the business. Too much is at stake to permit otherwise."

"It was a slave-spell," I said. "It would force me to take the throne, to follow orders."

Mandor licked his lips. It was the first time I'd ever seen him betray a sign of nervousness. It instantly made me wary—though I realized moments later that it may have been a calculated distraction. It caused me to guard against him immediately; and, of course, the attack came from Dara.

A wave of heat swept over me. I shifted my attention at once, attempting to raise a barrier. It was not an attack against my person. It was something soothing, coercive. I bared my teeth as I fought to hold it off.

"Mother—" I growled.

"We must restore the imperatives," she said flatly, more to Mandor than to me.

"Why?" I asked. "You're getting what you want."

"The throne is not enough," she answered. "I do not trust you in this, and reliance will be necessary."

"You never trusted me," I said, pushing away the remains of her spell.

"That is not true," she told me, "and this is a technical matter, not a personal one."

"Whatever the matter," I said, "I'm not buying."

Mandor tossed a paralysis spell at me, and I pushed it away, ready for anything now. As I was doing this, Dara hit me with an elaborate working I recognized as a Confusion Storm. I was not about to try matching them both, spell for spell. A good sorcerer may have a half dozen major spells hung. Their judicious employment is generally enough for dealing with most situations. In a sorcerous duel the strategy involved in their employment is a major part of the game. If both parties are still standing when the spells have been exhausted, then they are reduced to fighting with raw energies. Whoever controls a greater quantity usually has the edge then.

I raised an umbrella against the Confusion Storm, parried Mandor's Astral Club, held myself together through Mom's Spirit Split, maintained my senses through Mandor's Well of Blackness. My major spells had all gone stale, and I had hung no new ones since I'd begun relying on the spikard. I was already reduced to reliance on raw power. Fortunately, the spikard gave me control of more of it than I'd ever held before. All I had to do was force them to use up their spells, then all trickiness would be removed from the situation. I would wear them down, drain them.

Mandor sneaked one partway through, hurting me in a brush with an Electric Porcupine. I battered him with a wall of force, however, slamming him into a system of revolving discs that flashed off in all directions. Dara turned into a liquid flame, coiling, waving, flowing through circles and figure-eights, as she advanced and retreated, tossing bubbles of euphoria and pain to orbit me. I tried to blow them away, hurricane-wise, shattering the great porcelain face, uprooting towers, family groups with holes in them, glowing geometries. Mandor turned to sand, which filtered downward through the structure upon which he sprawled, became a yellow carpet, crept toward me.

I ignored the effects and continued to beat at them with energies. I hurled the carpet through the flame and dumped a floating fountain upon them. Brushing out small fires in my clothing and hair, I forced my consciousness through numbed areas in my left shoulder and leg. I fell apart and drew myself back together again as I mastered Dara's spell of Unweaving. I shattered Mandor's Diamond Bubble and digested the Chains of Deliverance. On three occasions, I dropped my human form for things more suitable, but always I returned to it. I hadn't had a workout like this since my final exams with Suhuy.

But the ultimate advantage was obviously mine. Their only real chance had lain in surprise, and that was gone now. I opened all channels on the spikard, a thing which might have intimidated even the Pattern—though, now I thought on it, it had gotten me knocked senseless. I caught Mandor in a cone of force that stripped him down to a skeleton and built him back up again in an instant. Dara was harder to nail, but when I blasted her with all of the channels, she hit me with a Dazzlement spell she'd been holding in reserve, the only thing that saved her from turning into a statue as I'd intended. Instead, it left her in mortal form and restricted to slow motion.

I shook my head and rubbed my eyes. Lights danced before me.

"Congratulations," she said, over a span of perhaps ten seconds. "You're better than I'd thought."

"And I'm not even finished," I replied, breathing deeply. "It's time to do unto you as you'd have done unto me."

I began to craft the working which would place them under my control. It was then that I noticed her small slow smile.

"I'd thought—we might—deal with—you—our-selves," she said as the air began to shimmer before her. "I was—wrong."

The Sign of the Logrus took form before her. Immediately, her features grew more animated.

Then I felt its terrible regard. When it addressed me, that pastiche-voice tore at my nervous system.

"I have been summoned," it said, "to deal with your recalcitrance, oh man who would be king."

There came a crash from downhill as the house of mirrors collapsed. I looked in that direction. So did Dara. Mandor, just now struggling to his feet, did also.

The reflective panels rose into the air and drifted toward us. They were quickly deployed all about us, reflecting and re-reflecting our confrontation from countless angles. The prospect was bewildering, for space itself seemed somehow bent, twisted now in our vicinity. And in each image we were surrounded by a circle of light, though I could not detect its absolute source.

"I stand with Merlin," Ghost said, from somewhere.

"Construct!" the Logrus Sign stated. "You thwarted me in Amber!"

"And a short thwart for the Pattern, too," Ghost observed. "It sort of balances out."

"What are your wishes now?"

"Hands off Merlin," Ghost said. "He'll rule here as well as reign. No strings on him."

Ghost's lights began cycling.

I pulsed the spikard, open on all channels, hoping to locate Ghost, give him access to its energies. I couldn't seem to make contact, though.

"I don't need that, Dad," Ghost stated. "I access sources in Shadow myself."

"What is it that you want for yourself, construct?" the Sign inquired.

"To protect one who cares for me."

"I can offer you cosmic greatness."

"You already did. I turned you down then, too. Remember?"

"I remember. And I will remember." A jagged tentacle of the constantly shifting figure moved toward one of the circles of light. There was a blinding rush of flame when they met. When my vision cleared, however, nothing had changed. "Very well," the Sign acknowledged. "You came prepared. It is not yet time to weaken myself in your destruction. Not when another waits for me to falter.

"Lady of Chaos," it stated, "you must honor Merlin's wishes. If his reign be a foolish thing, he will destroy himself by his own actions. If it be prudent, you will have gained what you sought without interference."

The expression on her face was one of disbelief.

"You would back down before a son of Amber and his toy?" she asked.

"We must give him what he wants," it acknowledged, "for now. For now . . . "

The air squealed about its vanishment. Mandor smiled the smallest of smiles, reflected to infinity.

"I can't believe this," she said, becoming a flower-faced cat and then a tree of green flame.

"Believe as you would," Mandor told her. "He's won."

The tree flared through its autumn and was gone.

Mandor nodded to me.

"I just hope you know what you're doing," he said.

"I know what I'm doing."

"Take it however you would," he said, "but if you need advice I'll try to help you."

"Thanks."

"Care to discuss it over lunch?"

"Not just now."

He shrugged and became a blue whirlwind.

"Till later then," came the voice out of the whirlwind, before it blew away.

"Thanks, Ghost," I said. "Your timing's gotten a lot better."

"Chaos has a weak left," he replied.

I located fresh garments of silver, black, gray, and white. I took them back to Jurt's apartments with me. I had a long story to tell.

We walked little-used ways, passing through Shadow, coming at length to the final battlefield of the Patternfall War. The place had healed itself over the years, leaving no indication of all that had transpired there. Corwin regarded it for a long while in silence.

Then he turned to me and said, "It'll take some doing to sort everything out, to achieve a more permanent balance, to assure its stability."

"Yes."

"You think you can keep things peaceful on this end for a while?"

"That's the idea," I said. "I'll give it my best shot."

"That's all any of us can do," he said. "Okay, Random has to know what's happened, of course. I'm not sure how he's going to take having you as an opposite number, but that's the breaks."

"Give him my regards, and Bill Roth, too."

He nodded.

"And good luck," I said.

"There are still mysteries within mysteries," he told me. "I'll let you know what I find out, as soon as I have something."

He moved forward and embraced me.

Then, "Rev up that ring and send me back to Amber."

"It's already revved," I said. "Good-bye."

". . . And hello," he answered, from the tail end of a rainbow.

I turned away then, for the long walk back to Chaos.

RETURN TO AMBER...
THE ONE *REAL* WORLD, OF WHICH
ALL OTHERS, INCLUDING EARTH,
ARE BUT SHADOWS

The Classic Amber Series

NINE PRINCES IN AMBER 01430-0/$4.99 US/$6.99 Can

THE GUNS OF AVALON 00083-0/$5.99 US/$7.99 Can

SIGN OF THE UNICORN 00031-9/$3.99 US/$4.99 Can

THE HAND OF OBERON 01664-8/$3.99 US/$4.99 Can

THE COURTS OF CHAOS 47175-2/$4.99 US/$6.99 Can

BLOOD OF AMBER 89636-2/$4.99 US/$6.99 Can

TRUMPS OF DOOM 89635-4/$4.99 US/$6.99 Can

SIGN OF CHAOS 89637-0/$4.99 US/$5.99 Can

KNIGHT OF SHADOWS 75501-7/$4.99 US/$5.99 Can

PRINCE OF CHAOS 75502-5/$4.99 US/$6.99 Can

Magic...Mystery...Revelations
Welcome to
**THE FANTASTICAL
WORLD OF AMBER!**

ROGER ZELAZNY'S
VISUAL GUIDE to
CASTLE
AMBER

by Roger Zelazny and Neil Randall
75566-1/ $10.00 US/ $12.00 Can
AN AVON TRADE PAPERBACK

Tour Castle Amber—
through vivid illustrations, detailed floor plans,
cutaway drawings, and page after page
of never-before-revealed information!

AVONOVA PRESENTS
MASTERS OF FANTASY AND ADVENTURE

BLACK THORN, WHITE ROSE 77129-8/$5.99 US/$7.99 CAN
edited by Ellen Datlow and Terri Windling

SNOW WHITE, BLOOD RED 71875-8/$5.99 US/$7.99 CAN
edited by Ellen Datlow and Terri Windling

A SUDDEN WILD MAGIC 71851-0/$4.99 US/$5.99 CAN
by Diana Wynne Jones

THE WEALDWIFE'S TALE 71880-4/$4.99 US/$5.99 CAN
by Paul Hazel

FLYING TO VALHALLA 71881-2/$4.99 US/$5.99 CAN
by Charles Pellegrino

THE GATES OF NOON 71781-2/$4.99 US/$5.99 CAN
by Michael Scott Rohan

THE IRON DRAGON'S DAUGHTER 72098-1/$4.99 US/$5.99 CAN
by Michael Swanwick

THE DRAGONS OF THE RHINE 76527-6/$5.99 US/$7.99 CAN
by Diana L. Paxson

ABOVE THE LOWER SKY 77483-6/$5.99 US/$7.99 CAN
by Tom Deitz